Praise for the Lords of Vice novels

Dusk with a Dangerous Duke

"Hawkins's writing is effortless, free-flowing, and very eloquent." —*Under the Covers Book Blog*

"*Dusk with a Dangerous Duke* [is] tantalizing and sexy." —*My Book Musings*

"A satisfying and good read." —*Rakes Rogues and Romance*

"I could not put *Dusk with a Dangerous Duke* down." —*ce Novel News*

All ... rquess

"I love thi... and its decadent heroes." —*Romance Dish*

"A good, solid choice for historical fans." —*Night Owl Romance*

"One of the best in the series." —*The Good, The Bad and The Unread*

"If you love historical romances, then this is a must-read." —*Romancing the Book*

Sunrise with a Notorious Lord

"Simply spectacular from front to back!"
—Fresh Fiction

"A clever and passionate story with a plot twist or two that grabs your attention and holds on right up to the wonderful ending." *—Romance Junkies*

"These Lords of Vice only get more and more interesting as the series goes on. They make sexy and sinful feel like satin sheets you want to roll around in until you're sated and exhausted."
—The Good, The Bad and The Unread

"Smart, sexy, and fun." *—Romance Novel News*

"Regency fans will enjoy the bold heroine and rakish hero." *—Publishers Weekly*

"Alexandra Hawkins writes some of the best stories set in the era!" *—Huntress Reviews*

"Charming, fun, and sexy." *—RT Book Reviews*

"Hawkins is pure magic that captivates her readers from cover to cover." *—Romantic Crush Junkies Reviews*

"There is never a dull moment when the Lords of Vice get together!" *—Romance Dish*

"*Sunrise with a Notorious Lord* is a fun and lively story."
—*Romance Reviews Today*

"This book starts on a fast pace and never slows down."
—*Reading Reviewer*

"Her Lords of Vice definitely live up to their names."
—*Limecello*

After Dark with a Scoundrel

"I absolutely loved *After Dark with a Scoundrel*. It is an amazing read and I could not put it down . . . I can't wait for the other Lords of Vice."
—*Night Owl Romance*

"Those sexy Lords of Vice return as another member is caught in a maze of love and danger. Hawkins's talent for perfectly merging gothic elements into a sexually charged romance is showcased along with the marvelous cast of characters taking readers on a thrill ride." —*RT Book Reviews* (4 stars)

"A 'must-read' . . . *After Dark with a Scoundrel* is a fast-paced Regency historical romance with a new and exciting surprise just about every time you turn a page. . . .as stunning as it is riveting. This story has it all . . . scorching." —*Romance Junkies Reviews*

"The sparks between Regan and Dare are beautifully written, so that you can almost feel them coming off the pages." —*The Book Reading Gals*

"4½ stars. The intensity between Regan and Dare sizzles on the pages." —*Romance Dish*

"Ms. Hawkins knows just how to pull the best from her characters to make you care for them, love them, get irritated with them, and all those other delicious emotions we romance readers need in our books." —*The Good, The Bad and The Unread* (A+)

"Perfect explosion of emotional fireworks blasted off the pages and set the rest of the tone for the book." —*Romantic Crush Junkies* (4.5 quills)

"Poignant, sweetly romantic, and sexy as can be." —*Reader to Reader*

Till Dawn with the Devil

"*Till Dawn with the Devil*'s romance is first rate with unusual characters and an underlying mystery that will intrigue readers." —Robin Lee, *Romance Reviews Today*

"A terrific second book in this series. I had it read in a day and then bemoaned the fact it was over." —*The Good, The Bad and The Unread* (A+)

"You will devour every sexy and intriguing morsel of this divine read." —*Romantic Crush Junkies* (4 stars)

A Duke
But No
Gentleman

Alexandra Hawkins

St. Martin's Paperbacks

This is a work of fiction. All of the characters, organizations, and events portrayed in this novel are either products of the author's imagination or are used fictitiously.

A DUKE BUT NO GENTLEMAN

For information address St. Martin's Press, 175 Fifth Avenue, New York, NY 10010.

ISBN: 978-1-250-06472-1

Printed in the United States of America

St. Martin's Paperbacks edition / July 2015

St. Martin's Paperbacks are published by St. Martin's Press, 175 Fifth Avenue, New York, NY 10010.

10 9 8 7 6 5 4 3 2 1

It is not enough to conquer; one must learn to seduce.
—Voltaire

Chapter One

March 4, 1792
Malwent Commons, England

Norgrave was a madman.

With one hand on the hilt of his sheathed short sword, and the other gripping the warm metal handle of a lantern, Tristan Bailey Rooke, Duke of Blackbern, watched intently as his friend parried his opponent's attack. The sharp, deathly clash of steel echoed in the night while Norgrave flirted as if the grim specter of Death was just another lady he needed to seduce into his bed.

No sane gentleman would duel in the fog at midnight, but too much brandy and pride had a way of dulling a man's wits. When Viscount Caxton knocked over the marquess's glass of brandy and issued his challenge, Norgrave eagerly accepted.

Caxton had been too blinded by his righteous anger to comprehend that he had been cleverly manipulated. If the gentleman had not been so generous in delivering his libelous insults not only to Norgrave, but to Tristan as well, he might have warned the man of his opponent's proficiency with both pistol and sword.

Instead he had remained silent.

Wronged or not, the pompous arse deserved the bitter

taste of humiliation for his insinuations, and Cason Brant, Marquess of Norgrave, intended to be the gentleman who forced every foul drop down the man's throat.

"Already winded, and your elbow keeps dropping." Norgrave made a soft sound of disapproval. "Do you wish to yield?"

Caxton bared his teeth at the suggestion. "Nay." He brought his blade down, but it only stirred the air when Norgrave stepped out of range at the last second. "Not until I hear an apology from your lips."

Tristan glanced over at the viscount's second who was staring at the fighting men with the excitement of a chained dog that longed to be free of his tether. He paced the edge of the circle, his sword unsheathed. Tristan didn't trust the man not to interfere to give his friend the advantage.

Norgrave grinned. "On the contrary, you should be apologizing to me for not being a worthy opponent. It is apparent you have been neglectful in keeping your sword skills honed for these unpleasant affairs."

The viscount responded with the resounding clang of steel against steel. He shoved to push the marquess away, but Norgrave was taller and slightly heavier. He held his ground, and it was Caxton who went stumbling.

"Hold, good sir!" Tristan ordered the viscount's second when he took a step forward. What the devil was his name? Prigs? Twigs? No, that did not sound quite right, but he was close. His lips curved in triumph as he suddenly recalled the man's name. "Briggs, your friend is fine. Do not interfere."

Caxton did not even glance at his friend. He charged Norgrave. "Stay back, Briggs. This bastard is mine!"

The marquess turned sideways and countered the man's blade. High and low, Norgrave's blows struck with accuracy and a ringing force that proved minutes later to be the thirty-eight-year-old gentleman's undoing. He had provoked the wrong man.

Norgrave shoved the viscount away from him.

"Are you satisfied, Caxton?" his friend taunted, his movements to evade his opponent swift and graceful. "Speak now, and you can return home to your sweet Audrey."

His brown eyes flared with indignation. "How dare you! You have no right to utter her name."

"I regretfully disagree. Audrey insisted that I take such liberties. As you know, it was just one of many," Norgrave said, his silky insinuation puncturing the other man's composure.

Anger strengthened Caxton's arm, and his blade sliced the marquess's upper arm. The viscount smiled at his small victory. "You might have caught her fancy, but her father accepted my offer of marriage, not yours."

Norgrave paused at the gentleman's words. "Who told you I offered marriage?" He cast an incredulous look in Tristan's direction. "Audrey's father accepted your timely offer because he knew—"

"Speak not another word!" the viscount roared as his expression darkened. "You are insulting my bride. If you continue, a mere scratch will not satisfy me."

"You truly believe you have the skill to best me, Caxton?"

"Love and justice will guide my arm."

"'Tis a noble declaration. A pity we did not invite a poet to our private gathering. He could compose a sonnet and deliver it to your widow."

"Enough, Norgrave," Tristan said in even tones. "An insult is not worth any man's death."

"Most evenings, I would agree," his friend said, his gaze fixed on his opponent's face. "However, I suspect Caxton is not planning to be reasonable."

"So you admit it," the viscount snarled.

The two men circled each other. "To what precisely? I have committed numerous sins . . . ah, but you are only interested in the ones that involve your delectable wife."

"Norgrave, cease provoking him!" Tristan pointed his sword at Briggs. "And you, back away. This duel is woefully unbalanced as it is."

Has everyone lost their head this evening?

"You seduced her." Caxton's mouth twisted with misery and pain.

The marquess's forehead creased in concern and disbelief. "Is that what she told you?"

If Norgrave had not spent several evenings regaling Tristan with titillating tales of his carnal exploits with the charming Audrey, he might have believed his friend was innocent.

Lord Caxton was also unconvinced.

The viscount shook his head. "She did not have to say a single word. I saw it in her eyes the moment you entered the ballroom."

A low chuckle rumbled in Norgrave's throat. "You poor gullible fool. You stand before me, willing to risk life and limbs for a duplicitous wench."

Caxton dragged his gloved hand through his dark brown hair. "You are wrong. My lady—"

The marquess slashed the air, cutting off the gentleman's words. "Cast her wiles in Blackbern's direction first. Is that not true, Tristan?"

"What transpired is no longer important." To Caxton, he said in apologetic tones, "It was a harmless flirtation."

Unhelpful as ever, his friend snorted in disbelief. "Audrey and her family had high aspirations to ensnare a duke's interest. Unfortunately for her, Blackbern was not attentive so she consoled herself in my arms."

Tristan frowned at Norgrave. His friend's retelling of last year's events was not quite accurate. He had been mildly smitten by Lady Audrey. If given the chance, he might have pursued the lady in earnest. However, Norgrave had swept her off her feet with his seemingly limitless charm, but he doubted the viscount would find comfort in the truth.

Nor did he seem to accept the marquess's half-truths.

"What are you saying?" The viscount lowered his sword as his fury increased. "That my wife seduced you? I refuse to believe such a preposterous claim."

"Oh, I seduced her, Caxton." The marquess closed the gap between them. "Did she claim that she was a virgin on your wedding night? Quite understandable since your valet is probably the only person who has handled your ballocks. Nevertheless, I can attest your devoted Audrey came to your bed with a bit of tarnish. I distinctly recall her crying out my name when I shoved my cock—"

Caxton bellowed, drowning out Norgrave's confession

as he rushed forward. He knocked the marquess's blade aside as the two men collided, fell, and disappeared into the fog.

"God's teeth and toes, this isn't bloody mud wrestling!" Tristan jumped out of the way as the fighting men rolled too close to his boots, his lantern swinging wildly. The duel had been reduced to fisticuffs if glimpses of Caxton's elbow were any indication. "Get up and show some dignity. The retelling of this over brandy will not be favorable for either of you."

He raised the lantern higher, attempting to discern the health of his friend. Norgrave deserved a few bruises for taunting the viscount about his wife's not-so-innocent past. However, it wasn't Caxton's face that was illuminated in the lantern's light. During the fog-shrouded brawl, the marquess had gained the upper hand and was pummeling his opponent with his fists. Tristan wasn't the only one who noticed.

With his short sword menacingly poised to strike, the viscount's second was striding toward them.

"Put down your sword, Briggs, and help me separate them before someone actually gets hurt," Tristan snapped, hoping the man was too used to following orders to ignore him. Without turning his back on the man, he sheathed his own sword and slowly set down his lantern.

"Stand aside, Blackbern. I have no grievance with you. Norgrave is violating the terms. He has no honor," Briggs said, discarding his lantern as he prepared to skewer the marquess in the back.

"Bloody hell!" Tristan ruthlessly kicked his friend in the upper shoulder, knocking him off balance as he retrieved his sword. Briggs's blade missed the marquess and found purchase in Caxton's chest.

The viscount howled in pain.

Tristan blocked the man's second attack. Sporting a visible bruise on his cheekbone, Norgrave gave him an appreciative lopsided grin. "Knew you couldn't resist showing off your skills," he said, before he scrambled to his feet to face his opponent with his sword in hand.

Fresh blood flowed like a sluggish spring down Caxton's white linen shirt as he stood. His chest was heaving for air, but he seemed oblivious to his injuries. The viscount was too intent on maiming Norgrave to call an end to the duel.

In the fog with four small lanterns to shed some light on the evening's violence, Tristan distracted Briggs while the other two men continued to battle. Norgrave was correct. He was eager to display his sword skills to a worthy adversary, but he preferred a less bloodthirsty setting. Usually, his reputation was enough to discourage most disgruntled rivals. However, Norgrave was driven to prove himself on the field of honor. He was never satisfied unless blood was spilled. His loyalty and longstanding friendship with the marquess placed Tristan at his side.

Briggs had some training, but it was apparent he had never faced a seasoned opponent. Although Tristan did not seek out battles, he had the skill to finish and win them. His persistent attacks and parries kept Briggs away from Norgrave, and it wasn't long before the man began to tire. Briggs was sweating, while his lungs were working frenziedly like inefficient bellows.

With a look of disgust, Tristan swiftly disarmed his

opponent and pressed the tip of his sword to Briggs's throat. "I trust you have the good sense to sheath your sword."

The man hastily nodded. "Aye, I do." It took him a few attempts, but he managed to put away his short sword. "Only a madman would continue."

"I cannot fault your reasoning. Now, if you don't mind, why don't you fetch the surgeon who had the good sense not to leave his coach. Caxton will need his skills since you managed to stab him."

His burly shoulders hunched as the man winced at the reminder that he had contributed to his friend's injuries. He picked up one of the lanterns. "What about them?" He gestured in the direction of the sounds of grunts and heavy breathing. "No one mentioned this was a battle to the death."

"It isn't. I have no desire to abandon my estates and flee England." Tristan glanced over his shoulder, and shouted into the fog. "Gentlemen, blood has been shed. Can we assume everyone is satisfied?"

Norgrave and Caxton staggered into view. The viscount had enough blood on his shirt to make it appear that he had sustained a mortal wound. Their short swords were nowhere in sight. His friend had fared better, but he was not walking away from this duel unscathed.

"What say you, Caxton? Are you satisfied?" Norgrave asked too cheerfully for their situation.

The man loved a good fight.

"I'm too tired to fight you," the viscount responded sullenly. "Aye, I'm satisfied—as long as you stay away from my wife."

Brazen bastard that he was, the marquess clapped the gentleman on the shoulder as if they were old friends. "A reasonable request I am happy to oblige. I have a bottle of brandy in my coach. What the surgeon cannot fix, a glass or two will help ease."

Tristan ruefully shook his head at Norgrave's mercurial mood as the two men headed for the coaches. Lord Caxton was never at risk of losing his wife's affections to the marquess. Norgrave had sampled Lady Audrey's charms and moved on to other conquests. No lady had ever claimed his friend's heart for long. He doubted such a female existed.

Hours later, Tristan and Norgrave were still celebrating their triumph at the marquess's residence. Along the way, they had collected two courtesans from their rented theater box. Jewel Tierney was an Irish beauty who had left her small village at sixteen and through a series of lovers had found her way to London. It wasn't long before she had secured a string of wealthy protectors. Both he and Norgrave had some history with the lovely Miss Tierney. He had been twenty when the dark-haired enchantress had cast a calculating glance in his direction. Their time together had been costly, but well worth it. Even so, he had been young and too wild to be tamed by any comely wench. His interest in her had quickly waned. There had been no recriminations. Ambitious and quite fickle in her affections, Jewel had moved on to other lovers—including Norgrave.

To Tristan's surprise, Norgrave and Jewel still shared a friendship of sorts, even though the fiery passion that had brought them together had burned out years ago.

Occasionally lovers, Norgrave had an amicable arrangement with the twenty-nine-year-old courtesan. Intimately familiar with his carnal predilections, Jewel often handpicked young women who had recently arrived in London and would be appreciative of the marquess's protection.

She had issued the same offer to Tristan, but he had politely refused. His title and the Rooke family's good looks ensured he had a willing female in his bed whenever he desired. He also did not want to be beholden to the courtesan. He had never inquired into the particulars of her arrangement with Norgrave, but Jewel was too shrewd not to demand a price.

"Tristan, I pray you are not spoiling my victory by passing out on us," grumbled Norgrave from the bed.

He had insisted that the four of them retire to his bedchamber so Jewel could clean the shallow scratches the surgeon dismissed as minor. The man had stitched up the wound on Norgrave's arm, and told him that he should confine his activities to his bed. His friend laughed and vowed to follow the old man's medical advice. Considering he was lying naked on the bed with only a sheet draped across his lean hips while two pretty women fussed over him, Tristan bemusedly wondered if Norgrave had bribed the surgeon for his opinion.

Reclining against the glassy blue silk cushions of the sofa, he did not bother opening his eyes when he replied, "More tired than foxed. It was a bloody long day and I had already developed a mild headache before we spent half the night drinking and playing cards. Not to mention our little adventure with Caxton." As an afterthought, he added, "And don't think I won't collect my winnings on that last game."

"You will forgive me for not beggaring you at the table as I often do."

His brows lifted in feigned outrage. "The devil you do!"

Jewel and her friend Eunice laughed.

"I was distracted by Caxton," his friend complained. "I had heard rumors at the club that he was working up the courage to challenge me."

"You deserved it," Tristan muttered without a trace of sympathy. "You were Audrey's first lover and then you made certain he knew it once he married her."

"Cason, that was terribly wicked of you!" Jewel admonished the marquess. The bed creaked as the woman moved closer to soften the sting of her words with a kiss.

"Do not tell me that Caxton didn't deserve it. Besides, it was his wife who caused all the fuss when she fainted at my feet. How was I to know that the lady still harbored feelings for me?"

The other woman sighed. "You poor man . . . it must be difficult to have all of your lovers fall in love with you."

Norgrave chuckled. "It is a curse."

Tristan groaned. The man's arrogance was boundless. "*Love* is not the appropriate word. Most of your former mistresses despise you."

When there was no sarcastic response from Norgrave, he opened his eyes and glanced over his shoulder at the bed. While he had been lightly dozing, Jewel and Eunice had disrobed and joined the marquess in bed. In spite of the colorful bruising on his body, Norgrave had positioned Jewel so she sat astride his hips. She slowly rode his cock while Eunice cushioned his swollen cheek with her breast.

"At least most of them do," Tristan said, dismissing Jewel and her curvaceous naked body as an aberration.

"I am certain they do, but their feelings are no longer my concern," Norgrave said, proving his passions and his thoughts rarely intermingled. "Over the years, how many of my former lovers have cried on your shoulder, Tristan?"

He shrugged. "I've lost count, you callous villain."

The marquess laughed. "And how many of those heartbroken and embittered wenches found solace in your bed?"

He grinned. "A few."

Tristan shifted his position so he could rest his chin comfortably on his bent arm. He felt no embarrassment in observing Jewel as she moved as gracefully as a dancer while stroking her lover. Norgrave did not possess a dram of shame when it came to amorous displays. He was proud of his body, and his prowess as a lover. It excited him when others watched him take a woman.

In truth, Tristan was not as immune to the couple's love play as he feigned. It was not difficult to recall the softness of Jewel's skin, the silk of her dark tresses against his face, or the quiet sigh that always escaped her lips when he filled her. His testicles tightened at the thought.

His hand moved to his thigh. What he felt was lust, but it wasn't Jewel or Eunice that he hungered for—any woman would do. His duties to his family and his lands filled his days and nights, and he had little time for a demanding mistress. It was unlike him to deny his appetites, but he had not minded his self-imposed celibacy. As he observed Norgrave with Jewel and Eunice, his thoughts turned inward and drifted as he considered searching for an amenable lady who would satisfy him in bed while he was in London. He was not as hardhearted toward his lovers as Norgrave, but he preferred an uncomplicated arrangement.

There was also Norgrave to consider.

Although he would be the first to heartily cheer if Tristan took a mistress this season, he would also place demands on his time. With his thoughts spinning in his mind like wooden puzzle pieces, he had not noticed that Eunice had left the bed at Norgrave's whispered request. It wasn't until she knelt beside the sofa that his gaze focused on her face.

"Your Grace, do I please you?" Eunice asked in a soft hesitant voice.

Tristan studied the naked woman offering herself. He had barely glanced at her when Jewel had introduced her, since he had only planned to toast Norgrave on his victory and retire for the evening. He wasn't surprised that his friend had other plans. As he took a closer look at Eunice's face, he could find little fault in it. He deduced her age fell somewhere between twenty and twenty-five, but it was difficult to tell with the cosmetics she had applied to her face. Her body was a bit too slender for his tastes, but her limbs were well formed and unblemished. He glanced at Jewel and wondered if this had been her strategy all along, since it was obvious the young woman was her current protégée. If he needed a mistress while he resided in London, why not invite Eunice into his bed? Her thoughtfulness would spare him the time it would take to find a willing woman on his own.

Unfortunately, Jewel was too busy pleasuring his friend to confirm his suspicions.

Since the woman was expecting some sort of answer from him, Tristan shifted his gaze back to Eunice. "You are quite lovely, my dear. Nevertheless, I am quite content with my brandy and thoughts. Nor would I wish to deprive Norgrave of your company."

Her face fell with disappointment. "But he said—"

From across the room, Norgrave seemed to choke with laughter. "Tristan, don't be an arse. If your cock gets any stiffer, the buttons on the flap of your breeches will pop."

"Tend to your own business," Tristan snapped, as he glanced down and noted the prominent bulge at the front of his breeches. It was pointless, but he tried to conceal his arousal with his hand. If he had the capability to blush, he would have in that moment.

The marquess snorted, and delivered a hard slap on the courtesan's buttock. "And you, to yours, my friend." Jewel gasped in surprise as Norgrave pushed her onto her back and covered her. He growled against her throat and she laughed in delight.

Tristan started at Eunice's touch. She had moved closer while he had been distracted. Her left breast brushed against his thigh as she reached for the buttons at the front of his breeches.

He placed his hand over her fingers as she worked the

first few buttons free. "Pray ignore my friend. I did not lie. I have no expectations. If you wish to return—"

"I do not, Your Grace." She tipped her face earnestly upward. The manner in which her hair tangled around her face was quite charming. His high opinion of her increased, when she boldly slipped her hand into his breeches and curled her fingers around his engorged cock. "You have your thoughts and brandy. Leave this to me."

His left leg slipped from the cushion as his legs parted until his foot rested on the floor. Eunice accepted his silent invitation, and crawled closer until she could press her breasts against the apex of his thighs. Tristan did not stop her when she pulled down the flap of his breeches and released the hot length she stroked with eagerness. There was no point denying the fact that he was aroused, and Eunice's shy offer had eroded his restraint.

Any female will do.

Norgrave, the arrogant bastard, had deduced his needs even before he had.

From his friend's point of view, the woman admiring his cock was merely a means to an end. Norgrave did not truly care which woman Tristan bedded as long as he ceased behaving like a bore.

The realization dampened his ardor.

He detested being manipulated. Eunice sharply inhaled when he abruptly grabbed her by the hair to stop her from lowering her head. Their gazes met. One held bridled anger and the other pain and fading lust.

"Let me pleasure you, Your Grace."

Without waiting for his reply, her tongue shot between

her lips and she licked the head of his cock. The muscles in his stomach rippled and he swallowed the groan forming in his throat.

"Bloody hell, woman. Are you trying to kill me?"

Eunice's eyes crinkled in mischief. "I'll give you my answer in the morning."

Her lips parted and this time Tristan gently guided her mouth to his straining arousal. Eunice opened her mouth wider and she took as much of his rigid length as she could. He clenched his teeth as she held onto the base of his cock to control the depth of his thrusts.

Tristan was dimly aware of Norgrave's perusal as sweet Eunice pleasured him with her talented mouth. The smug bastard knew he had won this battle. For now, Tristan was inclined to let his friend savor his small triumph because their battle of wills revealed one thing— he did not have the temperament for celibacy.

Nonetheless, when he returned to London, he would handpick his own damn mistress.

Chapter Two

June 1, 1792
London

"Imogene!"

The lady in question sat in front of her dressing table as her maid finished curling her hair. She did not consider herself a vain creature, but it was important that she look her best this evening.

"That is the third time Papa has bellowed your name," her younger sister said anxiously. "You know how he is. If he has to shout your name a fourth time—"

Imogene rolled her eyes. "Then he cannot be held accountable for the consequences," she said, echoing what her father always told them when he was close to losing his temper. "I know, Verity. Besides, Margery is almost finished dressing my hair. Is that not so?"

"Aye, my lady," the maid replied, setting aside the hot iron so she could fuss with the loose curls. "You will have every gentleman begging for a dance, I wager."

Verity, who had been watching for their father through the crack in the door, glanced sharply at her sister. "What am I? A wallflower?"

"More like a tenacious weed if you persist in your

whining," Imogene teased, though her tone held a subtle warning.

Always ready to soothe a budding quarrel between the two sisters, Margery replied, "No, sweetie, you are too comely to be a wallflower. The gents will adore you, as well, but we have to marry your sister off first."

"Why?"

"It wouldn't do to have you marry first," the maid replied, accustomed to Verity's complaints about the unfairness ruining her life. "People would think there was something wrong with your sister."

"There *is* something wrong with her," her sister muttered under her breath. "Everyone in the beau monde knows it to be true."

"Just like everyone knows you are a brat," was Imogene's exasperated retort.

Verity was eighteen months younger than Imogene, and the reality of her situation was not to her liking. Imogene sympathized with her little sister for feeling slighted by the family and being a tad jealous. On several occasions, she had pulled Verity aside to assure her that it was only a matter of time before she also would be displayed like a prized rose in the Duke of Trevett's hothouse, but her sister persisted to behave like a spoiled child.

Imogene stood. Giving her skirt a shake, she asked, "How do I look?"

"You'll be the bonniest lass at Lord and Lady Kingaby's ball," Margery declared.

She raised a questioning brow in her sister's direction. "No insults to hurl my way, Miss Brat?"

Verity huffed, and opened the door wider. "Mama

will not have to worry about you shaming the family. You'd better go. I predict Papa has worked himself into a fine froth over your tardiness."

In her sister's current mood, Imogene should probably accept her sister's words as a compliment. "I do not understand why everyone assumes I am late. We won't be leaving the house for another hour."

"Imogene!" The duke thundered her name.

"That's four. You'd better go before he takes a whip to your backside." Forgetting that she was annoyed with Imogene, she pushed her out the door.

"For all of his bluster, Papa has never taken a whip to anyone in this household." She halted abruptly and turned back. "Good grief! My reticule and fan!"

Verity waved her off. "Oh, just go. I'll bring them down later."

Imogene rushed down the corridor as swiftly as her dress would allow her. She slowed her pace on the stairs. A broken ankle would be worse than any punishment her father could deliver since she would likely spend the next few months confined to the house. Once she reached the front hall, she hastened into the library. The duke had left the door ajar, an obvious sign of his recent retreat.

He was standing near the lectern that displayed an old family Bible. This did not bode well if the impending lecture required a quick perusal of the Old Testament.

"Good evening, Papa." She curtsied, and offered him a smile that never failed to charm him.

"When was the last time you washed your ears, Lady Imogene Sunter?"

"I believe it was this morning." At his frown, she

amended, "Or rather, before bed last evening. Why do you ask?" she politely inquired.

"Why? I'll tell you why, my impertinent little miss. I called for you nearly twenty minutes ago."

"Forgive me, Papa." She leaned forward on her toes and kissed him on the underside of his jaw. At five feet and three inches in stature, it was the best she could manage. "Margery was curling my hair, and neither you nor I can rush her. I came downstairs as soon as she was finished."

"I shouted three times for you, young lady."

"Actually, it was four. Does that mean I get the whip?" she asked solemnly.

"The—what the devil?—I have never taken a whip to anyone." Her question befuddled him until he saw the twinkle of mischief in her dark blue eyes. "Although I might reconsider if you persist in exasperating your papa."

She slipped her hand around his arm and they walked to the sofa.

"You must be confusing me with Verity. I have been on my best behavior. Just ask Mama."

The duke sat down beside her. "What good will that do, I ask you? Your sweet mother coddles you and your sister. Spoiled to the marrow, you girls are."

Imogene laughed at his feigned woebegone expression. "And if I asked Mama, she would tell me that you are the one who is too indulgent with us." She resisted embracing him because Margery had gone to too much trouble with her coiffure; instead she settled on tugging on one of the buttons of his coat as she had when she was a little girl. "So you might as well accept with some grace that you had a hand in spoiling your girls."

"I will not," he said gruffly. "At least not outside the walls of this house."

"Your secret is safe with me," Imogene said, making a small cross over her heart. "It is the least I can do for the best father in all of England."

The duke's expression softened with love as he gazed at his elder child. He seemed to catch himself, and with a shake of his head, he said, "Oh, no you don't, my dear. You cannot dismiss your latest wickedness with flattery and sweet smiles."

"I have no notion of what you mean."

"Indeed you do, young lady, and it is the very reason why I insisted on speaking with you before you depart for your evening." He abruptly stood and began to pace in front of the sofa. "I have heard a troubling tale, and your name was mentioned."

Imogene bit her lower lip in contemplation. If her suspicions were true, word had reached her father's ears more swiftly than she had anticipated. "I cannot fathom what rumors you've heard since our arrival in town is too recent to warrant any speculation from strangers."

"Hmm . . ." Her father crossed his arms over his chest as he scrutinized her face. "If it were anyone else in the family, I would concur. Is it true that you had a private conversation with Miss Winall?"

Imogene resisted the urge to wince. "Lenora? There is nothing untoward in calling on an old friend."

The duke's eyes narrowed at her guileless expression and innocent tone. "Were you aware that her family has been quietly arranging a match between her and Lord Renchare?"

Of course she had heard about Lord Renchare's interest in her friend. Almost twice Lenora's age, the viscount had approached her friend's father more than a year ago to express his intentions. Since then, he had visited the country estate twice in an attempt to win the lady's heart. Unfortunately, for all involved, Lenora had already fallen in love with Mr. Hewitt—a gentleman she had been introduced to last spring.

"I have heard of Lord Renchare's interest," Imogene replied warily. She had received a note from Lenora within a day of her arrival to London, and learned that the family had hoped to announce their daughter's betrothal to the viscount this month. "More's the pity no one asked my friend's opinion on the subject."

The lines between the duke's eyebrows became more pronounced.

"Then you do not deny meddling in Miss Winall's affairs."

"It depends on your definition of *meddling,* Papa," she said with a shrug. "Lenora asked for my opinion, and as any good friend is wont to do, I gave it."

Her father's coloring did not look very good as he leaned forward. "Did you encourage this girl to spurn the affections of a worthy suitor and run off with her impoverished lover?"

"I would not choose those particular words." In fact, her father's summation of the facts sounded utterly dreadful.

He shook his head as he struggled to understand his daughter's part in this potential scandal. "Precisely how would you describe your part in Miss Winall's ruination?"

"Lenora is not a ruined lady," Imogene said crossly. "While it is true, Mr. Hewitt and Miss Winall eloped without her family's blessing, she is married to a man who holds her heart and will likely value his good fortune for the rest of his life."

"I am certain Miss Winall's family is comforted by the notion that instead of marrying a respectable viscount who will elevate their daughter's standing in polite society, their daughter is worshiped by the second son of a merchant."

Imogene stirred to defend her friend's husband. "Papa, Mr. Hewitt has many fine qualities to recommend. He—"

"Do not defend the man to me!"

Her father's harsh command forced her to swallow her rebuttal.

"You have yet to explain your part in the chicanery," he said, striving to control his temper, but it was apparent to Imogene that he had already deduced what she had done.

"Nothing too scandalous, Papa." She clasped her hands on her lap. "Lenora summoned me because she feared her family would not respect her decision to not marry Lord Renchare. She confessed her love for Mr. Hewitt and her despair that her family would not approve of their love match."

"Of course they would not approve of such a match. They love their daughter."

Imogene refrained from debating him on that point. If they loved their daughter, wouldn't they support her decision? "Lenora arranged for me to meet her Mr. Hewitt. And I found him quite earnest and honorable. So I—"

She hesitated.

The duke rubbed his eyes, his expression a mix of frustration and resignation. "You might as well confess to the rest of it, my girl. I already know the ending to your tale."

Imogene sighed. "Lenora was distraught at the thought of losing Mr. Hewitt. He had already approached her father for her hand in marriage and was rejected. He proposed eloping, and she turned to me for advice." Unable to meet the mute anger in her father's gaze, she stared at her clasped hands. "I told her if the notion of marriage to Lord Renchare was unbearable, then she should dash off to Gretna Green with Mr. Hewitt."

"Is that all?"

If she was fortunate, she would be banished to her bedchamber for a week. "I was the one who told Lenora to lie to her family. For the first few days, they believed she was staying here, though I assume that is how everything unraveled. Her father must have asked about Lenora and you—"

"I told him that I did not know what he was talking about." He scowled at her. "Can you comprehend the awkward and embarrassing situation in which you have placed me with your lies?"

"Forgive me, Papa. It was never my intention," she said solemnly. Imogene did feel awful that her father had been caught up in the web of lies. "When Lenora asked for my help, it never occurred to me that I should refuse. She is my friend."

"It was not your place to interfere, Imogene. I confess, I am disappointed in you."

Her lower lip trembled, the subtle sign of her distress. Imogene adored her father, and was sickened that he thought less of her because of her actions. "So shall it be the whip, after all? Or perhaps, imprisonment while I subsist on a diet of bread and water?"

Imogene glanced up, but he had already turned his back on her. She could not be certain, but she could have sworn his mouth had twitched as he tried not to smile.

"Nothing so dramatic, daughter. Locking you in your bedchamber would be kinder, because there is one thing you didn't consider as you helped Lenora plan her elopement."

"What is that?"

"The courage it will take to face her family. They quickly deduced who assisted their daughter and they are not pleased with you. Lord Renchare may not have been the sort of gentleman young ladies swoon over, but he is respectable, wealthy, shuns gambling and strong spirits, and would have been a tolerant husband to your friend." He glanced back at Imogene. His stern expression softened when he noticed the tears in her eyes. "Miss Winall married the man of her choosing, but there's no promise that it will be an easy life. Both of you will have to live with the consequences."

She sniffed as her nose burned with unshed tears. The duke handed her a handkerchief, and she mumbled her appreciation. "Should I make a formal apology to Lenora's family?" she asked, dabbing at the corners of her eyes.

"Only if pressed for one. Sir Horatio and his wife

would prefer not to draw scrutiny to the details of their daughter's recent marriage to Mr. Hewitt. It is fortunate that Lord Renchare is generous, and quite willing to overlook the insult of being rejected for a less favorable suitor."

Imogene nodded. "Am I allowed to join Mama and Verity this evening?"

"The King's birthday is in three days and the entire nation is celebrating. I see no reason to deprive you of the festivities."

"Thank you, Papa." She stood and approached her father. "You are kinder than I deserve."

He clasped her extended hand and lightly squeezed her fingers to silently let her know she had not lost his love. "I understand your loyalty to your friend. However, I must impress upon you that a daughter's loyalty is to her family."

Imogene loved her family. She could not fathom a day when her loyalties would be divided. "I understand."

He was visibly pleased with her reply. "Excellent! I pray you will remember our conversation when it is your turn."

"My turn." Her forehead furrowed slightly in puzzlement. "What does Lenora's predicament have to do with me?"

"The Winalls are not the only family in town who have high ambitions for their daughters." He placed a kiss on her forehead. "However, do not fret. You can trust your papa to find a proper husband for you."

A husband . . . for her?

Imogene smiled and nodded, but her stomach fluttered at the thought. She was young—a mere eighteen years old. Her mother had assured her that she should enjoy London this spring and that marriage would come later. Had her mother lied? Was there a much older suitor waiting for a proper introduction?

With undefined fears whirling in her head, Imogene excused herself and fled the library before her father noticed the distress his words had caused her.

Chapter Three

"Well, this is a most welcome surprise, Blackbern," Norgrave said, inclining his head in deference to Tristan's title. "I thought you were attending the theater since the play *The Suspicious Husband* is being performed this evening."

"Why attend a play, when the subject is being performed in every ballroom in town?" Tristan said blandly.

Norgrave laughed. "I thought that pretty actress who is playing the lead still had her hooks in you," the marquess teased, though his expression revealed he found the predicament appealing.

"Not quite. I showed my appreciation for her performance with a few bouquets. It was harmless flirtation," Tristan said dismissively. The actress had been spellbinding on stage, but in the proper light, she was older and less attractive in temperament when she uttered her own words.

"A pity you found her so lacking," his friend said, deducing what Tristan was too polite to admit. "I shouldn't mention it, but Eunice has inquired after you. Months have passed since she last enjoyed your company, and she is eager to renew your friendship."

He had been extraordinarily drunk the night Eunice had crawled between his legs and pleasured him with her skillful mouth and tongue. It had been a pleasant few hours, but he had decided to select his own mistress. If the gossip was accurate, the courtesan had not mourned his disinterest for long. She had had two protectors in his absence. What baffled him was Norgrave's casual attempts to push him back into Eunice's arms.

"What if I told you that I have sworn off courtesans and actresses this season?"

His friend pursed his mouth in contemplation. "I would have to call you a liar, Your Grace."

"There is no challenge in pursuing such greedy wenches, my friend." Together they threaded their way through the crowded entrance hall of Lord and Lady Kingaby's town house. "They can be tamed with a few coins."

"I heartily approve of the simplicity of such pleasurable transactions. Those few coins buy you a convenient female who will not burden you with guilt, demands, and tears."

"You can keep your gold if you use your hand."

Norgrave choked on his laughter.

Nearby, a gasp from an elderly matron and a censuring glare reminded him that he was not being discreet.

"I do beg your pardon, madam," Tristan said as he raised his hand to his mouth to hide his smile. "My comment was not directed at you."

"I doubt the dowager is acquainted with that particular vice," Norgrave muttered under his breath.

He wasn't being very helpful.

"Indeed it should not, Your Grace!" The lady halted, preferring not to walk beside them.

Norgrave glanced over his shoulder and winked at the elderly woman. "Her disposition might improve if someone taught her—"

"Enough." Tristan cursed softly. "Are you volunteering?"

"Christ, no!" Norgrave said, looking appalled at the suggestion. "I do have some scruples."

"Some? It sounds like you have just one clinking around in your empty head," Tristan teased.

"Arse."

"Blackguard," he replied affectionately. He caught sight of a familiar profile. "Ah, just the gentleman I was seeking."

"Who?" Norgrave peered in the same direction as his friend.

The man in question sensed he was the object of scrutiny, and searched the crowd around him. He immediately noticed the two gentlemen and lifted his hand in greeting.

"Jasper." Tristan raised his brows in acknowledgment, and nodded at the pantomimed instructions to meet outside the ballroom. "I have finally convinced the earl to part with his prized stallion."

"Liar. What's truly transpiring between the two of you?"

"Nothing," Tristan protested with a breathy chuckle. Numerous gentlemen had offered for that horse, including Norgrave.

"I do not believe you. Jasper treats his animals as if he had a hand in siring them."

"An improbable and disgusting notion." Not to mention one that could get you executed for consorting with beasts. "You are envious because he accepted my offer over yours."

"Naturally," Norgrave replied easily. "Have I mentioned how much I resent your damnable good fortune?"

"Too often. However, I doubt you will ruin our friendship over a horse."

Norgrave inclined his head. "Or women. Both are too plentiful for us to squabble over."

"I heartily agree." In spite of their differences, Norgrave was a man who could be counted on when problems arose. "I will seek you out when I have concluded my business with Jasper."

"Are you going to tell me how you bribed Jasper into accepting what I assume was a very generous offer?"

"Not a chance," Tristen said, already walking away from his friend. "I'm not giving you a chance to steal a prime piece of horseflesh right from under my nose."

Norgrave's laughter could be heard above the music as Tristan made his way toward the door Jasper had used to exit the ballroom.

This was not an auspicious beginning to her evening. Imogene stood still, but she couldn't resist glancing behind her as the servant applied needle and thread to the torn lace on her skirt.

"How bad is the damage? If I tarry much longer, I will never hear the end of it from my mother," she fretted.

There had been a minor mishap when she had been dancing with Lord Asher. The earl had stepped on the hem of her dress and accidentally ripped a sizable section of the lace trimming.

"It's not too bad, my lady," the maid said, only the top of her white cap visible as she focused on her task. "When I am finished, no one will even be aware that any damage was done to your beautiful dress."

"That is a relief," Imogene muttered under her breath. "Lord Asher offered to pay for the damage, but it is humiliating enough to contemplate that he views me as a pretty, albeit clumsy chit."

She was in London to make a good impression, as her mother often reminded her.

The maidservant giggled. "Most gentlemen don't see more than a fair face. Stepping on your skirt gives him an advantage over your other suitors."

Imogene had yet to acquire any suitors, but she saw no reason to mention it. "I do not see how."

The maid glanced up, her brown eyes twinkling with amusement. "That's 'cause you aren't thinking like a man. Your lordship is downstairs, likely pacing and plotting . . . wondering how he can catch you alone. Maybe even steal a kiss."

"That would be awfully wicked of him." Her cheeks heated at the thought of the handsome earl boldly kissing her.

"Every lady should be so lucky as to dally with such a man," the maid said with a wink. She bent down and snipped the thread with her scissors. "There . . . we're finished. The work as good as any Bond Street seamstress, I say."

Imogene glanced over her shoulder and slowly pivoted in a tight circle as she inspected the maidservant's efforts. "Excellent work. No one will ever suspect the hem had been damaged. Thank you." She retrieved her reticule from a small table with the intent of paying the young woman for her service.

The maidservant's expression brightened when Imogene offered her a coin. "You are very generous, my lady. Thank you," she said, the coin was tucked away within the folds of her dress. "I wish you luck with your wicked gentleman."

"Lord Asher is not my—"

The maidservant gathered up her sewing basket and walked over to another female guest who required assistance with one of her sleeves.

"Oh, bother . . . it is not important," Imogene said more to herself since no one was paying attention to her. Her hem had been repaired, and she was grateful to the kind maidservant.

Imogene was halfway down the corridor when she came across one of her childhood friends, Miss Cassia Mead. Her smile was genuine as the nineteen-year-old and her female companion drew closer.

"Cassia!"

The two women embraced.

Her friend was attired in the latest fashion, and Imogene thought London suited her. "No one told me that you were attending this ball. How long has it been? No, first, I owe you an apology. I received your last letter, but I have been neglectful in responding—"

"You can apologize to me later," Cassia interrupted. Her hazel eyes were welcoming, but there was a sense of urgency in her voice. "You have bigger problems. Where have you been hiding? Your mother is demanding that a search of the house be done. She fears you have been beguiled by an unscrupulous fortune hunter or possibly seduced by a dashing rake."

Imogene's lips parted in surprise. For a few seconds, she could not fathom why her mother would assume she would behave so foolishly. First she was chastised by her father, and now she sensed a future lecture from her mother. "Of all the ridiculous conjectures!" She gestured downward at her skirt. "My hem was torn so I asked one of the servants to repair it."

Cassia pouted. "Fine, don't tell me! Nevertheless, you might want to come up with a better explanation for your absence when you confront your mother."

Indignation stiffened her spine. "It is the truth. Just ask Lord Asher. He—I have to find my mother."

Imogene expected Cassia and her friend to continue their stroll in the opposite direction, but they chose to walk with her as she headed for the stairs.

"Aha! So a gentleman was involved. I thought that might be the case," her friend said, sending her companion a knowing glance. "Though I should warn you, Lord Asher is hunting for a wife. He has visited our house twice in the past fortnight, and has managed to charm my mother."

"We have had the pleasure of his company three times," the tall, plain-looking woman standing beside Cassia announced. "He has been making the rounds, calling on every nobleman who has an unmarried daughter. Rest assured, you have been added to the list."

Imogene was mildly startled that she had managed

to impress the gentleman so easily. "It was only one dance. I barely spoke to the gentleman," she protested. Their brief conversation had been cut short after he had stepped on the hem of her dress.

"It makes little difference," the woman confided. "You will soon discover that London moves at a different pace than what you are used to."

For a stranger, the woman was making quite a few assumptions about her. If it wasn't for Cassia's presence, Imogene might have taken umbrage at the subtly delivered insult that she had spent too much of her life in the country.

Imogene halted when they reached the staircase.

"I appreciate your sage observations, Miss . . . ?"

Embarrassed by her oversight, Cassia covered her mouth with her fingers as she giggled. "How dreadfully remiss of me. I do beg your forgiveness. Lady Imogene, may I present my good friend, Miss Faston. She is a distant cousin of mine so naturally she has heard all about you."

Imogene was not heartened by the news, but it was ingrained in her to be polite. She curtsied. "Miss Faston."

"Lady Imogene," she said cordially, curtsying as well.

"Good," Cassia said, her hazel eyes gleaming with satisfaction. "Now that the pleasantries are done with, I am certain the two of you shall become marvelous friends."

Neither she nor Miss Faston appeared to be excited by the prospect.

"However, we can discuss this later. You, my dear friend, need to leave us." At Imogene's questioning look, she added, "Your mother awaits you downstairs."

"Of course," Imogene said, resisting the urge to roll her eyes at her own foolishness since Miss Faston already had a low opinion of her intelligence. She embraced her friend. "I have missed you, Cassia. I will be disappointed if we do not plan an outing or two while I am in town."

"You can count on it," Cassia said, her friendliness contrasting sharply with the dourness of her cousin.

Imogene pulled away and waved farewell to the ladies. At the risk of showing too much ankle, she hurried down the stairs. She picked up her pace as she crossed the front hall. Her evening slippers slid sideways on the polished marble floor as she rushed through the nearest doorway. Was it a right or left turn? Without slowing her stride, she glanced over her shoulder at the door on the opposite side of the front hall and collided into an unexpected obstacle. The gentleman grunted, his arms instinctively wrapping around her waist as her momentum knocked both of them backward.

Whether it was providence or the man's quick reflexes, they landed on the firm cushions of a sofa instead of the marble floor. A faint breathy squeak escaped Imogene's lips on impact. Her chin bounced against his solid chest while the underside of his jaw struck the top of her head.

"Merde," her disgruntled companion murmured under his breath. "Are you injured? On fire?"

It was such an odd question that she lifted her head to get a closer look at the man who had saved her from a nasty fall. Any coherent response faded from her mind as she stared into the most beautiful eyes ever bestowed on a male. Long dark lashes framed blue-gray eyes that reflected curiosity and amusement. Imogene's gaze dropped down to his mouth as the corners curled upward into a smug grin, as if her reaction to his masculine beauty was not unusual.

The handsome stranger was patiently awaiting her reply to his question, and here she was gaping at him as if she had never encountered a man. "Did you ask me about a fire?" she asked, her tongue feeling thick and awkward in her mouth.

He smiled, and it was quite a magnificent sight. His teeth were straight and his breath was infused with his favorite brandy. "Aye. The manner in which you burst through the doorway, I was certain your skirts were ablaze," he said, his gaze lingering on her face. "Have you hurt yourself, darling?"

"No." She frowned, belatedly realizing their reclining position on the sofa. She tried to move and found herself anchored to his muscled chest. His arms were still around her waist and one of his hands was indecently low enough to touch her backside. "I—we . . . you should let me go."

"I disagree. I am rather comfortable having you draped over my body."

"Well, I am not," she said primly, flattening her palms against his chest in an attempt to push away from him. Or at least she tried to free herself. The wicked man seemed determined to hold her captive. "It is indecent, and you are no gentleman if you persist in delaying my departure."

Although she would never admit it to anyone, she could have rested her chin against her crossed arms and stared at him for hours. He was truly extraordinary. Unfortunately, the arrogant man was aware that his looks were a cut above those of most gentlemen, and the effect he had on women.

"Do you not get bored with following the rules?"

Of course she did, but she would bite holes in her tongue before she made such a confession. Especially to *him*. "No. Rules are put in place to protect us and ensure order in the world."

"It must have been your governess who filled your head with that nonsense," he said dismissively. His hands tightened on her waist when she struggled to slip from his hold. "Life is wonderfully messy, and no amount of structure changes that fact. So what have I done to deserve you, my lady?"

"Nothing." The roguish gleam in his eyes was a little unsettling. He was staring at her as if she was a gift and he was deciding how to unwrap her. "An accident that I have already apologized for—"

"Actually, you haven't."

"I—" She inhaled and silently went over their conversation. It grated that he was right, but she refused to admit that she had been dazzled by his handsome face. "You are correct, good sir. Forgive my oversight. If I may, I would like to offer you an apology. I sincerely regret meeting you."

His eyes widened in surprise. "Oh, darling, now you are simply being cruel—and you are a liar."

She stirred in his arms as her temper flared. "How dare you!"

"It pains me to insult a beautiful lady, but I think if we are to continue our friendship, we should be honest."

Her gaze narrowed. "Are you drunk, or is this some sort of prank you play on unsuspecting ladies?"

His laughter was just as appealing as the rest of him. Rich with genuine humor, it warmed her even as her stomach fluttered.

"If true, that was quite a feat on my part. Lest you forget, you were the one who tackled me?"

Imogene blushed at the reminder of her carelessness. "Ooh, it is unkind of you to remind me. Let me up at once, or I shall—"

"Is this our first fight?" he inquired, his expression easing into indulgence. "And here I have yet to have a taste of you."

"A taste?" she said blankly, before the healthy pink in her cheeks deepened into a scarlet hue. "I forbid you to kiss me!"

The charming rogue chuckled. "How can I resist such a dare?"

She felt his fingers curl around her neck. No man had ever been so bold as to touch her in this manner. Her skin tingled at his caress. He nudged her face closer to his.

Good grief, the man intended to kiss her!

"Imogene Constance," her mother said in icy, clipped tones. "What are you doing with that gentleman? Climb off him at once."

Her fingers curled into impotent fists. "See what you have done. That woman is my *mother*," she furiously whispered into the man's face. "Release me or we will both pay dearly for your mischief."

Imogene half expected him to dump her onto the marble floor since he was caught in what appeared to be a compromising position by an irate mother.

Instead he pressed his face closer and whispered for her ears alone. "Are you so certain? Your mother has known you longer than I have, and it is apparent that the blame has been placed squarely on your shoulders, you naughty wench. I look forward to learning more about your adventures."

"Oh, for goodness' sake," Imogene exclaimed, pushing away from him. Handsome or not, she could not tolerate another minute in his presence if the scoundrel was planning to throw her to the lions. Or, in this instance, a lioness.

"Mama, I can explain."

The duchess wasn't tapping her foot with impatience, but her expression revealed that she was close to dragging her daughter off and sending her home in the family's town coach.

Although he managed to hold on to her, he allowed her to pull away. He moved with her in tandem, displaying impressive strength and grace as he shifted his legs until his feet rested on the floor and she was sitting beside him on the green, upholstered, three-seat sofa.

Imogene glanced about the small alcove to ensure that her mother was the only witness to her humiliating tumble. Noting his gaze had dropped to her bodice, she gave the front of her dress an indelicate tug to conceal the flesh that had been exposed when she had collided with him.

Had he been staring down her bodice? Naturally, he had taken advantage of her vulnerable position. It was probably the reason why he had held her against his chest. "You are a terrible man," she muttered, shaking her head in disgust that she had thought him beautiful.

The source of her ire had the audacity to wink when she glared at him.

"Give me one reason why I should not send you home, young lady," her mother said, her thunderous expression switching between her and her companion.

Accepting that she was alone in this awkward predicament, she unflinchingly met her mother's angry gaze. "I tore my dress," she began, silently debating if she should mention Lord Asher. Imogene wrinkled her nose. "Not that the details of how I got here matter."

He crossed his arms, drawing attention to the substantial muscle filling out his coat sleeves. "On the contrary, I am intrigued. Any story that begins with a lady's dress being torn sounds promising," the Adonis seated beside her said, his voice warm and inviting as a cozy fire. "I cannot wait to hear how this tale ends."

She shivered at the thought of cuddling closer since her mother looked about as welcoming as a winter storm.

"It ends with you keeping quiet so no one challenges you to a duel," she snapped, wondering if she was dealing with a madman.

Unimpressed, he shrugged. "I am competent with all manner of weapons."

Of course he was familiar with all types of weapons. How many people had longed to shoot him minutes after meeting him? "I will shoot you myself if you lay a hand on any member of my family!"

"Does that include you, sweet Imogene," he whispered in her ear.

The whirlwind named Imogene Constance opened her mouth, and promptly closed it. She was an enchanting wench with large dark blue eyes, an elegant nose, and generous lips that taken as a whole did not make her a classic beauty, but she was quite fetching. Her light honey-blond hair had been frizzed, curled, and pinned high on her head. Someone had gone to a lot of trouble to give her some town polish when it came to her attire, but her slightly puzzled expression revealed that she was clearly out of her depths with a gentleman like him. It was her misfortune that he enjoyed teasing her. How could he resist? She was such a delightful mix of feminine indignation, curiosity, and innocence. If her mother had given them a few more minutes, he might have coaxed her into kissing him.

It surprised him how much he hungered for a chaste kiss. It would likely be a mediocre one at best since he doubted Imogene Constance knew how to properly kiss a gentleman. Even so, he was willing to tutor her.

His confidence was built on his experiences with the fair sex. Females of all ages adored him, and Imogene was not the exception. There was no doubt she was drawn to him, but she had the good sense to resist the attraction. Tristan admired her for it, because most of the ladies he dallied with were shameless wenches who longed to ensnare him for his title. When he had bedded his first female at the age of fifteen, he thought he could never tire of these eager conquests. By his early twenties, he began to crave women who offered him a little more challenge. The moment Imogene crashed into him and tumbled them onto the sofa, he deduced she might be worthy of his interest while he resided in London.

His respect for her increased a minute later.

With as much dignity as the young lady could muster, she rose from the sofa and walked toward her mother, most likely appealing to her assistance. Tristan did not blame her. Without a shred of modesty, he knew she had never encountered a man like him before in her sheltered world.

"Mama, appearances are deceiving. After my hem was repaired, I ran into Cassia. She told me that you were looking for me," she explained.

His thoughts turned inward as Imogene tried to explain to her mother how she had ended up in her current predicament. How they met was of no consequence to Tristan. He was content to admire her petite figure. The blue silk brocade dress she wore was modest in deference to her age, which he assumed was older then seventeen years and younger than twenty. Long sleeves covered slender, ivory limbs that ended with Dresden work lace engageantes at her wrists. Her waist was narrow, but he suspected the yards of fabric and bustle concealed the gentle curves of a woman's hips and well-proportioned legs he could easily envision wrapped around his hips. The thought did little to ease the arousal he had been hiding since her mother's sudden arrival. Having Imogene's body flush against his had whetted Tristan's appetite, and he wondered how he could lure her back into his arms.

Who was Imogene Constance? Her mother's reaction and the quality of their silk dresses led him to believe that the young lady was a nobleman's daughter. Not that he particularly cared about her lineage. She could have been a fishmonger's daughter, and he still would have been intrigued. In truth, there would be fewer complications if she had been the daughter of one of the servants. He could have enjoyed her company for a time, and eased her disappointment with a few dresses or a piece of jewelry. Young innocents with protective mothers were best avoided. A reckless gentleman who dallied with the wrong lady generally ended up leg-shackled. At his clubs, he had heard countless cautionary tales about these unhappy married fools who had allowed themselves to be castrated on the altar of Vesta. Duly warned, Tristan directed his carnal appetites elsewhere, but over the years, he had encountered a few ladies who tempted him to break his own rules.

Imogene Constance might be one such lady.

He belatedly realized that the young lady who had captured his interest had ceased talking, and both women were staring at him. Her mother's caustic stare was enough to take the remaining starch out of his cock, so he stood and crossed the short distance to join them.

"My lady, I pray you will not be too angry with your daughter. She speaks the truth. Our embarrassing tangle was an accident." He smiled benignly at the frowning Imogene. "Although I would be honored to receive a formal introduction to ease any awkwardness and allow us to greet one another as friends. With your permission, I would like to introduce myself. I am—"

"I know precisely who you are, Your Grace," Imogene's sour-faced mother said in clipped tones, unmoved by his civility. "No introductions are necessary since you will not be meeting my daughter again. Come along, Imogene."

The young lady appeared startled by her mother's rudeness. Torn between duty and etiquette, she hesitated, and for a moment Tristan wondered if the lady would defy her mother by offering her full name.

"Imogene!"

The blonde sent him a rueful glance as she curtsied. "Forgive me, Your Grace. I will show more care the next time I enter a room."

Tristan bowed. "Somehow I doubt it. I sincerely hope I will be nearby to cushion your next fall, my lady."

Imogene blushed at the reminder of their brazen embrace. She shyly smiled and walked away to catch up to her scowling mother.

It was a pity the lady had a dragon for a mother, Tristan thought as the two ladies walked away. Anyone who dallied with Imogene would not stroll away unscathed.

Chapter Four

"Mama, I beg you to stop. I cannot catch my breath at this pace," Imogene said breathlessly as she tried to pull free of her mother's firm grip as they entered the ballroom.

"It is the least you deserve for your latest mischief. Just wait until your father hears of this," the duchess hissed in her daughter's ear.

"I told you it was an accident," she protested.

"Ha!"

Undeterred by her mother's disbelief, she pressed her case. "Why would I throw myself at a stranger? The man could have been a footman or valet—"

"Oh, that gentleman is not a servant." The crowded ballroom forced her mother to slow down, a small respite for which Imogene was grateful. "Of all the potential bachelors in London, you had to throw yourself at him."

The duchess shook her head in disgust.

Imogene glanced back to the entrance of the ballroom as her mother tugged her hand to prevent her from stopping altogether. *He* had followed them. At least he had the decency to stop his pursuit near the doorway. The handsome stranger casually strolled to one of the green marble columns and braced his shoulder against it as he surveyed the guests.

A tingle shot through her the moment his blue-gray gaze met hers. Those beautiful lips formed into a knowing smile as the distance between them increased. She glanced back at her mother, angry that she had been caught gawking at him. It was one thing to be intrigued, but quite another for him to know it.

"Who is he? A fortune hunter? A murderer?" Imogene demanded.

Her mother expelled an exaggerated sigh before she suddenly halted and turned to address her. "I have no patience for your ill-conceived attempts at humor, my girl. Lord and Lady Kingaby have more sense than to invite a murderer to their house. I wish I could say the same for you."

The insult stung. "For the last time, I did not—"

"I believe you," the duchess said, effectively dousing Imogene's growing outrage. "The gentleman you encountered is Tristan Bailey Rooke, the Duke of Blackbern."

Imogene blinked in surprise. She assumed her mother would have been overjoyed that her daughter had caught the interest of a young and handsome duke.

Undoubtedly, there was something wrong with the gentleman. Perhaps even a hidden flaw in his character that could not be ignored by her mother.

"Oh, he is married," she realized, feeling a cooling wind of disappointment. "Does he have a string of mistresses? Is that why you were so upset?"

"He is a bachelor," her mother said, annoyed with her daughter's questions. "However, I insist that you stay away from this particular gentleman. I am uncertain what has brought the duke to the Kingabys' ball, but I can assure you that he is not here to find a bride."

Imogene automatically sought him out, but there were too many guests blocking her view. "How can you be so confident in your opinion?"

"The duke and his circle of friends have garnered a reputation for their decadence." Her mother's face softened, and she stroked her daughter's cheek with affection. "Imogene, your father and I have high hopes for your marriage prospects this season, but direct your gaze elsewhere. The Duke of Blackbern is headstrong and too young at five-and-twenty to be considering marriage. Like many of his peers, he drinks and gambles beyond what can be viewed as respectable, and he keeps company with courtesans. While his bloodlines may be impeccable, there is little I can recommend when it comes to character. I beg you not to encourage any flirtation."

Any residual anger toward her mother faded away. "Mama, if this gentleman is as notorious as you describe, I doubt he would be intrigued with me. I am nothing unusual, and my interests are rather mundane, do you not agree?"

"Not in the slightest. Your modesty will serve you well in catching a husband, but your beauty will draw all men to you, even the immoral scoundrels who think only of their pleasures. Your father and I will do my best to guide you, but you must heed our advice."

"Of course, Mama," she said, not understanding the

pang of sadness in her chest. She had not spent enough time in the Duke of Blackbern's presence to feel regret. "You and Papa only seek the best for me. You do not have to worry about me."

"Yes I do," the duchess said, laughing. "You and mischief have walked hand in hand for most of your life. I do not expect miracles from you, daughter. Now, come, I have a few people I would like to introduce to you."

From his position, it appeared the older woman had forgiven her daughter for being found in a compromising embrace. Arm in arm, the two women purposefully approached a small group of guests and were joyously welcomed. Was this Imogene's first season in London? Her enthusiasm and shy glances indicated that her family had sheltered her on one of her father's country estates. Small wonder her mother had had an apoplectic fit when she discovered her innocent daughter in his arms.

"How did your meeting go?" Norgrave asked, circling around to the other side of the column.

Tristan's gaze was fixed on Imogene's elegant profile. An absent smile lifted the corners of his mouth. "Quite satisfying. Have you beggared everyone with a hefty purse in my absence?"

"I did my best." Realizing he did not have his friend's complete attention, the marquess peered in the same direction as Tristan. "Who has caught your eye this evening?"

"No one," he said, redirecting his gaze away from Imogene. He knew Norgrave better than anyone, and a young innocent lady from the country was easy prey for his friend.

"Nonsense. One of these silk canaries has plucked your heartstrings." When Tristan snorted at the outrageous suggestion, his companion hastily amended, "Well, perhaps my aim was too high. Knowing you, Blackbern, any stirring likely originated in your breeches."

Tristan and Norgrave laughed.

Too competitive to be dissuaded from the subject Tristan was content to drop, his friend scrutinized the guests around them. "Come now . . . point the lady out. Who is worthy of your notice this season?" the marquess coaxed.

"I hate to disappoint you, but the fresh faces this year are rather disappointing," he lied.

"Truly? How very cynical of you, Blackbern. There are usually one or two ladies who are passable in looks." Norgrave sounded unconvinced as he scrutinized the females in the ballroom. "Ah, there . . . what of that fine creature?"

Tristan yawned. "Which one? The redhead?"

The marquess tilted his head in contemplation. "She is quite fetching in an unconventional way, but I was speaking of the blonde."

Naturally, Norgrave had honed in on Imogene even though there were at least fifty women in the ballroom. Tristan swallowed his annoyance. "The blonde in the green dress?"

"You never mentioned having problems with your eyesight," his friend said, frowning. "The lady in the green dress bests both of us in age. I am referring to the lady in blue. Do you see her?"

He saw her. Clearly, he and Norgrave were not the only ones who were captivated by Imogene's beauty.

Two more gentlemen were hastening to join her growing collection of admirers.

"Oh, the lady in blue." Tristan pursed his lips as he stared thoughtfully in her direction. "I will admit she is pretty."

The marquess's eyebrows lifted in incredulity. "Pretty? Such faint praise for a lady many would view as a goddess."

"You only consider them goddesses until they fall at your feet," he said, knowing his friend relished the chase. Once a lady surrendered, Norgrave quickly lost interest in his conquests.

"I prefer to have them on their backs," his friend countered. "Or on all fours. As for the petite blonde, I long to try her out in all my favorite positions."

Tristan shrugged. "If you say so."

Norgrave's eyes narrowed with suspicion, and it was then that he realized he had overplayed his indifference toward the lady.

"When did you meet her?"

His mild annoyance was not feigned. "I didn't—"

"You lie quite well, Blackbern, and are capable of fooling most people, but not me. I have known you since we were boys. We have no secrets between us. So tell me, how the devil did you gain an introduction?"

Feeling cornered, Tristan combed his dark hair with his fingers in agitation. "We were not properly introduced."

"Did her dragon of a mother snub you?" Norgrave's eyes brightened with glee. "How dreadfully humiliating for you, Blackbern!"

"Enough."

His friend was taking perverse pleasure in what he perceived as Tristan's failure to impress a young lady and her mother. "Ho! How the mighty have fallen if your handsome visage and title could not sway the ladies."

"I fear my reputation casts a long shadow," Tristan admitted, not particularly distressed by the notion. He had always managed to work around such hindrances in the past.

Norgrave clapped his hand on his friend's shoulder in sympathy. "Well, no one can say that the stories about you and me are untrue."

"Less entertaining as well."

"There is that." The marquess leaned against the column, and stared at Imogene and her mother as if they were a puzzle he desired to solve. "Not to boast—"

Tristan laughed. "When have you ever restrained yourself?"

"Never," he replied without hesitation. "I should warn you in advance—I saw her first. Not only that, I know the lady's name," was Norgrave's smug reply.

Imogene Constance. It was on the tip of his tongue to admit that he knew her name, however, there was a chance his friend was exaggerating. "You were in the card room. I doubt you had time to be introduced to the young lady."

Because Imogene was too busy pressing her body against mine.

"Arse. There are other ways to glean information," his friend said, enjoying their verbal jousting. "We are not the only gentlemen who have noticed Lady Imogene Sunter. Several gentlemen at the table were speculating on her dowry, now that her family is taking great pains to introduce her to all of the prominent families while they are in London."

"Sunter. So she is—" he said, his brows lifting as he realized that her lineage was almost as impressive as his own.

"The Duke of Trevett's elder daughter."

"Her father is well liked by the King," Tristan murmured, astounded that the Duchess of Trevett had not demanded his head on a platter when she had caught them, limbs entangled, on the sofa. If they had lingered undisturbed a few minutes longer, he would have kissed her.

Lady Imogene is the beloved daughter of a duke who has the King's ear.

He cursed under his breath. Unless he desired to be leg-shackled, the lady was most definitely off-limits.

"Shouldn't she be in a nursery or a nunnery?" Tristan muttered, his mood darkening at his friend's latest revelation.

Norgrave stared at the lady in question. He did not bother concealing his admiration. "She is old enough to marry. According to the gossips, her father had high hopes to match his little purebred mare with a princely stallion. His ambitions almost came to fruition, but I do not know which party cried off."

Although she had the bearing of a princess, Tristan could not imagine Imogene being happy to be presented as a brood mare for an ugly foreign prince or an infirm, elderly king just to gain a title. The very notion seemed a defilement of her beauty.

"Her father and mother indulge her," Tristan said, recalling how swiftly she was forgiven by the duchess.

"I plan on spoiling her as well."

His gaze abruptly shifted to Norgrave who appeared to be quite earnest. "I think the word you are seeking is *despoiling,* you heartless reprobate. The Duke of Trevett will geld you slowly if you so much as speak to the lady."

If the duke were to learn that he had already touched Imogene, the man would probably slice off Tristan's cock, too.

Norgrave dismissed his friend's concerns with a wave of his hand. "I'll admit that Lady Imogene presents some intriguing obstacles. I have every confidence that both of us could navigate them when the reward is worthwhile."

Tristan froze. He immediately understood the direction of his friend's thoughts. "No."

"Oh, why the devil not?" Norgrave said peevishly. "It has been ages since we've been provided with a worthy prize for one of our special wagers."

He and Norgrave had been born with competitive natures. Even when they were boys they had always sought to best one another, whether it was a footrace or who could swim across the pond first. They had taken turns as victors, but as they grew older, their wagers became more sophisticated and Norgrave's thirst for victory often took both of them down dark, ruthless paths. By the time they had reached Imogene's age, women they both had coveted had become fair game. For years, they had charmed, courted, and bedded countless females for the sake of victory.

"Why bother?" Tristan said, though the thought of seducing Lady Imogene was a temptation he was reluctant to dismiss lightly. "The game has grown stale, Norgrave. Not to mention quite boring since I tend to win these wagers."

"You do *not*!"

"It is hardly my fault that women prefer my handsome face over yours," he teased, deliberately baiting his companion.

Norgrave was not amused. "Those silly females may have swooned over the dimples in your cheeks and your soulful glances as you spun flattering lies, but when I have them under me, it is my cock that has them sighing and begging for more."

The thought of Imogene lying underneath the marquess chilled Tristan's blood. His friend had a reputation for not being a tender lover. It was the reason why his friend preferred to bed courtesans who understood the rules and were generously rewarded for their services. No, Imogene was too innocent, and bruises on her pale skin would be an abomination. If she was to take a lover, by God, it would be him.

"What are you proposing?"

Norgrave was one inch taller than Tristan, and he took advantage of it as he took a menacing step closer. "A wager."

Tristan longed to decline the outrageous proposition. He had outgrown such wagers, but he was willing to indulge his friend if the distraction would keep the marquess away from Lady Imogene. "Are we playing by our old rules or are you making up some new ones?"

Confident that he would get his way, Norgrave said, "Let's keep matters simple and limit our restrictions. This way you won't be able to claim our game has gone stale."

"Come now, there must be a few rules," Tristan protested. "Otherwise, I'll just bed the closest lady and declare myself the winner."

"Fine. If you insist." The marquess paused as he considered a few rules that might satisfy his friend. "Once the game commences, we grant each other equal time with the lady in question."

"What if the lady finds you repulsive?"

Norgrave grinned, displaying his perfectly aligned teeth. "They never do. However, I insist that we play fair with each other. For example, telling our quarry that I have the misfortune of suffering from the French pox will be viewed as unsporting and a violation of our limited rules."

It wasn't something he was proud of, but the tactic had proven highly effective. "To be honest, I only told one lady that you had the pox. Then there was that pretty brunette with the crooked teeth. I recall telling her that you accidentally shot your cock off while cleaning your dueling pistol."

His friend glanced at his shoes as if he was fighting to control his anger or laughter. When he met Tristan's eyes, his light blue eyes were clear and direct. "I have always wondered what you had told her. To this day, I sometimes catch that stupid wench staring at the front of my breeches with a puzzled expression." He shook his head in amazement at Tristan's audacity. "Your cleverness will not help you win this wager. If you tell our lady lies to discourage her from seeking out my company, the competition ends and I will be declared the winner."

"Fair enough. What are the stakes? Money? Property? My new stallion that you covet?"

"I was aiming for something more original. After all, we do not want you to grow bored. How about something so rare and precious to the owner that it can only be claimed once in a lifetime." Sensing he had captured Tristan's curiosity, he paused to heighten the anticipation. "The lady's maidenhead."

"The owner of the maidenhead might consider the price too high for a gentlemen's wager," Tristan said lightly, though his stomach was heavy with dread.

The ladies they had pursued and fought over had never been innocents. Some had been married and others widowed. There had been celebrated courtesans, actresses, and singers. All of them had been women who had surrendered their virtue years ago. Granted, these liaisons never lasted, but no one was truly hurt.

"The lady in question does not need to know about the wager. Her family is intent on placing her on the marriage market. No one will question our deliberate courtship."

Norgrave was a depraved bastard. "We are speaking of Lady Imogene Sunter, I presume," Tristan said bluntly.

"A most exquisite challenge, do you not agree?"

"Surely you jest. Do you recall the part of our conversation when I mentioned that her father is likely to castrate the fellow who lays a hand on her?"

"The danger adds spice to the chase."

Tristan hesitated. He despised the part of himself that was grudgingly intrigued by the challenge his friend presented. The wager gave him permission to seek out the lady and pursue her, because his attraction to Lady Imogene was far from honorable. Perhaps Norgrave sensed this depravity he tried to keep hidden, and was dangling the lady's virtue as a delectable temptation that he did not want to refuse.

Still, he resisted. "No, it isn't fair. Choose another lady. Another stake."

Norgrave grasped him by the chin. Instinctively, Tristan struggled to break free of his grip because he disliked being directed by anyone, especially his friend. However, it was not a battle worth winning and soon he found his gaze settling back on Lady Imogene.

"Look at the gentlemen hovering around her like drones around their queen," the marquess whispered in Tristan's ear. "Do you think any of them would not sample her charms if given the opportunity?"

He recognized many of the gentlemen vying for the lady's attention. The urge to stride across the ballroom and stake his own claim startled him. He blamed the man standing beside him. All of Norgrave's talk of wagers and seduction was awakening Tristan's protective instincts toward someone who was more vulnerable than she could possibly fathom. "With the intention of marriage, not ruination. You go too far, even for you."

The marquess parted his hands in a gesture of capitulation. "Very well. Then I shall declare myself victor of this wager."

Tristan's hands curled into fists. Their friendship was too competitive for him to yield without a fight. Through clenched teeth, he muttered, "If you must, to appease your pride."

"Scruples make you grumpy, my friend. However, you are correct. What is a triumph without the spoils? It all seems so hollow." Norgrave stepped in front of Tristan, blocking his view of Lady Imogene. "I have a brilliant idea. What if I honor the spirit of the wager before I declare my victory?"

"What are you planning to do?"

"Without your interference, it should be appallingly simple to seduce Lady Imogene. She will surrender her innocence, thus fulfilling the conditions of our nonexistent wager. Do not fret. When I coax her into my bed, she will be begging for my touch."

"The devil you say." Tristan's jaw hardened with mute fury. Whether he accepted the wager or refused, Lady Imogene would lose her maidenhead. Norgrave, the manipulative bastard, had backed him into a corner. He had a choice—stand aside and watch his friend seduce Lady Imogene or fight for the right to claim her for himself.

I had seduction in my thoughts long before Norgrave tossed his wager like a goddamn gauntlet at my feet. Why not take her?

It was a weak excuse for committing debauchery, and he silently cursed his friend for goading him into agreeing to his wild scheme. "I have reconsidered. I will accept your bloody wager, and I shall be the victor in your sordid little game."

Instead of being angry, the marquess appeared oddly satisfied with Tristan's declaration. He took a step backward as if he sensed his friend was resisting the urge to punch him. "You can try. However, Lady Imogene has her part to play. I am curious to see which one of us she will eventually choose as her lover."

Chapter Five

"I was told you attended Lord and Lady Kingaby's ball last evening," Lady Charlotte Winter said, after their hostess, Lady Yaxley, had introduced Imogene to the nineteen-year-old young lady since they were close in age.

She glanced over at her mother who was chatting with an older woman who was unfamiliar to her. As if sensing her scrutiny, the duchess halted her conversation and gave Imogene and her companion a brief appraising look before she returned to her conversation.

Her mother had told her that the connections she made in town were likely to follow her for the rest of her life. There were days when the weight of being born the daughter of a duke and duchess was a burden.

"Yes, I was there with my parents." She nodded, pleased that she had something to contribute to the conversation, though, so far, Lady Charlotte appeared to be capable of handling both sides.

The young lady loved to talk.

"I attended with my parents, as well," the blonde

said, her hazel eyes warming to her subject. "Did I mention that Lady Kingaby is a very close friend of my mother's?"

"No, I was unaware," Imogene murmured. As she listened to her new friend explain her family's connection to Lady Yaxley, she discreetly studied the other attendees.

They varied in age from the ten-year-olds who were helping themselves to the tarts and biscuits that were artfully displayed on one of the long tables to the elderly woman her mother had engaged in conversation. There were other young ladies her age and gentlemen who appeared in their prime. If variety heralded the success of a literary saloon, then Lady Yaxley's gatherings were destined to be popular this season.

"I have never attended a literary gathering. Were we supposed to bring our favorite book?" Imogene asked, praying she did not sound too provincial. "Mama did not fully explain what I should expect, and no one seems particularly interested in books."

Lady Charlotte giggled, though there was kindness in her hazel gaze. "These types of gatherings are common throughout the year, and depending on the guests, can be rather boring. Lady Yaxley can be relied on to invite all the right people." She leaned forward and whispered, "When I say the *right* people, I speak of ensuring there is a proper balance of males and females. Not too young and not too old."

"For what purpose?" Imogene asked, mystified. "Are you talking about people or books?"

"People, you silly goose!" Lady Charlotte stood

several inches taller than Imogene. At a passing glance, they might have been mistaken for cousins. "More to the point, the proper gentlemen. Lady Yaxley's literary saloon is a good place to inspect some of London's most eligible bachelors. An afternoon stroll in the countess's gardens gives us the opportunity to admire each gentleman's attributes. You would not believe the flaws that can be overlooked in candlelight."

Imogene pursed her lips as she contemplated her companion's words. "A brilliant notion. I had not considered—" Her thoughts abruptly shifted to the duke she had clumsily tackled. His body had been lean muscle and bone and his eyes had enthralled her. In candlelight, she had thought him quite beautiful . . . an Adonis, she thought, the god of beauty and desire. "So I should not trust my eyes if I meet a handsome gentleman in a ballroom?"

Enjoying that she could impart her knowledge to a friend, Lady Charlotte impulsively hooked her arm around Imogene's and they strolled the perimeter of the drawing room. "Not in the least. There are some bachelors residing in town who are divinely handsome. If you have doubts, I would recommend a stroll through a garden or a drive in a park."

Since everyone at Lady Yaxley's seemed content to visit, explore her house and gardens, or nibble on her tempting refreshments, Imogene was pleased she had encountered Lady Charlotte. If she was expected to pick a respectable husband, she needed all of the sound advice she could collect.

"Tell me more," she entreated.

* * *

"Since this was your brilliant notion of how to waste an afternoon, tell me again why we are attending this gathering," Tristan grumbled. It was the third time he had complained in five minutes, and knew he was drifting steadily toward being the type of person he detested—a fellow who whined.

"It is a literary saloon, Blackbern, not an execution," Lord Norgrave replied, seemingly in a fine mood considering their less than stimulating surroundings. "Intellectual, like-minded individuals who discuss and debate their favorite books. I have been told it is quite invigorating."

Tristan glowered at the solemn affair. "Did you imbibe several bottles of wine with your meal? The only invigorating debate going on in this drawing room is whether or not to try a millefruit biscuit or the rather bland cake that brown-haired fellow to our right is crumbling into a pile of sweet rubbish on his plate." He leaned in closer, ignoring the fact that his friend was fighting not to laugh. "And have you noticed that not a single person is actually carrying a book? For a literary gathering, one might expect to encounter at least one tome, do you not agree?"

"Oh, Blackbern, thus far, your observations have provided the most entertainment at an otherwise dull affair. However, my friend, our mutual pursuits have led us down somewhat unusual paths and sacrifices must be made."

Tristan scowled. "What the devil are you talking about?"

Norgrave's tolerant expression as he searched the drawing room blanked as a sudden stillness overtook him. Something or someone had caught his attention. "Ah, the true reason why we are here, since it is pointless to attempt to broaden your literary tastes."

"Leave my literary tastes alone. They do not need to be improved upon, thank you very much. I like books as well as anyone else. While I may have little interest in pontificating on the symbolism of Chaucer, it does not mean I—" He realized Norgrave was not listening. "You were about to tell me the reason why I am not outdoors, enjoying this good weather."

"Lady Imogene," his friend said succinctly, causing a subtle tension to steal into Tristan's limbs. "The difference between you and me is that I am focused when presented with a particular task. It gives me the advantage, and while I do regret ruining your afternoon, I feel compelled to tell you that this will be your downfall. I will win our wager."

Tristan's gaze moved from female guest to female guest until he found the lady he was seeking. Of course, she was wearing white this afternoon, unknowingly looking like the virginal sacrifice that Norgrave had set her up to be. She was in a deep conversation with a pretty blonde. The other woman was monopolizing the conversation. Lady Imogene nodded, and her attention shifted to the window. One could see a glimpse of the sun-drenched gardens. The lady stifled a yawn with her gloved hand.

Tristan was not the only person present who found their afternoon amusement less than stimulating. He grinned when she yawned again.

"Who is the lady with her?" he asked, not particularly caring if his friend knew her name.

It was Imogene who intrigued him.

"Lady Charlotte Winter, I believe," Norgrave said, priding himself on knowing the names of every eligible lady within the radius of London. "You have been introduced to her twice."

Tristan did not bother to respond to the dry comment from his companion. He recognized the lady's name, and had spoken to her sire on several occasions, but the conversations had involved politics and trade. The daughter had not been mentioned.

"I had forgotten her name."

"Lady Charlotte is an amiable creature. Fair in face, but no great beauty. Knowledgeable, and her father's connections could be a useful asset to an ambitious gentleman." Norgrave's eyes narrowed as he coldly dissected the lady's positive and negative qualities. "Virtuous and eager to please, which are beneficial if one hopes to take a wife, though she has an annoying habit of talking too much."

"I assume you have experienced this personally?" Tristan asked, amused by the annoyance in his friend's voice.

"Yes, unfortunately." The marquess frowned. "Like most females, Lady Charlotte is quite smitten with me."

Tristan shook his head at the man's arrogance. "You think all females are in love with you."

"It is because all of them are," he said in a suspiciously bland tone. "Where are you going?"

He paused and glanced at Norgrave. "To reacquaint myself with Lady Imogene."

"You never precisely explained the circumstances which brought you and the lady together," Norgrave said, joining his friend as they headed in the lady's direction. "It is unlike you to keep an amusing tale to yourself."

"There is little point. There is no story to tell," he lied. "Besides, since we are competing to win the lady's favor, I am hardly inclined to divulge my secrets."

The marquess's lips curled into a smile. "As your best and closest friend, I can attest that I am acquainted with your numerous flaws and sins. We have no secrets between us, Blackbern."

"True," Tristan conceded, though it rankled him. Norgrave had an uncanny knack for uncovering information if he stirred himself to make the effort. "Still, it will not stop me from winning our wager."

Satisfied he had the final word, he headed in the direction of the captivating young lady who had unwittingly created friction between him and the marquess.

"I would also suggest writing down in your journal the names of the gentlemen you meet indicating those who have made a favorable impression," Lady Charlotte said, fully engrossed in a subject near and dear to her heart. "It would not hurt to note attributes and your opinion on each one."

"You have put an impressive amount of effort into this task," Imogene said, not offering the lady a feigned compliment. "How do you use this information? Do you submit it to your father?"

Lady Charlotte giggled in a manner that made her sound like a bird. "Good heavens, no. The details are for my own use, though I have been generous with my knowledge. There have been a few occasions when I have spared a lady the heartbreak of placing her high hopes on the wrong gentleman."

It was no wonder her mother and father thought she was too lighthearted about her marriage prospects. She studied one of the male guests whom she deduced to be close to their age. "Can you tell me something about this gentleman?"

Her new friend quirked her lips as she studied the gentleman with the medium-blond hair. "He is one-and-twenty years of age. Second son of an earl. Educated. Enjoys his wine and horse racing. His flatulence is humorous. Is a subtle dinner companion, but has a bad habit of spitting and making an awful clicking noise when he picks his teeth."

Not wanting to draw attention to herself, Imogene covered her mouth to conceal her laughter. "Good grief, you learned all of those details in one conversation?"

"Not exactly. I deduced this through years of observation," Lady Charlotte said blithely. "The gentleman is my older brother."

Imogene's shoulders shook as she struggled to compose herself. "I consider myself forewarned. Shall I pick another gentleman?" she asked, warming up to their new game until she noticed the approach of a familiar dark-haired gentleman and his blond-haired companion. "It appears we have two willing volunteers."

She did not believe it was possible, but her friend's smile grew wider and she unconsciously began to play with one of the curls near her right ear as she recognized the two gentlemen.

"Your Grace and Lord Norgrave," Lady Charlotte

said, visibly struggling to contain her excitement at their presence. She curtsied and Imogene swiftly followed suit. "I was unaware that you two gentlemen would be taking part in Lady Yaxley's gathering."

The blond-haired gentleman attired in a light brown frock coat and breeches who her friend addressed as Lord Norgrave offered them a disarming smile. "It was an impulsive decision on our part." His gaze shifted to Imogene, and something akin to anticipation warmed his light blue eyes, making the contrast startling. "Nevertheless the best experiences are usually the ones unplanned."

Imogene smiled in agreement. "I have often found it to be so, my lord." She could feel the Duke of Blackbern's gaze on her, and the embarrassment of the previous evening smothered her like a humid summer breeze. It would have been rude to ignore him, so she deliberately turned to address him. "Do you not agree, Your Grace?"

He surprised everyone, especially Imogene, when he grasped her hand and brushed the top of her hand with a kiss. "I have never squandered the opportunities that tumble into my lap, my lady."

If he meant to fluster her then he would part company from her disappointed. However, there was little she could do about her blush, and it had not gone unnoticed by Lady Charlotte and Lord Norgrave.

"So you and Blackbern are acquainted?" Norgrave asked, making it seem as if she and His Grace were keeping secrets.

"No," Imogene replied at the same moment the duke replied, "Yes."

She glared at him. Only she, her mother, and the Duke of Blackbern knew about the humiliating encounter. While the amusing little tale might entertain his friends, it would not place her in a flattering light.

Lady Charlotte glanced from Imogene to the duke. "So which is it?"

Unhappy with the direction of their conversation, she had a desire to accuse the gentleman of lying. "We were not formally introduced," Imogene said, hoping the explanation would satisfy her new friend. She looked for her mother, but she was nowhere to be seen.

'Tis a fine time for her to abandon me.

Understanding lit Lady Charlotte's eyes. "Then you have not been—Oh, where are my manners. Forgive me," she said, placing her hand on Imogene's arm in a friendly manner. "Lady Imogene Sunter, may I introduce you to Cason Brant, Marquess of Norgrave."

"My lord," she said, curtsying. "It is an honor."

The marquess bowed. "The honor is all mine, my dear lady."

Imogene reluctantly turned to his companion. He patiently waited for a formal introduction which was a blessing. She certainly did not wish to explain their first meeting to anyone.

Lady Charlotte was oblivious to undercurrents of tension. "And may I formally present Tristan Rooke, Duke of Blackbern."

"Your Grace." She curtsied, but a childish part of her wanted to stick her tongue out at him.

"Lady Imogene," the duke drawled. "I trust your mother is in good health."

"It is kind of you to inquire, Your Grace," she said,

before a mischievous thought occurred to her. "Perhaps you would prefer to express your compliments to the Duchess of Trevett. She insisted on joining me this afternoon."

Blackbern's eyes narrowed, knowing full well that her mother would not be pleased to see him at Lady Yaxley's little gathering. "I look forward to improving upon my first impression."

Imogene could not prevent herself from grinning. "It should not be difficult."

Since her opinion of you is quite low.

The duke acknowledged her unspoken comment with a slight nod as though he had deduced her private thoughts. For Lady Charlotte's and Lord Norgrave's benefit, she added, "The duchess is very forgiving."

Blackbern made a soft choking noise that he concealed behind his fist. "Pardon me. I will take your word for it, my lady."

"Lady Imogene and Lady Charlotte, since Lady Yaxley has yet to begin, would you ladies be interested in stepping outdoors to enjoy the gardens?" Lord Norgrave asked, successfully distracting them. "The dust is irritating Blackbern's lungs, and a little fresh air would benefit all of us."

"So kind of you to think of my health," muttered the duke.

Lord Norgrave gave him a guileless smile. "How could I not, when you are like a brother to me."

Imogene was surprised when the marquess extended his arm to her. Lady Charlotte and the duke frowned at them.

"Will you do me the honor, Lady Imogene?"

Since walking with Lord Norgrave was the safer choice, she placed her hand on his bent arm. "It would be my pleasure, my lord."

"Lady Charlotte," the Duke of Blackbern said behind her.

Norgrave resisted the urge to glance back and smirk at Blackbern as he and Lady Imogene took the lead strolling through Lady Yaxley's back gardens. It was one of the benefits of friendship that extended into boyhood. A lifetime of experiences had given him insight on how his friend thought. He had become adept at anticipating the other man's thoughts and reactions, and he was quite certain the duke was gnashing his teeth over the fact that he had not invited the ladies to join them in the gardens.

After witnessing Blackbern's flirtation with Lady Imogene, he had mentally readjusted his own plans for the lady. Either he had underestimated his friend's interest in their beautiful prize or the lady was more intriguing than he had credited.

He was determined to find out.

"Imogene is such a lovely name. Is it a family name?" Norgrave asked.

"I was named after a great-grandmother on my father's side of the family," she said, averting her gaze in what he assumed was shyness.

How refreshing.

With her face bathed in sunlight, the lady in question was without a doubt a tribute to her sex. Delicate, flawless features, full unpainted lips, and expressive eyes that revealed intelligence as well as discomfort since she was clearly unused to spending her afternoons with potential suitors. Norgrave privately wondered if she would manage to retain that air of innocence after he had bedded her.

Nothing fired his blood more than taking something that did not belong to him.

"Tell me about yourself," Lady Imogene invited. Her curiosity about him was a loving stroke to his pride and cock.

"Hmm . . . what could I share that would not make me sound like a braggart?"

"Your family name is unfamiliar to me. Where did you spend your boyhood?" she asked.

"Northwest of London. It is a four-day journey," he said, deliberately quickening his stride to add distance between him and Blackbern. "My turn. Is this your first visit to London?"

"Ah, no," she said, tightening her grip on his arm when she stumbled.

He sent her an apologetic look and slowed his pace.

"I have been to London numerous times with my family. However, this is the first season I have been permitted to enjoy the evening amusements."

"So young. You make me feel like a doddering old man."

"You cannot be that old," she said with a laugh. "I cannot believe you are older than thirty."

"Bless you, my lady, for not guessing a higher number. No, I am twenty-seven years old and many years have expired since the night of my first town ball."

She grinned up at him. "You are holding up rather well for a gentleman of your age."

"Why, thank you, Lady Imogene. I do my best, and there are benefits to considering an older, more experienced gentleman when you are entertaining suitors."

The lack of a delicate blush coloring her cheeks reminded him that he was flirting with an innocent. She stepped away from him to examine a flower that had caught her fancy. Perhaps Lady Imogene was still more girl than woman, but her stay in London would be more educational than a room filled with tutors.

"We have only recently arrived, and I have no suitors," she shyly admitted when he moved next to her.

"I must respectfully disagree, my lady. If you confess to having no one dancing attendance in your drawing room, then allow me to be your *first*," Norgrave purred, amused that she would not appreciate his double entendre.

"You have set yourself an impossible task, old man," Blackbern said, as he and Lady Charlotte joined them. He was angry with him, and if the ladies had not been present, Norgrave might have been obliged to dodge the duke's fist. "If anyone is Lady Imogene's first, it is I."

Chapter Six

It was unlike Tristan to hold a grudge, but his temper had not faded in the hours since he and Norgrave had bid farewell to Lady Imogene at Lady Yaxley's literary saloon. The two gentlemen had gone their separate ways, because he had not trusted that he could hold his tongue after watching his friend flirt with the lady.

Gullible chit, he thought uncharitably.

Lady Imogene had smiled and nodded, believing every word uttered by the marquess. There had been an occasion or two that she recalled he was present, but she had not offered him any encouragement. Who knew what the devil the blackguard was telling her. When Norgrave had picked a flower and tucked it in her hair, she had blushed prettily and laughed as he complimented her beauty.

By the time they had reentered the countess's drawing room, Tristan had been in a rotten mood. He had not been the only one who was not amused by Norgrave's antics. Lady Charlotte's expression had grown withdrawn during their stroll through the gardens, and their conversation suffered for it. There had been pain in her gaze as she watched the other couple, and he could only pity the poor woman. If Norgrave ever married, his ambitions were loftier than an earl's daughter.

A duke's daughter would be more to his liking.

To prove he was not jealous of Norgrave, Tristan had agreed to meet his friend at the Green Goose to observe a bare-knuckled match in the courtyard. As he and Norgrave watched the two pugilists fight, the knot in his gut eased as if the punishing blows had been delivered by his own fists.

"How much did you wager on the match?" Norgrave shouted over the noise of the spectators.

"Twenty-five guineas on Ivie," Tristan replied.

"You are too young to be that miserly. Or perhaps you do not have much faith in your man," Norgrave teased. "I have wagered eighty guineas on Herring."

"And you are too careless with your wealth. You risk much for a pugilist you do not know or care to know," he replied, reminding himself that he was not the marquess's steward or his father. If the man wanted to beggar himself then it was his choice. He could not resist adding, "And that is why you will lose our wager."

Norgrave raised his eyebrows as if he was surprised Tristan had mentioned their wager for Lady Imogene's virtue. "Lose? Did you not see how the lady chose me over you? She thoroughly enjoyed my company, and if we had been alone, I might have slipped her away so I could kiss her in private."

Thinking of all of the women his friend had bedded in Tristan's presence, he muttered, "When has an audience stopped you from taking what you wanted?"

"Careful, Blackbern," the marquess chastised in a mocking tone. "One might think you were jealous."

Tristan scoffed at the very notion. "Do not be ridiculous. I am not jealous. I was merely disappointed the chit was fooled by your gallantry. I had credited her with more intelligence. However, if she remains in town she will learn that your reputation with the ladies is warranted."

"As is yours, my friend," he countered, unperturbed that he had been insulted. "I am not the only one participating in this wager . . . or the ones that came before it." He tore his gaze away from the fight and gave Tristan a hard look. "Unless you are having second thoughts."

Ivie took a hard hit to his square jaw. The pugilist staggered back a step. The spectators roared, some cheering the man to remain standing while others were screaming for him surrender.

Norgrave knew how to prod Tristan's competitive nature. It did not sit well with him to yield to anyone, especially his friend. "Not at all. Besides, you are getting ahead of yourself. You are not going to talk her into lifting her skirts just because you charmed her by picking a damn flower."

"It just galls you that she chose to walk with me this afternoon."

"Lady Imogene was simply satisfying her curiosity about you. It is to be expected, considering her family has high hopes that she will find a husband this season." He scratched the underside of his jawline and winced as his fighter took another hit to the face. "In fact, there is a chance that we will both fail if her family gets wind of the wager and warns her off."

"It is always a possibility," Norgrave conceded, but he appeared unconcerned.

"It occurred to me that we should refine our rules."

The marquess cupped his hands around his mouth and shouted. "What did you say? Rules?"

The unruly crowd was making any attempt to have a civil conversation impossible.

Tristan leaned toward his friend so he could speak into his ear. "I said that we should refine the rules when it comes to courting Lady Imogene. If we are together, we should share her and allow her to judge for herself whom she would prefer to spend time with."

"Are you demanding that I play fairly, Blackbern?"

Tristan placed a companionable hand on the marquess's shoulder. "I doubt you are familiar with the concept. What I propose is that we publicly court the lady. No one, not even her family, will question our presence when she is surrounded by numerous suitors. Nor will it seem odd if we approach her separately."

"You will not stand in my way if she prefers my company over yours?"

His eyes narrowed at the thought of Lady Imogene alone in the marquess's company. "If she does, I will have to persuade her to see the error of her ways. Oh, and one more rule. No matter who is declared the winner, we do not speak of it publicly. It costs us nothing, and she deserves to marry without worrying that her association with us has cast a shadow on her reputation."

Norgrave slowly nodded. "Careful, Blackbern. You are beginning to sound like an honorable gentleman."

"Not really. After all, I intend to be the one who claims her maidenhead," he said, the mockery in his

voice solely directed inward. "Let me remind you, her
father is the Duke of Trevett. He could be a powerful
political enemy whom I have no interest in provoking."

"Even though I disagree with you on whom will be
her lover, I cannot fault your logic about her father," the
marquess said, already losing interest in the conversation as his gaze returned to the spectacular display of
bare-knuckled violence.

"I propose another wager between us. A hundred
guineas on Ivie being the winner."

Norgrave gaped at him as if he was mad. "Only a fool
would make such a wager. Ivie is slipping in his own
blood."

"A reckless wager it is, but I am feeling lucky," Tristan
said, thinking the hundred guineas wasn't the only prize
he would be collecting from the marquess.

Norgrave grinned and clapped him on the shoulder.
"It will be a pleasure to relieve you of your gold. I accept your wager."

"What are you about, daughter?"

Imogene sighed and glanced up from the book in her
hands. "I am reading the first chapter of the book Lady
Yaxley entertained us with this afternoon. If we join her
literary saloon again, it would be helpful if one of us was
familiar with it so we can participate in the discussion."

The countess had selected *Modern Chivalry* by Hugh
Henry Brackenridge. Imogene was unfamiliar with the
author, but his satirical tale about the quixotic Captain
Farrago and his servant was humorous. Lady Yaxley
had been kind enough to loan her the first volume after
she had complimented the lady on her selection.

Her mother had been content to remain home this evening since they had spent most of the afternoon at the Yaxleys'. Imogene had enjoyed the gathering, and had managed to make a few new friends. The duchess should have been pleased, but her mother had seemed distracted at dinner.

Verity looked up from the sheet of music she had been pounding her way through for the past hour. "That silly book was the worst part of the afternoon," her sister declared with a pout.

"How would you know? You were too busy stuffing your face with pastries," Imogene said, annoyed that her younger sibling found fault with everything she seemed to like these days.

The admission had her mother's disapproving frown switching to the girl. "Verity, I told you one tart. You have your figure to consider."

"Mama," her sister whined, loathing to be the focus of their mother's displeasure. "I only had one."

"One tart, a piece of cake, and several biscuits," Imogene said, shutting the book. "And those were the sweets you managed to eat during the reading."

"Imogene," her mother said, sounding exasperated. "Tattling is beneath you."

"I am astounded you even noticed what I ate since you were flirting with the Duke of Blackbern and Lord Norgrave," her sister said, reminding her that revenge was swift and not entirely painless.

Her eyes glittered with anger. "Brat!"

"Coquette!"

Verity stuck her tongue out at Imogene and she returned the childish gesture.

"Girls!" Her mother put aside her embroidery and removed her spectacles with a deliberation that revealed the depth of her annoyance. "I have raised you to be ladies, and this petty squabbling is beyond the pale. It will not be tolerated, do you understand me?"

Her outburst drew a reluctant "Yes, Mama" from both of her daughters.

Before her mother could command her, Imogene said to her sister, "I should have not mentioned the pastries. Forgive me, Verity."

The tendered apology only stiffened her sister's spine. "As well you should, Imogene. It was very—"

"Verity!"

The duchess's inflection was harsh enough to make a sinner repent.

Chastened, her sister bowed her head. "Yes, Mama. You are forgiven, Imogene, and I offer my apologies."

"You are forgiven," Imogene said quickly, hoping this was the end of the discussion. Something in her mother's expression hinted that they were far from finished.

A few minutes later, she was proven correct.

"Verity, you have practiced that composition enough for the evening," the duchess decreed. "Why do you not pay Cook a visit and perhaps she will make you a cup of hot chocolate."

Her sister was cheered by their mother's suggestion. "A brilliant idea, Mama." She pushed away from the harpsichord and stood. "Perhaps a biscuit or two would complement the hot chocolate?"

Her mother did not roll her eyes, but she came close to it. "One biscuit. Not a crumb more."

"Yes, Mama." She curtsied and hurried to the door. Belatedly, she recalled that Imogene was being left behind with their mother. Sensing a lecture in her sister's future, she asked, "Imogene, do you wish to join me?"

"Yes—" Imogene placed the book on the table and began to rise.

"Sit," the duchess ordered her elder daughter. "Run along, Verity. Your sister and I have a few things to discuss. She will join you later."

"Do not tarry or I shall eat your share of the biscuits," Verity warned, and Imogene smiled, appreciating her tenacity for once.

"I said one biscuit, daughter," the duchess said, giving her younger child a meaningful glare.

"Oh, very well," her sister huffed, and then she was gone.

"What did you wish to discuss, Mama?" Imogene said, accepting that no amount of evasion would deter her mother.

The duchess studied her daughter before she spoke. "Specifically? The Duke of Blackbern and the Marquess of Norgrave."

"Ah, yes, they were Lady Yaxley's guests. Lady Charlotte was on hand to make formal introductions."

"How convenient," her mother muttered under her breath. "Do you recall our conversation about avoiding Blackbern?"

How could I forget? "Yes, Mama," she said, lowering her gaze to her lap. "You were quite clear on the subject."

"Excellent. The same advice applies to Norgrave." She picked up her embroidery and retrieved her glasses.

"I do not wish to be disrespectful, but how do you propose that I avoid these gentlemen?"

"You might begin by not strolling with them in Lady Yaxley's gardens."

Imogene winced. It had been too much to hope that her mother had been too distracted to notice. "It was a benign request and I did not wish to offend Lord Norgrave. Lady Charlotte accompanied me and she spoke highly of the gentlemen," she added to her weak defense.

"Lady Charlotte is blind when it comes to the marquess. The young lady is smitten, and if her father had any sense, he would discourage the friendship."

She had not noticed that Lady Charlotte had a deep affection for Lord Norgrave. How had she missed this? Perhaps because the marquess had offered his arm to Imogene instead of her companion. She mentally cringed at her thoughtlessness. "I have to disagree, Mama. Lady Charlotte appeared to possess a general fondness for both gentlemen." Recognizing that particular look on her mother's face, she hastily added, "It was a pleasant exchange and His Grace and Lord Norgrave were respectful. You have nothing to worry about."

"What's this?" her father said, entering the music room. "Good evening, my girls." He walked to his duchess and kissed her lightly on the cheek. "Are you quarreling?"

"No," Imogene said swiftly.

The duchess gave her daughter an indecipherable look. "Not yet," was her mother's reply.

"I was introduced to His Grace, the Duke of Blackbern, and Lord Norgrave this afternoon," she explained, assuming she might as well be honest with her father. She valued his opinion. "Mama has told me to avoid these gentlemen at all costs."

Her mother frowned. "Those were not my precise words."

"The gentlemen are friends with Lady Charlotte and Lady Yaxley's welcomed guests. I saw no harm in accepting an invitation to explore the countess's gardens."

"Nor I." Her father walked to her and stopped to kiss her on top of the head.

"Husband," her mother said sharply.

"Wife, I agree, Blackbern and Norgrave are not the best suitors for our girl." He glanced down at his daughter. "They have run wild for years and some of the gossip is not fit for a lady's ears."

"Some?" her mother muttered.

"No worse than I was at that age," her father countered. "They are a bit too seasoned and jaded for someone your age. Have they expressed an interest in courting you?"

She felt the weight of her mother's and father's stares as they awaited her response. "I believe so, Papa. What should I do?"

"Husband, you are not possibly considering allowing her to—" her mother said, rising with her embroidery clutched in her hands.

"Imogene could do worse than catch the eye of a duke and marquess," he said, speaking over her protest. "News of their interest will spread and encourage other gentlemen to seek introductions. I am well pleased with your efforts, daughter."

"Thank you, Papa," she said, not quite certain what she had done to deserve their attention.

Her mother was far from satisfied with the duke's decision. "You are willing to overlook the gossip about Blackbern and Norgrave?"

"I refuse to condemn a gentleman over gossip," was her father's dismissive reply. "Besides, a courtship is not the same as a betrothal."

The duchess stuffed her embroidery in her sewing basket. She glowered at them. "Exactly. It is something you should consider while you dangle our daughter in front of those rakes like a tempting sweet morsel!"

Her mother marched out of the music room.

"Mama is upset," Imogene said, biting her lower lip. "Perhaps I should keep my distance from the duke and his friend."

The duke touched her on the shoulder. "Rubbish. If you favor these gentlemen, you may encourage their courtship. However, I feel obliged to warn you that Blackbern and Norgrave have gained notoriety, and that is what troubles your mother. You are a beautiful young lady, but do not pin your dreams on such gentlemen. They are fickle with their affections, and content to remain bachelors. Enjoy their flattery, but look beyond them to the gentlemen who follow. One of them will step forward and become your future husband."

Chapter Seven

For all of her father's assurances, neither Lord Norgrave nor the Duke of Blackbern had left his calling card with their butler that week. As Imogene had sifted through the pile of cards with their butler, Sandwick, she had to admit her father had been correct that the gentlemen's interest would encourage other suitors. Much to her sister's amusement, she had too many of them—so many she could barely recall most of their names.

Her mother had declared the attention her elder daughter was garnering as encouraging.

Faint praise indeed from a lady who, in her time, had captured the Duke of Trevett's eye and eventually won his heart.

To celebrate Imogene's rise within the *beau monde*, more dresses, bonnets, fans, shoes, and stockings were ordered. A dancing master was employed to refine her dance steps and arms so she moved as if she was one of the nine muses: Terpsichore, the goddess of dance who had stepped down from Mount Olympus with a laurel crown adorning her head and a lyre cradled in her arms.

This evening's amusements would begin at the King's

Theater. Imogene and her mother were sharing the theater box with her friend Cassia and her mother, Lady Golding. They were attending the first performance of the opera *Dido, Queen of Carthage*. The music had been composed by a Mr. Storace and the lead character would be played by Madame Mara. Even if not a single gentleman visited their private box, Imogene was too excited to let it ruin her evening.

Cassia inclined her head. "Imogene, is that not Lord Asher?"

To her left, she noticed the gentleman who was partially responsible for her colliding into the Duke of Blackbern. The gentleman raised his hand in greeting. She acknowledged him with a soft smile.

"It is."

"Oh look, he is leaving his box. I wonder which box he is planning to visit?" Cassia teased.

Lady Golding touched her daughter lightly on the arm with her shut fan. "Even if you know the answer, you and Imogene will display your surprise at his appearance. It is to your advantage not to seem too eager, ladies."

She turned her attention back to the duchess when Cassia and Imogene nodded.

"I pray Lord Asher will keep his heel off my hem," Imogene whispered to her friend. "If I go over the balcony, I will do more than tear the hem."

They giggled, earning a silent warning from the duchess.

Imogene sighed. In London there were so many rules to follow.

* * *

Tristan would have preferred to pass the evening at one of his clubs, but his concerns over Norgrave's next move with Lady Imogene left him edgy and in pursuit of his unpredictable friend. A brief stop at the marquess's residence and a chat with the butler revealed that the man had planned to enjoy the theater this evening. Norgrave rarely secured his own private theater box for such occasions because he preferred to circulate from box to box. In the past, Tristan often joined him on these outings, but the wager had turned them into friendly rivals.

The first private box he visited was Jewel Tierney's, since she and Norgrave still managed to have an amiable arrangement even though she was no longer his mistress. The dark-haired courtesan was seated with four female companions. He immediately recognized Eunice, but he was not acquainted with the others. Any man who hoped to have a private introduction to one of Jewel's protégées would not approach the box until he was invited.

"Good evening, Jewel," Tristan said, inclining his head. "Ladies. My apologies for intruding, but I am looking for Norgrave. Have you seen him?"

"Your Grace," Jewel said, extending her hand to establish that they were old friends. She had deliberately used his title to alert her companions that they had captured the attention of a gentleman who was worthy of their interest. "This is a delightful surprise. I have not seen you in months. You have neglected your good friends."

Eunice was shyly glancing down at her shoes as if she was a young innocent who was too overcome with excitement to gaze into the eyes of a potential suitor. She played the role quite well. Tristan might have been fooled if the young courtesan had not proven she was quite skilled with her mouth.

"Alas, I have had little time for amusements," he said apologetically, his voice laced with feigned regret. There were other gentlemen who would claim these women for the evening, and he had no intention of ruining their prospects by rudely dismissing them.

Jewel frowned as she studied his face. "You work too hard, Blackbern. Perhaps you would like to sit with us. The five of us could undoubtedly help you forget your burdens."

Tristan laughed. "Of that, I have no doubt," he said, recalling past evenings that he had enjoyed with Jewel and her friends. The woman knew how to cloud a man's head with lust and leave him pleasantly exhausted. "Unfortunately, I must regretfully decline since I must find Norgrave."

Jewel arched her right brow. "What if I could direct you to Norgrave? Once your business with him has concluded, you and the marquess would be most welcome in my private box."

Her catlike grin let him know that the courtesan was not referring to the theater.

"You are very generous, Jewel." If he gave her any encouragement, he could spend a very invigorating evening in her bed. "Once I find our friend, I will mention your invitation."

She pouted at his polite rejection. Jewel had made several attempts to coax him back into her bed, but he had lost interest years ago when they had parted ways.

"Very well. If you direct your gaze up one tier and to the right, you will see him."

Tristan nodded, his gaze already searching the dimly lit theater boxes.

However, it wasn't Norgrave who caught and held his gaze, it was Lady Imogene. Delight washed through him like a tropical breeze. It cooled when he recognized one of the women as the Duchess of Trevett. He was unfamiliar with the other ladies seated on either side of her.

The ladies were not alone.

Four male admirers had charmed their way into the private box. Although they were being respectful and engaging of the women, Tristan suspected that all of them were there for Imogene. He recognized them, but it was one gentleman in particular that had him gnashing his teeth.

Norgrave.

That lying bastard!

What was the point of setting ground rules if the man intended to ignore them?

"Is something amiss, Your Grace?" Jewel asked, using her gilt scissors-glasses to peer at the private theater box that he was glowering at. "Who is the owner of the box?"

Jewel only concerned herself with the gentlemen of the *beau monde*.

Unaware if Norgrave had confided in the courtesan about the wager, Tristan preferred to avoid mentioning Lady Imogene's name. "The Duchess of Trevett is likely the owner," he said carefully, watching for any signs of recognition.

He saw none.

"It appears our Norgrave aspires higher than his rank," Jewel said, unconcerned how it might influence her relationship with the marquess.

"He always has," Tristan replied, his gaze lingering on Norgrave. "I will give him your regards, Jewel." He inclined his head, ignoring the look of disappointment that flashed in Eunice's eyes. "Enjoy your evening, ladies."

Tristan left the courtesans' box, and was not surprised that several gentlemen were waiting just beyond the closed curtains for admittance. His first inclination was to head directly to the duchess's private theater box and separate Lady Imogene from the marquess. Norgrave was not to be trusted. It was a flaw he was intimately acquainted with, but the stakes seemed significantly higher.

He had no intention of letting his friend win this wager.

Indignation carried him halfway to the private theater box before logic overruled his anger. His steps slowed. He did not have to ruin Norgrave's plans. The dragon—uh, Her Grace—would ensure no harm would come to her daughter. The duchess was too shrewd to be swayed by Norgrave's considerable charm. Imogene was safe from his friend's machinations for the moment.

The marquess had done him a favor. If he could break the rules, so would Tristan.

He smiled in anticipation.

The realization that her life was about to change began at breakfast when their butler, Sandwick, brought in a bouquet of roses from Lord Asher. Thirty minutes later, a bouquet of chrysanthemums from Mr. Scropes arrived, followed by a basket of fruit from Lord Coddington, and a single rose from Lord Barrentine.

"You carried yourself well last evening, daughter," the duchess had told her as she read the notes sent with each token of affection. "Your father will be pleased when he learns that Lord Coddington has formally declared his interest in you."

The earl was a distant cousin of the King, and his father was a friend of her mother's family. Imogene had known the gentleman since she was a child, but he had always treated her as if she was an irritating younger sister. Until the basket arrived, she had assumed his brief visit to their private theater box had been based on nothing more than friendship.

Leaving her mother and sister to their morning repast, Imogene left the breakfast room so she could ponder these new developments in private. Sandwick managed to catch her before she reached the stairs.

"Another bouquet has arrived for you, my lady."

Imogene was about to instruct the butler to give her mother the bouquet, when curiosity got the better of her. There had been one other gentleman who had lingered in their private box.

The Marquess of Norgrave.

He had flirted with all of the ladies, but she caught him staring at her numerous times. Had he also sent her flowers?

"Is there a note or card, Sandwick?" She glanced at the bouquet. Her admirer must have emptied one of the flower carts in Covent Garden. The butler's arms were filled with gladiolus, rhododendrons, bleeding hearts, roses, freesia, and geraniums. "Never mind, you have enough to manage. I will get the card."

A slow smile spread across her face as she glanced at the calling card. The bouquet was not from Lord Norgrave as she had assumed. It was from the Duke of Blackbern. He had scribbled something on the back of the card.

> *Have you taken a drive through Hyde Park?*
> *I will come for you at one o'clock.*
> *—B*

"Presumptuous," she muttered to herself, though she had half expected to see him at Lord Norgrave's side.

"Is something wrong, my lady?" the butler inquired.

"No . . . it is nothing," Imogene assured the servant. "It appears I have an engagement this afternoon."

"Have I mentioned how much I appreciate a lady who is prompt?" Blackbern said three hours later as they entered the park.

"During our brief acquaintance, I do not believe the subject has come up," Imogene said, still dwelling on the duke's reaction when she descended the staircase. She was wearing her new carriage dress and bonnet, and the masculine focus in his eyes had warmed her blood and sent her heart racing.

"I tend to get distracted when a lady is wiggling on top of me," he said dryly. The corners of his mouth curled as she huffed and sputtered over his outrageous remark. "Nevertheless, I would have eventually gotten to the finer points."

"I wish you would stop referring to our accident as something wanton," Imogene said. This time the warmth creeping up her neck was embarrassment. "You make it sound as if I deliberately ambushed you."

"It was a memorable encounter," he said, the source of her discomfort sounding too pleased with himself. "I have never had a lady throw herself at me in such a manner."

"Good grief," she exclaimed. "What will it take to make you stop mentioning it? My mother—"

"A kiss."

Imogene gaped at him. She could not have heard him correctly. "Your Grace—" she began.

"You asked my price," Blackbern reminded her as he signaled the horses to halt. Still grasping the reins, he met her stunned gaze. "I must admit that I enjoy teasing you, but if you wish me to stop, you must silence me with a kiss."

"No."

"A simple kiss. What is the harm, Lady Imogene?" he asked, sounding as if he demanded kisses from every female who crossed his path.

The notion of kissing the duke made her tremble. Her gaze dropped to his mouth. She thought of his full, firm lips pressing against her mouth. Unconsciously, she licked her lips to moisten them. His eyelids narrowed as he watched her and waited for her to decide.

The choice was hers.

"I do not know. We should not," she said, trying to think of a good reason why she should not kiss him.

"You know you want to . . . and we should," he said,

his eyes silently daring her to take the risk. "Just lean forward and kiss me. It is not overly complicated."

Imogene was torn. She knew she should tell him to go to the devil for tormenting her with his childish dare. However, the woman in her wanted to know how his lips felt against hers.

"Your word."

He grinned at her. "I promise it will not hurt."

Before she could choose the coward's path, she leaned forward and kissed him. Hastily, she withdrew.

"I am not your cousin or father, Lady Imogene," he teased. "You can do better."

Imogene sighed. Naturally, he would not make this easy for her. She leaned forward again, her gaze resting on his mouth. He had a beautiful mouth. She closed her eyes and lightly brushed her lips against his.

Once. Twice. Thrice.

Soft featherlike kisses. On the fourth pass, she lingered a few seconds as if to test them both. When his lips parted, she pulled away.

"Are you satisfied, Your Grace?"

Blackbern shut his eyes as if he was struggling to find the right words. When he opened his eyes again, what she glimpsed had her stomach fluttering.

"You are full of surprises, Lady Imogene," he murmured as he shook his head. "Your kiss has granted you a reprieve." He gave her a long side-glance. "For a few days."

Imogene stifled a groan as he urged the horses forward. She should have expected the duke's reprieve would only be temporary.

Chapter Eight

Almost five days had passed before she encountered the Duke of Blackbern and Lord Norgrave again. She might have believed the gentlemen had lost interest in her as her father had predicted. There had even been moments when she was so distracted by her growing circle of admirers that she forgot to search the other theater boxes or the ballrooms for them.

A part of her would have relished tossing her betrothal to another gentleman in their faces. She could just imagine Blackbern's reaction to the news. He and Norgrave might not be in love with her, but they were too arrogant to accept that she preferred someone else's company.

She glanced at her dance card and noted the name written down. Before she could move away from the marble column, an arm came around her waist and lifted her slightly off her feet to gain her compliance. Her backside was pressed against a warm, muscled wall that was unquestionably male.

"Miss me?"

"Ugh, no, I did not!" Imogene turned her face away, but she could not avoid Norgrave's quick kiss on her cheek. "Release me at once," she said, prying his arm away from her waist. "Do you lurk behind pillars to waylay unsuspecting ladies?"

She had missed him, but he did not deserve to know the truth.

"A desperate man resorts to unsavory measures when he has neglected his lady." Satisfied that he had her attention, he freed her and stepped back to admire her. "Why, Lady Imogene, you look positively scrumptious. If you would like to take a stroll with me in the gardens, I am certain we could find a quiet spot for me to test my theory."

He waggled his eyebrows at her.

"I believe I will reject your generous offer, my lord," Imogene said haughtily. "And let me be clear. I am decidedly *not* your lady, so practice your unsavory measures elsewhere. Now if you will excuse me, I have promised Mr. Edgecomb my next dance."

Her chin high, she started to leave, but he grasped her hand and halted her escape.

"Edgecomb is a dilettante and his hand is as limp as his—"

"Not another word," Imogene ordered. She covered her mouth with her hand, her eyes gleaming with mirth. "You are a very wicked man, Norgrave."

"Coming from you, my dear, I take that as a high compliment." Before she could protest, he hooked his arm through hers and escorted her to the middle of the ballroom. "You can do much better than Edgecomb, my dear Imogene."

"I never said that he was courting me," she said

mildly. "I merely accepted his invitation to dance the minuet."

"Dancing with the wrong gentleman would hurt your reputation." Norgrave's expression darkened as he noticed Mr. Edgecomb's nimble approach. "My apologies, Edgecomb. Your tardiness has cost you dearly. If you hurry, you might find another dance partner."

The marquess silenced the man's objection with a cutting glance. He nodded to Imogene and headed in the opposite direction.

"Mr. Edgecomb was not late," she whispered as they joined two other couples. "What you did was unkind."

"I disagree," Norgrave replied. He stood opposite her and bowed. "And I saw you first."

Actually, Blackbern had met her first, but she refrained from mentioning it.

Imogene and the two other ladies curtsied to their partners. She placed her right hand within the marquess's and they faced forward. With a spring in her step they took several steps forward, and then backward. The three couples pivoted to face each other. They stepped right and left, and circled in place. The ladies joined hands and the gentlemen mirrored their actions. In a line they stepped forward and retreated. In perfect formation, the men claimed their lady's left hand and Imogene walked with Norgrave between the lines they had formed. He released her hand and she bowed her head to walk under the arch the two ladies had formed with their arms. The marquess did the same, and they took their new positions at the end of the line.

The couples repeated the dance steps, each pair

alternating their positions. Imogene was pleased with her performance. Her skills had improved under the critical eye of her dancing master. Norgrave was a competent partner. More than one lady was watching him as they danced.

With a parting grin to her partner she bent her head to walk under the arch her female companions had formed. The sudden appearance of a new lady flustered Imogene. Without thinking, she accepted the woman's hand and stepped forward as she was prepared to circle about to join Norgrave, but her hand was suddenly released and the unknown lady assumed her place in the line.

Her dancing master had neglected to mention this part of the dance. Before she could pout, the two ladies from a different set grasped her hands and stepped forward so they could greet their gentlemen.

Her mouth fell open when she realized the Duke of Blackbern was her new dance partner.

"Is that an invitation to kiss you, Lady Imogene?"

"Certainly not!" she said, ignoring the chuckles from her companions. Only her hours with the dancing master kept her from muddling the steps required. She offered the duke her hand and they promenaded and separated. "Did you conspire with that woman to get her to switch places?"

"Naturally," he freely admitted. "You should have seen Norgrave's thunderous expression when I had you plucked from right under his nose. I thought he might challenge me on the spot."

She and Blackbern moved gracefully together. At a glance, they gave the impression of familiarity.

"You could have waited your turn."

His eyes were brimming with appreciation as his gaze lingered south of her face. "I was growing impatient. Besides, I have a habit of taking what I want."

Imogene rolled her eyes as she stepped away from the duke. She had not made up her mind what her dance partner desired more—her or baiting the marquess. "Does the rivalry between you and Norgrave ever get tiresome?"

She squared her shoulders and then slid into a graceful curtsy and he formally bowed, a signal that the dance had ended. Before she could walk away, he stalked toward her. He grasped her by the elbow and escorted her in the opposite direction from Norgrave.

"I need to apologize for your rudeness," she said, although she allowed him to direct their course because her struggles would have drawn attention to them.

"Later," he said, his face a rigid mask of determination.

She could hardly fathom that she had thought she missed these two scoundrels.

The duke abruptly spun her in a half circle and she felt a solid wall against her back. "Blackbern—"

"Hush!" he ordered before he sealed his mouth over hers.

Imogene did not try to avoid his mouth. He murmured his approval when she lifted her chin and parted her lips. Her tongue met his and she sagged against the wall where he had pinned her. The duke knew how to kiss a lady.

Blackbern seized her by the shoulders as he tore his mouth away. He was out of breath and there was something in his expression that made her want to flee from him. "Little fool, you are not supposed to encourage me," he exclaimed, behaving as if she was tormenting him.

Imogene smiled. "I like encouraging you, Your Grace."

His expression was incredulous, as if he could not believe she was daring him to kiss her again. "You have caused me enough trouble, Lady Imogene. Now run back to Norgrave and offer him an apology. You can thank me later for distracting him. He is too angry with me to consider any mischief with you."

Her spirits plummeted at his explanation. "You kissed me to provoke your friend?"

"Of course," he said carelessly, seemingly oblivious to her pained expression. "When I kiss a lady, I prefer to do it in private so I can take my time."

Imogene's lips betrayed her by trembling.

Blackbern noticed and took a hesitant step toward her. "Lady Imogene."

"Thank you for the dance and the lesson in ballroom etiquette," she said, slipping under his arm so she could put distance between them before she disgraced herself by crying.

"Imogene!"

She ignored his plea to return to him. He was a true scoundrel and she had to remind herself of that fact. Blinded by self-loathing and fury, she stepped right into Norgrave's arms.

"Sweet lady, has someone upset you?"

Imogene was in no mood to indulge either gentleman this evening. "Not in the slightest," she lied. "If you will excuse me, I intend to spend some time upstairs in the drawing room set aside for the female guests."

Norgrave cast a speculative look over her shoulder. She refused to glance back to see if the duke was observing them. "Of course, my dear. We will talk later after you have recovered from your upset."

Her gaze focused on the floor, she resisted the urge to run toward the nearest door. If she was fortunate, she might find something to purge the foul taste of Blackbern from her mouth.

"Feeling better?"

Imogene had not expected to find Norgrave waiting for her when she reemerged from the ladies' saloon. He unfolded his crossed arms and straightened from his slouched position against the wall as she approached.

"You did not have to wait for me, my lord," she said, her emotions too close to the surface to fence words with the marquess.

He frowned at her. "You were upset. If I were to wager a guess, I suspect Blackbern had something to do with it."

"I do not wish to speak of it," she replied, her mouth thinning at the reminder that the duke had kissed her to bait the gentleman walking beside her.

"Of course," Norgrave said solicitously. "It was not my intention to distress you further by mentioning a certain gentleman."

He guided her along a passageway she had not explored earlier, and down the stairs. She was not quite ready to return to the ballroom. Nor was she ready to face the duke.

"What is it?" he asked, noticing that her pace had slowed with each step.

"I cannot—" She shook her head, unwilling to explain her feelings about his closest friend. The two gentlemen were behaving as if they were rivals for her affection, but she did not trust the marquess not to reveal their conversation to the duke. "You go ahead. I am not quite ready to return to the ballroom."

Her admission pleased Norgrave.

"Perhaps I can offer you a compromise," he said rather mysteriously, before he led her through a side door. Instead of opening into another room, the door opened into a narrow gallery above the ballroom. "This way, you can enjoy the ball and my company."

Imogene returned his smile, knowing she should not encourage him. Between Norgrave and Blackbern, she could not decide which gentleman was more arrogant. She was certain if she asked her companion for his opinion, he would view her complaint as a compliment.

"Do you often spend your evenings observing people?"

"You would be amazed what some people will do when they think they are not being observed," he said, wiggling his eyebrows in an exaggerated manner.

Imogene laughed, and continued down the gallery that circled the ballroom. They were not the only spectators. She stopped from time to time, and took a moment to view the guests below. Norgrave was correct. It was amusing to watch the awkward introductions, the groups of matrons sharing gossip as they observed their daughters from a distance, the fortune hunters seeking out potential heiresses, and the young couples stealing a few minutes of privacy in the alcove.

"You are quite brilliant, my lord. This is more entertaining than the theater," she declared.

"I have always thought so," he said, staring at her with an indulgent expression on his handsome face.

They had moved away from the dancers, and were positioned above the open doors that led to the back terrace. Imogene glanced across the ballroom and casually noticed a man and woman. A potted tree obscured the couple, but they appeared to be engaged in an intimate conversation. She braced her gloved hands on the railing to see what would happen next.

Any amusement she was feeling slipped away when the gentleman turned his head to reveal that she was staring at the Duke of Blackbern. The marquess stepped closer until her body was caged by his.

"Ah, I had wondered where Blackbern had gone," he said, tilting his head as if he was attempting to discern the identity of the duke's companion. He did not seem particularly surprised that his friend had lured his female companion into one of the alcoves. "I had not realized—" He broke off as if he was reluctant to finish his thoughts.

"Realized what, Lord Norgrave?"

"Norgrave will suffice, my dear lady," he said absently, his hand covering hers. The marquess nodded in the couple's direction. "Blackbern and Lady Flosham. It appears our mutual friend is keeping secrets."

"Secrets?" she echoed weakly. Imogene watched as the duke lowered his head. It was impossible to discern if he was kissing the lady or merely speaking to her.

"The Countess of Flosham," Norgrave said, oblivious

to Imogene's growing disquiet. "She and Blackbern shared a very close friendship five years ago. Although their liaison lasted only a few months, our friend was quite smitten with her. She was the one to break their connection out of respect for her husband. There was some speculation a few years ago when her husband perished in an accident that the duke would renew his acquaintance with his former love. I suppose he was giving her time to mourn the loss of her husband."

"I see," Imogene said, not understanding the grief and disappointment welling up within her. She had no claim on the Duke of Blackbern. He had flirted and kissed her, but it had been her misfortune to assume he had been developing feelings for her. When he had kissed her earlier to make Norgrave envious, she had naively assumed his devotion had been genuine.

"It is quite admirable of the duke to take into account the countess's feelings for her husband," she said, striving not to reveal her own feelings on the matter. "She is a fortunate lady to find two good gentlemen in her life."

The curious look Norgrave sent her hinted that he was not entirely convinced that she was as unmoved by Blackbern's fickle affections as she appeared.

"You know, when I first saw you, I thought you superficially resembled Lady Flosham. You are both blondes and close in stature and looks," he said, his keen perusal studying her from head to toe. "When Blackbern expressed an interest in meeting you, I had wondered if he was thinking of his countess."

His countess.

The thought of their earlier kiss sickened her. Had he been thinking of Lady Flosham all along?

"I can see that I have been thoughtless," Norgrave murmured, drawing her away from the railing and blocking her view of the couple. "Until I saw your face, I had no idea that you had developed feelings for Blackbern."

"No," Imogene denied, appalled that her affection for the duke was so apparent. "I do not love him."

The marquess nodded at her fierce declaration. "Very wise of you. Blackbern is a decent fellow, but he is unable to resist a fair face. I do what I can to shield young ladies from my friend's flawed nature, but there is little I can do for a bruised heart."

"You are a good friend, Norgrave," she said, her throat feeling scratchy and raw. "I appreciate the warning, but I see Blackbern for the scoundrel he is. I do not have a bruised heart," she lied, desperately wanting to believe it.

Norgrave nodded with approval. "You are a sweet, clever girl, Imogene. I realize Blackbern saw you first, but it is my fondest wish that you might consider me a worthy substitute when it comes to matters of the heart."

"My lord, I do not know what to say," Imogene whispered, wondering if she might have felt differently if Norgrave had been the gentleman she had crashed into the night of the Kingabys' ball. "I do not view you as any man's substitute."

His grin widened. "Then I am a fortunate man."

Before she could guess his intentions, the marquess kissed her. With the image of Blackbern and his lady-love burned into her brain, Imogene eagerly tipped her chin up so their mouths met in hopes Norgrave could wipe away the lingering trace of the duke's kisses.

For a few minutes, the marquess actually succeeded.
When Norgrave stepped away and her head cleared,
Imogene realized how far she had fallen for Blackbern—
and she did not know what she was going to do about it.

Chapter Nine

Days earlier, she had been disappointed by Lord Norgrave and the Duke of Blackbern's absence. Now she wished they would find another lady to tease and play their wicked games. The marquess left his card two days in a row with Sandwick, when their butler had told him that Lady Imogene wasn't receiving visitors. The duke had also left his card with the promise that he would call on her this afternoon. On the back of his card, he had scrawled in his distinctive handwriting:

> *You cannot avoid me forever.*
> *—B*

Blackbern would be astounded what she was capable of when she was annoyed. It was precisely the reason why she had accepted the invitation to join her friends on a picnic. No one with the Blackbern or Norgrave titles had been invited. She had made inquiries in advance. After being manipulated into kissing both men, she came to the realization that she lacked the sophistication to be much of a challenge for such jaded gentlemen.

Unless they coveted her because she was a daughter of a duke. An alliance with her family would be prized, she thought. However, her mother was convinced that marriage was not what interested the duke and his friend.

Imogene was determined to banish both gentlemen from her thoughts.

"Lady Imogene," Lord Asher called out, distracting her from her dour musings. "I would be honored if you would walk with me."

Her friend Cassia nudged her when she failed to immediately respond to his invitation. She had been sitting on a blanket with Cassia, Miss Faston, and two other ladies. Lord Asher had accompanied the recently married Mr. and Mrs. Hewitt. Cassia viewed the earl's efforts as dreadfully romantic, and she predicted the gentleman would declare his intentions to Imogene's father in the near future. Lord Asher was clumsy around her, but he was courteous, intelligent, and the consummate gentleman. The thought would never occur to him to drag her off in a scandalous manner and then kiss her senseless.

Imogene frowned. Some hours, she truly despised the Duke of Blackbern. When she reached the point that she could hold on to her hate for an entire day, she would finally be cured of him. And Lord Norgrave, too, she silently added. His kisses were not as devastating, but he was equally dangerous.

"Imogene," Cassia whispered.

She shook her head and smiled at the earl. "Forgive me, Lord Asher. Of course I would love to join you. A stroll will shake off the lingering lethargy of our meal."

She offered her hand and he rushed forward to assist her. The toe of one of his shoes caught the edge of the blanket and the poor man lost his balance. Several ladies shrieked in dismay as he fell and landed on Miss Faston.

"Good heavens!" Imogene exclaimed as she and Cassia grabbed the humiliated earl and struggled to help him to his feet. Lord Asher and his unfortunate victim were not helping matters by flailing about. "Miss Faston, are you hurt?"

"No harm done," the lady wheezed. "My lord, if you could just remove your elbow from my middle."

Imogene watched in fascination as Lord Asher's face deepened into a dark red hue.

"I do beg your pardon," he rasped, struggling to free himself from the awkward tangle of limbs. "Lady Imogene and Miss Mead, if you could release my arms, I may actually be able to do more than flop about like a fish."

She and Cassia dropped his arms as if they had been stung.

Masculine laughter drifted behind her. Imogene's eyelids narrowed into slits. She recognized that voice.

Blackbern.

Imogene cocked her head to the side so she could glare at him. "Why do you not be useful for a change and help us, Your Grace?"

Everyone froze at her waspish tone. She supposed it was highly disrespectful for her to order the duke about like a footman, but he deserved it for chasing after her as if he was pursuing a fox on a hunt.

The duke greeted her anger with his usual aplomb. "Not sleeping well, darling, or is it your monthlies?"

"You fiend!" Imogene shouted, too vexed to be polite. She stepped away from the duke before she threw something at him.

"If I was a betting man, I would wager it was her monthlies." Blackbern braced his hands on his knees as he crouched down. He sent an apologetic glance to Miss Faston. "I beg your pardon, dear lady. Your patience is about to be rewarded." He seized the earl and effortlessly hauled him off the blanket. "Let me guess what happened. You were distracted by Lady Imogene's smile."

"Something like that," Lord Asher muttered, refusing to look at anyone.

Imogene could sympathize with the gentleman. She was appalled that the duke had humiliated her in front of her friends and Lord Asher, not to mention the false intimacy he inferred discussing personal matters such as her monthlies.

As if he had the right to know!

Blackbern was kind enough to assist Miss Faston to her feet. She stiffened when he glanced in her direction. "Come along, Imogene. You have caused enough mischief for the afternoon."

"Me?" Imogene took a step back. Everyone was watching her and the duke as if they were players on a stage. "I was attempting to help."

"You might begin by scrubbing a little soot on your cheeks or perhaps consider wearing a sack over your head when you are strolling about in public. Your beauty is giving us mortal men heart failure, and casts other ladies in an unflattering light."

"Hear, hear," mumbled Miss Faston.

"Miss Faston," Imogene exclaimed, dismayed that she had lost an ally. "Do not encourage him."

Blackbern thinks I am beautiful?

The woman shook her head. "I have the right to complain since Lord Asher failed to see me until he actually fell on me like a mighty oak tree."

"Permit me to apologize again for my clumsiness," Lord Asher said, recovering some of his dignity when Miss Faston complimented his impressive physique.

"Bid your friends farewell, my goddess," Blackbern said, capturing her wrist as if he expected her to cause him more trouble. "We have an appointment to keep."

Cassia was the only one who appeared uncertain about leaving Imogene to the duke's tender mercies. "What should I tell your mother?"

"Tell her nothing." The distance between her and her companions was widening with each step. "I will explain everything."

Blackbern had the audacity to laugh. "Not very skilled at lying, are you?" Without asking her permission, he lifted her into his carriage. "If you need a tutor, I am available. I am well versed in this particular art."

"I will pass on your offer," Imogene said, rearranging her skirt.

"You might be amazed what I can teach you," was the duke's enigmatic reply. The carriage dipped as he settled in beside her. "I know I am curious to see how brave you are."

His challenge had managed to silence Imogene. She was still angry, her posture seemed to convey her defiance and contempt toward him for sins real and imaginary. Tristan had never found troublesome chits appealing, but there was something about Imogene that made him want to ruffle her sleek feathers. He wondered what would happen if he taught her to channel her outrage into passion. The results might be worth facing the dragon's wrath.

It was obvious Imogene had inherited her fierce temper from her mother.

Their companionable quiet lasted ten minutes.

"I am not talking to you."

He bit the inside of his cheek and offered no opinion.

She huffed and muttered under her breath. "I cannot believe you speculated on my monthlies." Her lower lip quivered as if she was contemplating to sulk about it the entire drive.

To spare himself the grief, he said, "In my experience—"

"As far as I know, you do not have a mother, sister, or wife," she said, tapping her fingers as if each one was important. "Do not presume to share your opinion on the subject because any knowledge you possess likely came from other gentlemen."

Her uncharacteristic bluntness hit close enough to the mark for him to wince, but she had forgotten another sort of female—a mistress. Since there was no benefit to winning the argument, he held his tongue. However, there were other ways to bait his prickly companion. "So was I correct? Is that why you were so angry with me?"

"The subject is not open for discussion," she said in forbidding tones. "As for the reason why I was angry . . . you embarrassed me in front of my friends. You spoke to me as if we were—we were—" She audibly swallowed and shook her head.

Her shy, awkward manner disarmed him. His expression softened as he took pity on her. "I implied a certain intimacy."

Instead of pouting, she nibbled on her lower lip. "That we are lovers? Yes. It was cruel of you and it was wrong to give them a false impression about our friendship."

"Why do you assume it is false?" he softly countered, tugging on the reins to slow his horses. Securing the reins, he turned until his knees brushed against her skirt. "I am beguiled, my lady." He allowed her a minute to ponder his declaration. "If given the slightest encouragement, I would seize it. I would tutor you in the carnal arts, and we would become intimate. Lovers. I could show you a side of your nature you have been forced to bind with whalebone and layers of linen and silk. I would show you pleasure beyond your wildest dreams, drugging your senses with my lips, my fingers, and my cock."

Her cheeks turned pink at his frank language. "You are not supposed to speak to me like this." She was only beginning to comprehend what he had sensed from their first meeting.

"Why? I am offering you a glimpse of the future. It is your choice."

It won't be if Norgrave has it his way.

She shook her head as if denying their attraction would quell it. He desired her. The damn wager might have spurred him into action, but she had unknowingly sealed her fate when she had accidentally collided into him. Each meeting whetted his appetite, leaving him yearning for a few more minutes with her, a flirtatious glance, and the sound of her laughter caressing him like a lover's hand.

Lust nibbled at his restraint until he thought he might go mad if he did not bed her. He had seriously contemplated losing himself in another woman, but he had dismissed the notion the moment she had kissed him.

Imogene was unaware of the power she had over him. His virginal goddess had placed a spell on him, and a part of him resented her for it. He felt as if she had gelded him, because no other lady would do until he could break the enchantment.

Her sudden wariness made him realize that he had been staring at her lips. He retrieved the reins, and they continued the drive. This time, he was heartened by her silence. She was not screaming at him, demanding that he return her to her parents.

"I am astounded you have thought of me at all," she finally said. "The last time I saw you, you were kissing a redheaded woman."

Tristan did not have to guess how she felt about it. His gaze unerringly found hers, and he was not immune to the hurt in her dark blue eyes. "The redhead is an old friend."

"Norgrave told me that she was your mistress."

He silently cursed his friend for his helpfulness. "The lady and I have some history," he said, treading carefully. "And for the record, the lady kissed me."

"I felt nothing but pity as I watched you fight her off," she said dryly.

He grinned at a hint of jealousy in her voice. "Well, I did not wish to be rude. There was a time when she was a good friend. A *very* good friend," he teased.

Imogene's chin tilted a degree north. She shrugged. "It is your business."

Tristan chuckled. "Have you not been listening, Imogene? The redhead is an old friend, and whatever our arrangement, it was a long time ago. Norgrave implied otherwise in hopes that you would turn to him for comfort." An unpleasant thought occurred to him. "Did he succeed?"

She suddenly found the countryside fascinating. The faint blush on her cheeks confirmed his suspicion.

Norgrave was a cunning bastard.

"You kissed him."

Tristan wanted to quietly murder his friend for touching her. Nor was he happy with her behavior, though he conceded that the marquess could be quite convincing. If given a choice, Norgrave preferred lies over truth.

Ten minutes later, she and Blackbern had arrived at their destination. She glanced at her dress in dismay. She was properly attired for social visits.

"What are you thinking?" she asked guardedly.

"I am tempted to paddle your backside," the duke confessed. He disembarked from the carriage and took a few minutes to secure the horses. "Though I am willing to forgive you for a price. A kiss will suffice."

The man was incorrigible. It was difficult to remain annoyed with him when Blackbern was so determined to tease her out of her foul mood. During the drive, Imogene had already decided to forgive him. She accepted his hand, and mischievously grinned up at him once both shoes were firmly planted on the dirt road. "If you want a kiss, you will have to catch me first!"

She grasped her skirts and rushed toward the lake in the distance. Needless to say, she ignored his command to slow down. In Blackbern's company, she felt her first taste of freedom. He encouraged her spirited nature, and dared her to explore boundaries she had never considered crossing until she had met him. Glancing over her shoulder, she noted the duke had grabbed a blanket and basket before he chased after her. His burdens had not slowed him down because he was quickly catching up to her.

"Keep running, darling," Blackbern said, his laughter making her shiver with anticipation. "Though I should warn you that I always catch what I pursue."

She had no doubt he spoke the truth.

Pulling on the ribbons under her chin, she tugged off her bonnet and threw it over her shoulder. The duke swore as he dodged to avoid trampling it. She followed the edge of the small lake, heading for the taller grass where she glimpsed what appeared to be an old red brick folly. It was an impressive three-turret structure with a stone veranda that nature had been slowly claiming.

Before she could reach the folly, strong arms encircled her waist and the landscape tilted and whirled as he spun them about.

"Caught you," he growled, his lips brushing her ear as he embraced her from the back. "What shall I do with you?"

She noticed the wicker basket and the blanket had been discarded several yards away. "You could always feed me since it appears you have brought me on my second picnic for the day."

"You should have been waiting for me in your mother's drawing room, not flirting with Lord Asher." He pulled her closer. "Besides, I hunger, my lady, but not for food."

Imogene trembled in his embrace. His words did not merely fill her ears. His voice slipped beneath the layers of clothing and caressed her skin like warm smoke. Her nipples tightened in response. She danced out of his arms and turned around to face him once she was beyond his reach.

"Kissing you always leads to trouble, Blackbern," she teased, even though she was eager for him to kiss her again. "I would not wish to give you the wrong impression."

The duke casually removed and discarded his coat. "And what impression would that be, my sweet Imogene?" His striped waistcoat landed on his coat.

The only gentleman she had seen without his coat was her father. Her eyes widened as she stared at the white linen stretched across his chest. In the sunlight, the whiteness was almost blinding.

"I would not wish you to think that I will surrender my virtue to you."

And have you treat me as casually as you did the red-head.

Blackbern stalked toward her. "I like how you flirt with me."

"You do?" She smiled and moved again, keeping out of his reach.

The duke grinned as they circled around each other. "Indeed." He feinted left, and she gleefully squealed when his fingers brushed her hip. "You tease me until I would sell my soul for a taste of you."

Imogene smirked at him. "That does not seem very sporting of me."

"You are worth the challenge and the torture."

He abruptly lunged for her. Imogene shrieked and ducked under his outstretched arms. She ran in the direction of the folly, but Blackbern was close on her heels. He easily caught her against him and they tumbled onto the grass. She was breathless from the chase and her side ached from laughing.

Imogene was grateful he had ruined her outing with her friends.

Blackbern rolled onto his side and she reclined on her back. He tenderly smoothed away the strands of hair covering her face.

"I must look frightful," she said, her discomfort growing at his serious expression.

"Not in the slightest. In the sunlight, the hair curling around your face looks like spun gold and honey. Your eyes remind me of a cloudless sky, and your lips—"

"My lips?" she echoed.

"Forbidden fruit," he murmured, tracing the contour of her shapely lips with his finger. "Which happens to be my favorite sweet—and the one temptation I cannot resist."

To prove it, he leaned forward and kissed her. His mouth was gentle and coaxing against hers. She felt his hand on her shoulder, and he pulled her closer so her body molded against his. Blackbern tasted like salt and sunshine, and a flavor that seemed to belong uniquely to him. Her lips parted, and to her delight he took advantage of her silent invitation. His tongue speared into hers and dueled with hers, the soft press of flesh against flesh making her lightheaded.

A wordless sound of disappointment hummed in her throat when he stopped.

"Blanket," he muttered. He grasped her hands and pulled her to her feet. "Your dress is too lovely to ruin, and I know the perfect place for our picnic."

"Your Grace," she said, when he left her to retrieve their basket of food and the blanket.

"Tristan," he corrected, over his shoulder. "You can call me Blackbern in front of others, but it would please me to hear my name upon your lips."

His stride was purposeful as he returned to her. His fingers tangled with hers, and he led her to the folly that had intrigued her.

"How old is it?" she asked, squinting against the sunlight.

"The foundation dates back to the sixteen hundreds," he said, not even glancing up as they climbed the stone steps. "The main structure was built ninety years ago by one of my ancestors. I was told my grandfather used it as a hunting lodge, but it was already in disrepair when I was a young child."

Imogene stood on the stone terrace, and admired the view. "Perhaps you should be the one to restore it?"

"Perhaps," he said agreeably. He shook out the blanket and smoothed the fabric with the edge of his boot. "I have other estates that have required more of my attention. Like my father before me, I have been content to rent the house and surrounding lands to tenants." Once he was satisfied with his efforts he joined her and took a moment to enjoy the lake view. His arm curled around her waist. "I had forgotten the beauty of this old place."

They stood in comfortable silence, watching as several ducks glided over the mirrored surface of the lake. Imogene was also keenly aware of the duke's closeness. She could feel the heat of his body against her back, the quiet intimacy of his hand on her left arm, and the light caress of his jaw as it brushed the side of her head.

She was wholly aware of him—and the fact that they were alone.

"You have no tenants?" Imogene asked. She had not seen any signs of a family in residence on their arrival.

"The house has been empty since January. The new tenants will be moving in next month," he said, turning her until she faced him. "Does it concern you that we are alone?"

"Not in the slightest."

Blackbern frowned at her swift reply. "Maybe it should. Your company inspires some rather wicked thoughts."

"I trust you, Tristan," she said coyly.

He groaned in exaggerated despair, as he captured her hand and led her back to the blanket. "What am I to do with you, Imogene? Such blind faith makes me long to prove to you that I am deserving of your high regard."

"You are an honorable gentleman," Imogene said, her voice ringing with conviction. "You cannot convince me otherwise."

It had been Norgrave who had lied to her about the redhead.

"No, I am not," he countered, dragging her closer. "If

you could read my thoughts, you would be demanding that we return to town immediately."

"If you wish to kiss me again, you have my permission to do so," she invited, though she refrained from admitting that she was eager for more of his kisses.

"Little innocent," he said, shaking his head, his expression tender with amusement and affection. "And what if I demanded more?"

He had told her that she had a choice, so she was uncertain of what his current demands would entail. Imogene had not been lying when she had revealed that she trusted him. In spite of his arrogant boast that they would eventually become lovers, Blackbern appeared to be in control of his appetites. He would not press her for more than she would not offer him willingly.

"I fear you might think me wanton if I answer your question truthfully."

Her innocence would be the death of him. If he had any sense, he would escort Imogene back to the carriage and return her to the safety of her family. She stared up at him, a decadent confection of sweetness and light, and it was all he could do not to drag her to the ground and give her a taste of the pleasure he had promised. He no longer gave a damn about Norgrave or their foolish wager. He simply wanted the lady in his arms.

Though Norgrave intended to have her, too. Otherwise he would not have lied about the redhead.

Even if Tristan sent her away, his friend would laugh at his sentimentality. Nor would it end his pursuit of Imogene. The only way to stop his friend was to claim the lady himself.

Selfishness cloaked in nobility.

Tristan almost snorted at his cleverness. Leave it to him to rationalize that he was more deserving of Imogene than Norgrave—that by winning the wager, he was sparing her the marquess's fickle and not-quite-so-gentle affections.

He cupped the left side of Imogene's face with his hand. "You can be as wanton as you like. Nothing is forbidden."

"Nothing at all?" she echoed, her expression as transparent as glass as she contemplated such freedoms. In her cherished and protected world, she had no concept of the possibilities or the risks.

"Allow me to show you," Tristan said, his voice deepening with desire. He bent his head and kissed her, a small test of her commitment.

His initial plan when he had lured her away from her friends was no longer relevant now. The attraction crackling between them like invisible lightning was mutual. As far as he was concerned, he and Imogene were equals as curiosity manifested into something tangible, as intimacy and friendship entwined to create something new for both of them.

Imogene's eyelashes brushed her cheeks as she tentatively parted her lips, another invitation for him to deepen the kiss. When it came to the woman in his arms, he needed little encouragement. His tongue pushed against hers, even while he tugged her close so he could feel her body rub against his. The connection was giving him all kinds of naughty ideas, but her inexperience had him mentally tethering his lust. He desired her, but he had no intention of pouncing on her like a mindless beast.

"More," she murmured breathlessly against his mouth.

He groaned and pressed his forehead lightly against hers as he prayed for strength. "I am not a saint, Imogene. Push me away or tell me to go to the devil."

She offered him that shy half-smile that always made his testicles tighten within their sac and his cock harden. If she had more experience, he would have thought she teased him deliberately. "I thought you said that nothing is forbidden."

Tristan silently bid his good intentions adieu as he used his weight to draw her down with him. "You are truly a very wicked lady," he said, meaning it as a compliment, as he guided her onto her back. "What am I to do with you?"

Imogene gazed up at him, her cheeks rosy and her eyes bright with anticipation. "Kiss me again, Your Grace."

She was a delightful imp, he thought, happily rewarding her with another enthusiastic kiss. As he lay stretched out beside her, the hand he had placed on her abdomen slowly moved up her body until he felt the comforting weight of one of her breasts. As Tristan lightly squeezed, he had a liberal glimpse of the soft flesh peeking above her bodice.

"And what do we have here?" he asked, his right brow angling upward.

"What are you—" She gasped as he caressed her breast with his mouth. "Oh my!"

Tristan tasted the soft swell with his tongue. "Mmm . . . just as I suspected—you taste as good as you look." His fingers slipped beneath her bodice, peeling back the layers of fabric to reveal more of her flesh.

A rosy nipple, plump and inviting as a berry, popped free.

He felt her hands on his shoulders. "My God, you are so lovely." Without asking her permission, he lowered his head to suckle the first signs of her arousal.

Imogene dug her fingers into his shoulders. "Your Grace . . . Tristan. W-what are you doing?" she asked, her voice taut with nerves and uncertainty.

"Worshiping you as you deserve, my golden-haired goddess." Tristan licked the nub with his tongue, swirling and teasing it until he could suckle the firm flesh. He could feel the tension in her body and her halfhearted protests as he moved to her other breast.

He lifted his head from her damp flesh and met her anxious gaze. Her expression revealed her shock at his intimate ministrations, and her hand reached for her bodice.

He placed his hand over hers to stop her. "Leave it. I am not finished with these lush beauties."

"What if someone sees us?"

"I do not take kindly to trespassers." Or anyone who dared to glimpse her half dressed. He had no interest in sharing her with anyone, and that included Norgrave. The realization should have sobered him because he had never felt so possessive about a female, but he was too enthralled to pull away. "Here . . . allow me to cover you," he said, using his own body to blanket hers.

His cock was thick and hard, and his flesh ached as he pressed it against her hip. Imogene seemed unaware of the effect she was having on his unruly body. If she thought his mouth kissing her breasts was indecent, then she would be truly scandalized if he freed the rigid flesh from his breeches and pressed the swollen head of his cock against her maidenhead. The mere thought of breaching that fragile barrier and filling her made him lightheaded with desire.

"Tristan?" she politely inquired, her brow furrowing at his stillness as he fought down the clawing need to claim her.

"Give me a moment," he said tersely.

"What is it?"

He took her hand and brought it to the front of his breeches. She tried to retreat when her fingers came in contact with his cock, but he was stronger. Her hand molded over the rigid flesh. "You are not the only one aching, darling," he said. His mouth felt stiff as he tried to make light of his needs.

"I did this?" she said, sounding appalled. "Does it hurt?"

Only Imogene could make him laugh at a time such as this. "Aye, lady, but it is a good sort of hurting."

"I do not understand."

"Do you recall how you felt when I put my mouth on your breasts?"

Imogene nodded. "I felt a kind of warmth here." She touched the cleft between her breasts. "Also—"

When she appeared reluctant to finish her confession, he pressed, "Where else did it hurt?"

She wrinkled her nose and shook her head, too embarrassed to admit the truth.

Tristan guided her hand from his straining cock to the front of her skirt. "Does it ache here?"

"Yes," she shyly admitted. "There is a kind of curious warmth and it sort of tingles."

"Aye, it is the same for me," Tristan said. He needed her to understand that the sensations were not aberrant and she was not alone in feeling them.

"I can ease you, if you will let me." Tristan released her hand, and did not try to stop her from tugging on her bodice. Instead, he moved his hand lower and buried it under her skirt.

Imogene squirmed to avoid his hand, but he grasped her knee to calm her. "There is nothing to fear. Trust me." His hand slid higher on her inner thigh. "This is one particular ache that I can ease with just a gentle caress."

"You need not go any further," she said, squeezing her thighs together and capturing his hand between them. "The ache is gone. Truly."

"Liar," he contradicted. "It is just the beginning. Do you know why? Because it is the same for me." Tristan shifted and straightened his spine until his mouth was inches from her lips. "Relax your legs. I promise this will not hurt."

Tristan nibbled on her lower lip. She was as stiff as a statue. Even her mouth was unyielding. He would have stopped if he had glimpsed genuine fear in her eyes. Imogene was wary of the unknown, but she was not frightened of him.

"Think about my hands on you," he murmured enticingly against her throat. He kissed her neck. "My lips on your lips . . . down to your breasts. Do you remember the warmth you felt?" Her thighs loosened enough that his hand was free. "That's it, sweet love. My hand on your knee . . . your thigh."

Imogene made a soft sound of surprise at his first tentative touch.

"Aye, even there," he whispered encouragingly. "The soft down between your legs. A fine soft pelt for me to pet over and over until you are wild for my caresses."

Tristan kissed her firmly on the mouth, swallowing any protests she might have at the liberties he was taking with her body. His cock throbbed in his breeches, but he ignored the discomfort. Imogene would never accept him until he conquered her fears—not of him, but of her own body. Her needs were as great as his, but she was unfamiliar with satiating her desires. He wanted to be the man who wholly awakened her. Ignited and fanned her carnal needs.

His finger dampened with her arousal as he emboldened his strokes. Wariness faded as she raised her head in distress. Tristan comforted her with a few low wordless sounds and a kiss to her cheek.

"The warmth and wetness is a natural response to my touch," he assured her, keeping his touch light. "Your body is welcoming me. Encouraging me to be bolder." His thumb sought the hidden nubbin of flesh and he gently stroked it. She sucked in her breath and tensed, fighting her body's response. "Breathe, darling. Let the caress of my fingers flow over you and through you."

Usually, when he seduced a lady, he managed to get her out of her clothing. Imogene's gaze was unfocused and her cheeks were flushed, either by the sunlight beating down on them or the wicked things he was doing to her body. Tristan preferred to believe the high color in her cheeks was because of him. He had lost track of time as he concentrated on the lady in his arms. Soft compliments, kisses designed to coax and tease her, and his hand between her legs—stroking her wet yielding flesh as he enticed and tamed her to his touch. The heady musk of her arousal filled his nose, and perspiration dampened his brow.

He demanded nothing, but was silently asking for everything.

Minutes later, his patience was rewarded. Imogene tensed and shuddered, her face pressed against his shoulder. She whispered his name in wonderment. It was a small response, but it might as well have been as shattering as an earthquake. The increased wetness coating his fingers was another sign that she had found pleasure at his touch.

His own arousal thundered back into his consciousness. Tristan had been so focused on Imogene that he had buried his needs. His hand withdrew from Imogene's hot, welcoming flesh and he wiped the wetness on his fingers on the outer thigh of his breeches. In his mind, he could see himself freeing his cock and thrusting into her womanly sheath. She had found her pleasure with his hand, and it would be twofold with his cock. He could see to both their needs. She would not regret surrendering her maidenhead to him. He would make certain of it. The need to finish what he had started pounded like a drum in his head.

Every muscle in his body tightened as he fought against his instincts. He closed his eyes and concentrated on steadying his breathing and heartbeat. When he opened them, he noticed she was staring at him. She reached out and caressed his cheek.

"Tristan?"

He had accomplished what he had set out to do. The next time he touched her, she would not fight her body's response. She would let him pleasure her again. With a ragged sigh, he smoothed her skirt down over her legs. "I do not know about you, but I am famished. Shall we see what Cook packed in our basket?"

"Of course."

Imogene's gaze shifted to the front of his breeches. Oh, how could he have forgotten about his cock? His need for her was on prominent display. Perhaps he should stand up and head straight for the lake, though he doubted the water would cool his ardor.

Tristan turned away and climbed to his feet. He needed a strong drink, though he suspected his cook had packed nothing stronger than apple cider.

Chapter Ten

Lord Norgrave had added another card to Sandwick's silver salver while Imogene was enjoying her picnic with Tristan. A note had been included with an invitation to join him at one of the tea gardens. She was still annoyed with him for speculating on the duke's friendship with his former mistress, but she had decided to forgive him. His invitation reminded her that she had injured Lady Charlotte's feelings when she walked with Lord Norgrave in Lady Yaxley's gardens, and she wished to make amends so she decided to play matchmaker for her friend and the marquess.

The next afternoon, Imogene and Lady Charlotte enjoyed their surroundings while they waited for Lord Norgrave to join them.

"This was a terrible idea," Lady Charlotte muttered as she fidgeted with her jewelry. "You should have mentioned that I would be intruding."

"For the fifth time, you are not intruding," Imogene said, resisting the urge to groan in frustration. "You and I are friends. The marquess will not be upset that I have not come alone."

"I have overheard rumors that he and the Duke of Blackbern are courting you." The blonde looked as if she was on the verge of crying. "He likes you, you know. I noticed almost immediately when he asked you to walk with him."

Good grief, Imogene thought. Lady Charlotte was not smitten—she had fallen in love with the marquess.

"Is he aware of your feelings?" she asked, feeling guilty that she had inadvertently added to her friend's pain.

"I—" Lady Charlotte started as she glanced up to see the gentleman whom she coveted above all frowning at her. "Lord Norgrave, it is good to see you again."

Two hours later, Imogene returned home. Initially, she and Lady Charlotte had made tentative plans to visit Bond Street after taking tea with Lord Norgrave. The strained conversation that had ensued had dampened the lady's spirits and had given Imogene a slight headache.

Lord Norgrave had been impatient and condenscending. All in all, she was relieved the entire visit was over.

"Good afternoon, Sandwick." Imogene greeted the butler as she walked through the door.

"I trust your outing with Lady Charlotte was enjoyable?"

"Sandwick, it was dreadful and it was my fault." She paused and rethought her decision. "No, it was Lord Norgrave's fault. Well, parts of it anyway."

"What precisely is the marquess's fault?" her mother asked, descending the stairs.

"Lord Norgrave invited me to join him at the tea garden," Imogene explained while she removed her bonnet and gloves. "I invited Lady Charlotte in a clumsy attempt at matchmaking."

"Oh, Imogene," the duchess lightly chided her. "I told you that young lady was besotted with the marquess. It is plainly obvious to all that Lady Charlotte cares too much, and Lord Norgrave barely tolerates her."

"I wanted to help her, Mama," she said glumly. "All I did was upset Lady Charlotte and Lord Norgrave was obnoxious and deliberately rude to us. The next time he tries to leave his card, I have a mind to order Sandwick to tear it up and shower the marquess with the pieces."

Her mother laughed. "He was that terrible?"

"Positively beastly," Imogene replied. "Lady Charlotte did not deserve his callous regard. Neither did I." She rubbed her forehead with her fingers. "I am tempted to retire to my bedchamber and sleep the rest of the day away."

"I have something to show you that will make you reconsider."

She followed her mother into an alcove where a small trunk seemed out of place. "Who is it from?"

"I have my suspicions, but the boy who delivered it refused to give me the name of the person who hired him. You have been invited to the masquerade at Ranelagh Gardens. There are several groups planning to attend. Cassia has already asked that you ride with her."

"Perhaps she was the one who sent the trunk."

"The note within implies you have received two invitations to the masquerade."

Imogene glanced back at her mother. "Did you look inside?"

The duchess shook her head, and handed her the

note. "I assume it is a costume. If not, then you will need one unless we have something suitable buried in an old trunk."

Imogene folded the note and tucked it away. She recognized the handwriting as Blackbern's.

"Who sent the note?"

She ignored the question and opened the trunk. She pursed her lips as she scrutinized the vibrant patchwork dress. At the bottom of the trunk she discovered a black half-mask and a tambourine.

"Someone wishes that you dress as Columbine for the masquerade," her mother observed. The duchess did not appear to be pleased with the choice, but she was not threatening to burn it. "Hmm . . . who could be so thoughtful, I wonder?"

The duke was responsible for the costume. Only he would insist that she dress as Harlequin's mistress. The man had a peculiar sense of humor.

Chapter Eleven

"Norgrave will be vexed with us for leaving the masquerade without telling him."

Tristan silently agreed, but not for the reasons Imogene assumed. He and Norgrave had often shared a woman or two. Bending a female to their will and overwhelming her with their passions had been adventurous and extremely satisfying. He could not summon any regrets about his past, or the countess females with whom he had honed his skills as a lover. If he had suggested to the marquess that they forget about the wager and slowly introduce Imogene to the carnal delights of taking multiple lovers, he had little doubt that Norgrave would have eagerly amended the terms of their wager.

Even so, Tristan had kept his mouth shut. He had lied to the man who was almost a brother to him, and he would continue to do so. When it came to Imogene, he had discovered that he was a selfish man. The thought of Norgrave kissing and touching the lady sitting beside him could provoke him to violence.

Imogene was not one of the nameless and faceless fucks that he and his friend had shared when they had figured out what they could do with their cocks. She was a goddess among women, and she deserved to be worshiped.

He was her devoted acolyte if she would have him.

Imogene had been concerned about abandoning Norgrave, because they had arrived together. Tristan observed her and his closest friend together, and he noted only friendship in her gaze. Occasionally, regret flashed across her expressive face, but it occurred when the marquess tried to coax a kiss from her. In public, she was content to have two gentlemen court her, but there would be only one man in her bed—and that man was him.

Imogene leaned back against her seat and sighed. She had not removed her black half-mask when they had slipped away from Ranelagh Gardens, and he was content to leave the disguise in place so she would not be recognized when they disembarked from the coach.

He kept his hands to himself until they had reached their destination.

"Where are we?" she asked sleepily.

"A quiet place where no one will try to steal you from me," he said, his voice gruff as he recalled Norgrave's attempt to pull her into an alcove. He did not want to contemplate what his friend had in mind, when he was filled with his own lusty thoughts.

The coachman opened the door, and he took her hand to help her descend the few steps. Imogene yawned. "Is this your residence?" she asked, squinting at the house that was barely visible in the darkness and lamplight.

"When it suits me," he said, reluctant to reveal that the house was where he had built his reputation with the notorious balls he had held over the years and the many lovers he had escorted through the front hall and upstairs to one of the bedchambers. "I inherited the house from my mother. Before her, my grandmother used it as her dowager house. It has a rich history."

Most of it she would never hear from his lips.

Even in the shadows, the colorful patches on her skirt were visible as he escorted her up the walkway to the front door. He paused to remove the key from his waistcoat, and used his fingers to find the keyhole.

"I am surprised you do not rent the house this time of year," Imogene said, resting her cheek against his arm.

"Over the years, I have considered it," Tristan admitted. He grunted with satisfaction when the lock yielded. "Most of the furniture belonged to my grandmother. My mother had her bedchamber decorated to her tastes, but she did little else to the house. No one resides here, but the servants visit once a week to keep the floors and furniture clean for when I invite guests."

Her sudden stillness made him apprehensive. He wondered if she had guessed the reasons why he brought people to this house instead of his private residence. "How often do you entertain guests here?"

Tristan shrugged. "It depends on the year." He paused. "Norgrave has a key and my blessing to invite whomever he wants."

"What about you?"

"You are the first guest I have invited here in over a year," he answered truthfully. "I sometimes come here when I need to think. The quiet is soothing, and no one would think to bother me here."

She stepped into the house, and wrinkled her nose at the slight staleness scenting the air. "Not very recently."

"No," he said, shutting the door and turning the key. "I have been too distracted by an enchanting blonde who knocked me off my feet."

Imogene's laughter filled the front hall. "How long do you plan to tease me about our first meeting? I cannot believe I was so clumsy!"

Tristan lit a candle behind her before he pulled her into his arms. "You were perfect. I have never been so flattered, even though the dragon caught us together."

She winced. "You have to cease calling my mother a dragon. She has enough reasons to dislike you."

"Is it important to you that she likes me?" he asked, untying her half-mask so he could see her face.

"Yes."

The simplicity of her reply understated how complicated their relationship had become. Nor would it deter him from what he longed to claim.

Picking up the candleholder, he took her hand and led her toward the stairs. "Come with me."

Hand in hand, they made their way up the stairs. Tristan had lit the candle for her benefit. He had lost count of how many times he had climbed the stairs, only to fall into bed with or without a lover. Abruptly he halted and startled Imogene.

"Is something amiss?" she whispered.

How could he tell her that he had made a mistake? He did not want to lay her on the same mattress where he had bedded so many women in the past.

"For a minute, I lost my way," he lied. "This way."

His mother's bedchamber had the newest furniture, but he avoided the room. He released her hand so he could turn the doorknob of one of the spare bedchambers that had been used for guests. If the servants had been shirking in their weekly duties, he would sack them all.

Fortunately the room was free of noticeable dust and the room smelled faintly of freshly laundered linens. He set the candle down on a table beside the bed and he reached for the woman who often invaded his thoughts when he should have been working.

"Come closer, my lovely and impudent Columbine. Your Harlequin has been hungering for a taste of your honeyed lips," he growled against her mouth.

Playing along, she rubbed her hips against him. "My husband might protest," she whispered, tilting her head and offering him her neck.

Norgrave had considered dressing up as Columbine's husband, but he disliked the notion of being the cuckolded husband to Tristan's Harlequin. The plotting Pantalone held more appeal, but he had also been deceived.

"If we are careful, no one will ever know about us," he said, nipping her ear with his teeth. He did not know if he spoke for Harlequin or himself.

Without warning he swept her off her feet and into his arms. Imogen gasped and instinctively wrapped her arms around his neck. "Harlequin—Tristan!"

"Right on both counts," he said, teasing her mouth with his. He carried her to the bed and eased her down until her backside settled onto the soft surface. "Do you trust me?"

She nodded.

His hands shook as he removed the red spencer, peeling her slender bared arms from the snug sleeves. Tristan went to work on the buttons of her dress. Proficient at his task, he set about removing layer after layer of clothing and discarding them until she sat in her shift.

Imogene crossed her arms over her breasts, but she had only managed to draw attention to the mounds of flesh. "Are you undressing, too?"

"Aye, my love. Soon," he promised, lowering himself onto his knees so he was positioned between her legs. His hands slid up her calves to the garters tied above her thighs. He undid the bows, and slowly revealed her pale, shapely legs and bared feet.

Tristan pressed a kiss to the inner portion of her right knee. His mouth lingered and teased, a hint of what he longed to do. "I want to start with the arch of your foot and nibble my way up your body."

It was obvious she was nervous, and her mouth trembled as she attempted to smile. "Am I allowed to do the same to you?" she asked.

"Only if you wish to see me spill my seed before I have the opportunity to make love to you properly." Beneath the garish Harlequin costume of triangular patches, his cock had thickened in anticipation. The patterned fabric concealed his arousal, but once he removed it she would be aware of the power she had over him. "You can torture me later."

Tristan moved closer and gently pried her arms from her chest. Her nipples poked enticingly through the thin linen, begging for his attention. Without asking for her permission, his mouth covered one of her breasts. He suckled her nipple, dampening the fabric while his hands slid higher, lightly caressing her outer thighs until he found her hips.

"Tristan?"

He tugged her closer so he could rub his body against hers. The subtle musk of her arousal was an intoxicating scent that had him salivating for a taste.

"Aye, darling." The strap slipped free from her shoulder, revealing a glimpse of her rose-colored areola. He nipped and pulled the fabric with his teeth, revealing more until her puckered nipple was exposed.

She started at the initial contact of his tongue curled around the delicate bud and he opened his jaw wider so he could draw more of her flesh into his mouth. Her hands were not gentle when she pulled his head closer, begging him to take more.

Tristan unexpectedly released her breast and bowed his head as he strived for control over his unruly body. Imogene was more responsive than he could have ever anticipated. He covered his cock with his hand. Hard and aching, he squeezed the flesh, knowing the relief he craved could be found within the depths of her body.

He looked up and their gazes locked. "I am trying to be gentle," he said, already sensing he would have to apologize later because he was impatient and the demands he would make on her were beyond her experience. "You deserve a tender lover."

Imogene touched his face. "You are everything I want. Everything I need."

"What do you need, Imogene?"

"You," she coyly replied.

Tristan felt the invisible tether snap within him as he rose and coaxed her onto her back. His eyes focused on hers, he tore at the fastenings of his costume and hastily shed them and kicked them aside.

Imogene caged him with her legs. Her shift had ridden higher on her thighs with her movements, presenting him with a wanton view. Tristan glimpsed the honeyed curls between her legs and the beckoning dampness. He stroked his cock and shuddered; the rigid length was almost too sensitive to touch. Leaning closer, he used the broad head of his arousal to tease the folds between her legs. Although the lady in his arms was innocent, her body instinctively reacted to his proximity. His teeth clenched as he moved his hips, his cock pressing against the opening of her silky sheath.

His head bowed, he moaned as he mentally separated the sensations threatening to overrule his good intentions. Imogene tensed, feeling the first stirrings of discomfort as his demands manifested in a defining moment when he claimed her maidenhead and filled her.

"Kiss me," he entreated, straining forward so he could taste her. The subtle adjustment drove his cock deeper and her sharp gasp told him that it would be kinder to be swift. He withdrew just enough to allow him to thrust, the action driving his cock through the fragile resistance of her maidenhead and burying him deeply within her.

She expelled a soft strangling sound that could have been a protest against the unexpected pain, but that part was over.

"You are mine," he said harshly. It was not the poetic words she deserved but he was beyond words. Need and instinct welled up within him. Her silken sheath resisted his slow retreat and the exquisite sensation threatened to send him over the edge as he thrust fully, grinding his hips against hers. He was a man who prided himself on his control and his ability to prolong his lover's pleasure. With Imogene, he felt as if it was his first time as well. He did not dwell on the meaning, but he was determined to give her a glimpse of the pleasure ahead of them. He slipped his hand between their bodies, blindly seeking the small knot of flesh hidden beneath her intimate folds. She started as his fingers caressed and circled the sensitive nubbin as the hard length of him stroked her from within. The fleshy sac hanging beneath his cock was firm to the touch and primed for his impending release.

Imogene bit her lip. "I feel—I feel . . . you need to stop," she said as an unfamiliar tension invaded her body.

Tristan kissed her lower lip, which she was abusing. "You do not really mean it. In fact, you want me to quicken my pace." He was pushing his control to the very edge, but if Imogene was with him, he would happily fall.

"No . . . wait!" she pleaded, panic coloring her voice. "W-what are you—" She held her breath and her entire body tensed as she tried to make sense of the unfamiliar flutters of her first release. "Ooph!" she said as she released the air in her lungs.

Tristan wrapped one arm around her as the other sought her hip. Sweat burned his eyes and the steady hammering of his hips faltered and then slowed as the delicate muscles of her sheath rippled and squeezed the full length of his cock. A spark of common sense flickered in his brain and he began to withdraw, but Imogene pressed herself against him. He could not fight both her and his needs. With a strangled growl, he dragged her hips flush against his and surrendered to the release he could not hold back. His teeth snapped together as the force of his seed bursting from the head of his cock was unlike anything he had experienced.

A wave of exhaustion swiftly followed and he collapsed with his cheek resting against her shoulder. Their limbs entwined, neither one of them spoke. If he had not been crushing her into the mattress, he would have been content to fall asleep in her arms.

Tristan clasped her to him and rolled until she reclined on top of him. His cock had softened within her, but he was reluctant to break their connection. He brushed strands of hair from her face, and offered her a tender smile.

"You are a dangerous woman, Lady Imogene," he teased, feeling too good to regret his loss of control.

"Is that something good or something bad?" she asked, unable to conceal her vulnerability from him.

"Oh, darling, it is something very good," he drawled, too sated to do little more than place his hand at the back of her neck to draw her close for another bone-melting kiss. "If this was not your first time, I would dedicate the rest of the night proving it to you."

His cock twitched within her, obviously offering its opinion of his suggestion. It was with some regret that he eased out of her. She winced at his withdrawal, confirming his suspicions.

"What do you intend to do with me?" she asked, her dark blue eyes gleaming like polished stones in the candlelight.

Tristan shifted and tucked her body against his side. She cuddled against him and used his chest as a pillow. She still wore her linen shift. The next time he took her, she would be wearing only him. The carnal thought did nothing to cool his cock's enthusiasm. To conceal the evidence of his arousal, he reached over and pulled a sheet over them.

"Do with you?" he echoed, realizing he had not answered her question. "If you do not mind, I would like to stay like this for a while."

Imogene sighed. "I would like that."

His arms tightened around her waist as he considered the consequences of what they had done. He had won the wager. Another spring, a different woman in his arms, he might have pulled out of her, dressed, and sent her home while he sought out Norgrave to gloat about his victory.

With his free hand, he pinched the space between his eyebrows. *Merde.* When had he become such a ruthless bastard? If he were honest, the more intriguing question was why he had no intention of treating Imogene so callously.

The victory he often craved had been found in coaxing her first release from her virginal body. In the roar of his release as his cock filled her with his seed. The bliss he was feeling just holding her.

Tristan could not share the truth with Norgrave.

The wager had given him an excuse to approach Imogene and he was reluctant to see it end. As long as his friend believed there was a chance Imogene could be seduced, he would continue to court her. He and Norgrave were at an impasse. Tristan was even more determined to protect her from the marquess's advances, and anyone else who dared to pursue her.

A fierce feeling of possessiveness rose within him. He had never felt this way about any of his lovers, and it worried him because keeping her had never been part of his plan.

Tristan sensed the moment Imogene fell asleep, her breath tickling his chest. He silently willed himself to leave the bed. Remaining would lead to complications and hurt feelings.

Get up.

Instead he turned his face toward hers and kissed her on the head. He was not leaving her. Not this evening at any rate. He closed his eyes and shared another first with Imogene.

His worries faded away as he drifted off to sleep with his lover at his side.

Imogene was wide awake on the drive home. She had slept for two hours before Tristan had awakened her by caressing her back. He had brushed aside her embarrassment by confessing that she had thoroughly exhausted him and he had slept as well. She had been half expecting him to continue their lovemaking, but he had surprised her once again by carrying a basin filled with tepid water to her bedside. Ignoring her protests, he washed away the evidence of his seed and her maidenhead. The cool water soothed the soreness between her legs, while it aroused and warmed her.

Imogene could tell Tristan was quite aware of her reaction, but he told her that he had been too rough with her and she needed time to heal. She yielded to his experience in such matters. His touch was impersonal as he helped her dress into her Columbine costume, and he became once again her Harlequin. No promises were uttered, and if she felt slighted by the oversight, it was her fault not his. She had come willingly to his bed. She refused to feel any regret about it.

It was self-preservation that had her sitting on the opposite cushioned seat of the coach, but Tristan had seen through her attempt to put distance between them. He deftly tugged her into his lap and he held her while she quietly wept. Imogene could not fathom why she was crying, but the duke did not seem to mind her tears. He cradled her in his arms and whispered words of comfort and tried to calm her.

Her eyes were dry once they had reached her residence.

"You will offer Norgrave our apologies for abandoning him, will you not?" Imogene said, striving for a cheerful note. She did not wish to ruin what they had shared.

"Norgrave will survive," was Tristan's dry response.

"Well, good evening, Your Grace. I—oomph—"

Tristan cut off her blithe dismissal by grabbing her and kissing her until she felt faint from the lack of air.

"That is better," he said arrogantly. "Before you leave, I have something for you."

Her forehead furrowed in puzzlement. "You do not have to—" If he presented all of his lovers with a token of his gratitude, she might be half tempted to hurl it in his face.

"Stop scowling at me." He grinned at her as if he deduced her thoughts. "I do not offer this casually. Only one other person can claim such a gift, and you are prettier than Norgrave."

He opened his hand and revealed the key in his palm.

"What is this?"

"The key unlocks the front door of my mother's house," he explained, his carefully blanked expression not revealing the importance of his gift. "It is yours to use as you please."

Imogene accepted the key. She was gripping it so tightly, the key would likely leave an impression on the palm of her hand. "Thank you. I will not abuse the privilege."

"I place no conditions on its use," he said, offering her a crooked smile. "Though I would prefer to be waiting for you on the other side of the door."

"I would like that very much, Your Grace," she admitted, shyness creeping into her expression.

"Tristan," he corrected. He kissed her on the nose. "I enjoy hearing you say my name, and you do not use it often enough."

Her heart felt so light, she could almost believe she could fly. "I will endeavor to mend my ways."

"Excellent." He escorted her to the front door. "I look forward to instructing you in all things," he whispered in her ear, causing her to shiver. He cupped her backside and gave her buttock a playful squeeze. "Now get inside before I lose my head and kidnap you. I rather liked having you in my bed."

He sighed with regret and stepped away. Imogene turned away to hide her smile. Tristan had not uttered the words she longed to hear, but the key he had given her was a measure of his feelings for her.

In time, he would declare himself to her and her family.

Imogene entered the house, feeling as if her feet were barely touching the ground, secure in the knowledge that she could lay claim to the duke's affection.

Chapter Twelve

Lord Norgrave's boorish behavior at the tea gardens and her very personal decision to become Tristan's lover had resulted in her avoiding the marquess for eight days before he realized that if he wanted to catch her alone, it would require a little trickery.

The moment arrived when Imogene had been invited to join Lady Ludsthorpe in her private box. Blackbern had made his apologies to her in advance because he had other plans for the evening. He did, however, warn her that his aunt would most likely question her since the news had reached her ears that her nephew was courting the Duke of Trevett's daugher.

In between the play acts, she had expertly dodged the countess's not-so-very-subtle inquiries about the duke and the other gentlemen who subjected themselves to her mother's relentless scrutiny. Eventually, the older woman gave up and switched the conversation to the various snippets of gossip that she had overheard in the card room the previous evening.

It had been an usher who had approached her with the request that she follow him. She had initially thought

Tristan had been able to join her and his aunt after all, so she apologized to Lady Ludsthorpe and followed the servant to the private sitting room.

Instead of Blackbern, Lord Norgrave was waiting for her.

Swallowing her disappointment she entered the small room to properly greet the marquess. "Good evening, my lord." Imogene curtsied. "I was unaware that you were attending the play. Perhaps you would join me and Lady Ludsthorpe?" She took a breath and gave him an excuse to decline her invitation. "Unless you have other plans."

"You appear disappointed, Imogene." Norgrave took her hand and guided her to the narrow sofa. He sat down next to her. "Were you expecting Blackbern?"

"Since I am sitting in his aunt's private box, it was a natural assumption," she said, still feeling guilty that she had allowed Tristan to whisk her away from Ranelagh Gardens. "I thought the duke might be with you?"

The marquess offered her a sympathetic smile. "I regret I do not know his plans this evening. The man can be secretive at times. This usually occurs when he is besotted with a new mistress."

Lord Norgrave's aim was wickedly accurate when it came to mischief. The sharp stab to her heart was bloodless, and it took her a minute to remind herself that if the duke was secretive about a new mistress, it was because she was the lady in question.

"If you are correct, then I will have one less suitor to worry about," Imogene said, slipping her hand free from his.

His brows furrowed in puzzlement. "You surprise me. I was concerned the news would be upsetting."

"In many ways, it is a relief," she confided. "My father is disappointed in my progress, and has threatened several times to pick a husband for me if I do not reduce my choices to several possible candidates."

"It is a difficult decision." Norgrave placed his hand over hers in a comforting gesture. His fingers tightened over hers. "When you present your candidates to your father, I would be honored if I was one of your final candidates."

"Lord Norgrave." Imogene blinked, unaware that he had harbored any real feelings beyond friendship for her. He had displayed more passion when it came to his rivalry with Blackbern. "Forgive me. I was told that you had little interest in marriage."

His grip tightened painfully over hers. "Who told you that?" he demanded. "Your father?" Norgrave calmed at her quick nod. "My lovely lady, most fathers would discourage their daughters from seeking my affection. It is understandable. Blackbern and I have not always been discreet, I fear."

She preferred not to discuss the duke's former mistresses with Lord Norgrave.

"I have tarried too long. I should return to Lady Ludsthrope," Imogene said, pulling her hand free as she stood. "I am not prepared to make a decision, but I will thoughtfully consider your offer."

"I am not inviting you to dance, Imogene," Norgrave said, not hiding his frustration. "I am asking you to be my countess."

"I know," she said, her thoughts drifting to Lady Charlotte. "I need more time."

"Perhaps this will help."

The marquess grasped her wrists and pulled her into his arms. He tasted of brandy and desperation as he kissed her so hard that she tasted blood.

"No," she murmured against his lips.

He twisted her arm and dragged her down so they collapsed onto the sofa. Did he plan to seduce her with Lady Ludsthorpe just beyond the shut curtains?

Gathering her strength, Imogene shoved Lord Norgrave away from her. "I told you to stop. If you cannot respect my wishes, then I must regretfully decline your generous offer."

Lord Norgrave staggered to his feet. "Forgive me, Imogene. It was not my intention to frighten you."

Imogene nodded, edging toward the curtain. "I cannot be your countess, my lord. If you would open your heart, there is another who would happily accept."

"Lady Charlotte." He sneered. "Do not insult me further by telling me who I should marry. My apologies for interrupting your evening."

Norgrave stalked away. Shaken by the encounter, Imogene sat down and covered her face with her hands.

Norgrave was so furious he could not recall leaving Imogene. One minute he was fighting the urge to throttle her for tossing Lady Charlotte at him as if the timid creature was a worthy substitute for the lady he desired, and the next he was standing in the middle of the street.

Before he could take a step forward, a coach thundered by him. His hesitation had saved his life. If he had taken one step, the wheels of that coach would have cut furrows into his back.

"Stupid arse," the witness to his near death jeered.

The compassionate fellow shook his head in disgust. "Are you drunk or a simpleton?"

Norgrave offered him a taunting smile. "Are those my only choices? Come closer and decide for yourself."

The man waved him off. "Go sleep it off."

The marquess made a soft mocking sound. "It is just my misfortune that when I think I have found a man with stones in his hairy sac, I realize he has nothing but common sand."

Norgrave deliberately turned his back on the man. He shut his eyes and waited for his quarry to assume he was vulnerable.

People often underestimated him.

He silently counted the man's footfalls. The stench rolling off his unpleasant companion's unwashed body alerted Norgrave to when he should strike.

His first punch caught the man in the throat. "What? Nothing clever to say?"

Fighting for his next breath, the man grasped his throat and staggered sideways as he tried to evade his attacker. Norgrave's next punch struck the man's left ear, and then his right.

"Can you hear me over the bells, you mouthy rat?" the marquess shouted after him. "That's right, my good man. Scurry away like a good rodent."

Norgrave waited until the man had put enough distance between them that he would assume he was safe from further retribution. He calmly walked up the street and picked up a discarded wine bottle. Testing the weight of it against his palm, he glanced at the dark alley the rat had raced down.

It was time to show the man how wrong he had been.

*   *   *

Tristan sensed he was not alone before he saw Norgrave's hand on the bottle of wine. The marquess refilled his half-empty glass before he filled his own to the top and it overflowed onto the table.

"Are you planning to get drunk?" he mildly asked. He did not care one way or the other. In fact, getting drunk sounded like a good way to finish off the evening.

"Aye, so save your lectures," Norgrave muttered, sitting down on the opposite side of the table in the noisy tavern.

"You have been fighting."

The marquess blinked in surprise. "How can you tell? There isn't a bloody mark on me."

Tristan nodded to Norgrave's hands. "You have removed your gloves, I assume, because the unfortunate gentleman's blood ruined them. Also, your knuckles are beginning to swell."

"Impressive," his friend said, saluting him with his glass. More wine spilled on the table. "What else can you deduce?"

He chuckled. "That isn't your first glass of inferior wine this evening."

Norgrave snorted. "That is obvious."

"So what did the unlucky gentleman do to warrant a thorough thrashing with your fists?" Tristan asked, too used to his friend's mercurial temperament. In truth, the other man might have done very little to ignite Norgrave's wrath.

His companion finished his wine before replying. He glanced around the large public room, probably looking for a female or two to soothe his sour mood. "He insulted me."

"That was incredibly foolish of him. Does he still live?" Tristan asked, taking his time with his wine.

"He was still breathing when I kicked his unconscious arse into the middle of the street," the marquess confessed in his usual unrepentant manner. "I am not at fault if a coachman drives his horses and wheels over the fellow."

"Of course." In Norgrave's mind, only a foolish man would dare to insult him. The results were on the other man's head. "So tell me the real reason why you unleashed your temper on this stranger?"

The marquess signaled for another bottle of wine as he considered the question. "You know me too well, Blackbern." Norgrave scrubbed his face with his bare hand. "You might as well know the truth. It was Imogene."

Tristan's grip on the glass tightened. "You saw Imogene?" He swallowed thickly at his friend's curt nod.

"It shames me to admit it, but I cannot seem to win the lady's favor." Norgrave stared at him. "What about you?"

Relief rushed through his arteries and veins at such a speed that he thought his heart might burst. "I am experiencing similar results," he lied, and then scowled as he contemplated the reasons for his failure. "I believe the lady finds us charming, but she is intelligent enough to deduce that we are not to be trusted."

"A pity, do you not agree?" His friend laughed, pleased to learn that Tristan had not fared any better with the lady they both coveted. "I prefer a pretty, silly wench over one who has filled her head with intellectual pursuits."

The barkeep placed a bottle of wine between them.

Tristan raised his glass in a toast. "To silly wenches."

Norgrave filled his glass and raised it. "To willing wenches."

"Who believe a scoundrel's lies," he added, clicking their glasses.

They finished their wine and refilled their glasses again.

"The perfect woman," Norgrave said, slightly slurring his words. "So Imogene can resist that pretty face of yours."

It wasn't a question, but Tristan replied anyway. "There is no shame in declaring the wager a draw."

The marquess dismissed the suggestion with a grimace. "No lady has defeated me. I will think of something."

That was precisely what concerned Tristan the most.

"The wine is palatable, but I am craving a little female companionship to soothe my bruised pride." He tried to brace his chin on the palm of his hand, but it took three attempts before he succeeded. "The doxies in this tavern will give us the pox."

"What do you suggest?"

"The Acropolis," the marquess replied, naming a notorious club that catered to all types of carnal appetites. "My membership is in good standing. We could select a half dozen or more of their finest whores, drink and fuck until our cocks lose their steel. What say you, Blackbern? We haven't done anything so wild in years."

His unruly cock twitched between his legs at the thought of bedding and losing himself in a willing woman, but Tristan did not want a nameless whore beneath him.

He wanted Imogene.

Fortunately, he was sober enough not to confess his true desires to his friend. Tristan shook his head. "You will have to continue without me. I am heading home."

He braced his palms on the table to help him stand.

"Alone?"

Tristan nodded. "Enjoy your orgy, Norgrave," he said, ignoring the man's pleas to stay.

Even though he knew he should order the coachman to take him home, his thoughts kept drifting back to Imogene.

His need for her.

In the short time he had known her, Imogene had become important to him.

Tristan had yet to decide what he intended to do about it.

Chapter Thirteen

Tristan watched Imogene as she bade his aunt farewell. He was more than slightly drunk, and if he had any sense he would go home and sleep off the brandy in his cold, empty bed. He had Norgrave to thank for stirring his appetites this evening, however, there was only one lady he desired.

It took her a few minutes to notice that he was standing in the street. Imogene gaped at him. "Tristan, what are you doing here?" Forgetting about appearances, she ran to him. "I did not expect—"

He silenced her with a kiss. She seized him by the cravat and tugged him closer. He punished her by biting her lower lip and then rewarded her for her wanton ways by pushing her against the side of the coach.

Tristan grabbed a fistful of her skirt before his coachman cleared his throat as a polite reminder that anyone could stumble across them. "Take us home," he ordered as he guided Imogene into the compartment.

"I had a lovely evening with your aunt."

"I do not want to talk about Ruth," he said, reaching for her again. The interior of the coach was not as public as the exterior. He must have spoken the words out loud because Imogene stilled his hand that was currently resting on her knee.

Imogene cradled his face in her hands and peered at him. "Are you drunk, Your Grace?"

"Utterly," he confessed. "Do not fret, my lady. I am fully capable of seducing you. I do not need my wits, though in your case, it definitely helps. All I need is my c—"

She pressed her mouth to his to prevent him from finishing his boast.

"I cannot wait," he muttered, balancing her on his thigh so he could unfasten the buttons on his breeches. It took some effort because his coordination was off, but he managed to free his cock and work Imogene's skirt and petticoat above her knees.

His fingers sought and found the soft slit between her legs. He was pleased she was wet and ready for him.

"Perhaps we should wait until we—Ahh!" She moaned as he filled her with an impatient thrust. "What about the coachman?"

"He will have to find his own woman. I do not intend to share."

Tristan could not be certain, but he thought he heard the coachman's soft chuckle.

Then Imogene lifted her hips and his thoughts were wholly focused on her as she rode him. His lovemaking lacked his usual finesse, but his lover did not seem to mind their rough and hasty coupling.

Tristan slipped his hands under her skirt and caught her hips so he could set a dizzying pace. His cock plunged into her, his hip grinding against hers until he literally saw stars. He and Imogene found their release together. She cried out as his fingers left bruises on her flesh. He pulled her against him and counted the pulses as he spilled his seed deep within her.

Imogene held him as he shuddered. Tristan rested his face against her breasts while he savored the small residual twitches and jerks as the head of his cock was nestled against her womb. A part of him was appalled by his behavior. He had taken her as if she was a courtesan he had handpicked for a few hours of amusement. She deserved tenderness and a patient lover, not a wild fucking in his coach. The realization sobered him enough for him to struggle for an appropriate apology.

"Imogene, I have no words—"

"Nor do I, Your Grace. That was sinful, decadent, and wonderful." She licked his ear and giggled. "When can we try that again?"

His brain was so fuzzy with wine and lust, he was almost convinced that he was in love. "You are insatiable. Mortal men should be warned that dallying with goddesses is hazardous. At this rate, I will never celebrate my next birthday."

The coach slowed to a full stop.

"I would have never considered doing such a wicked thing in a coach," she said, carefully lifting her hips so she could fix her skirt. Tristan liked her where she was so he tried to pull her back onto his lap, but she evaded his hands. "Go home and sleep, Blackbern. If you think to dally with me in my father's house, I can guarantee that you will not have to worry about me or your next birthday."

Imogene kissed him and opened the door before the coachman. Tristan cursed as he tugged up his breeches and tucked his cock back into place. He fastened a few buttons on his breeches. "Wait for me. Damn it."

She blocked the doorway. "Tristan, this is not my father's house," she said, gazing over her shoulder at him.

"No, it is mine," he said as he placed his hand on her back to nudge her down the steps. When she remained speechless, he felt the need to clarify. "My private residence."

This was the one place he refused to share with any of his lovers. Tristan was too intoxicated to question the reason why he wanted to bring her to his home. Make love to her in his bed.

Tristan quietly accepted that he craved her—her smiles, her touch, the sound of her voice, and the way she looked at him. He needed her in his life. It was more than he offered any of his former lovers, and he prayed it was enough for Imogene.

Anticipation thrummed through her as she stepped through the front door and into the front hall of the Duke of Blackbern's town house. Imogene had already deduced that he valued his privacy. She had learned firsthand that he preferred to entertain his guests in his mother's old house. Most of the interior was cast in shadow, but what the glass lanterns mounted on the mahogany-and-rosewood staircase revealed hinted at the wealth and grandeur that she was certain he took for granted.

"Are you planning to give me a tour?" she teased, when they crossed the alabaster marble floor worthy of a Renaissance palazzo.

"Another time when I can show it off properly," he replied, brushing a light kiss against her lips. Instead of pulling away, he captured the delicate curve of her jaw with his large hand. His blue-gray eyes met hers, and his expression was both tender and vulnerable. "You are so incredibly beautiful. There are times I feel unworthy to touch you." He stepped away, allowing his fingers to trace the line of her jaw before his hand fell to his side. "It's too late. I cannot fight it—nor do I wish to any longer."

Imogene sensed that the brandy or wine he had imbibed before he approached her this evening was ruling Tristan's tongue. "What are you fighting?"

The duke responded with a careless shrug. "You . . . and me. Fate. Does it matter? I have surrendered."

Imogene laughed at the outrageous comment. She doubted her companion yielded to anything or anyone. "Now I know you are drunk. You are speaking nonsense."

She gasped when Tristan knelt, his knees pressed into the unforgiving marble floor. His hat tumbled to the floor as he grasped her hips and pulled her closer. He pressed his cheek against her stomach. "I may have had too much wine, but my thoughts have never been sharper."

"About what?"

"About you, Imogene. All I can think about is you. Thoughts of you consume me." Tristan held her tighter and sighed. "The poets would call it love."

Imogene held her breath as she placed her hand

lightly on his shoulder. Tristan thought he was in love with her? He did not seem particularly thrilled by the prospect. "Since you are not a poet, what do you call it?"

Tristan pulled back so he could meet her steady gaze. His lips parted as if he intended to explain his feelings for her. Instead, he shook his head and said, "I prefer to show you."

With more grace than a gentleman in his inebriated state should have had, he stood and took her by the hand. "Come."

Imogene placed her foot on the first step and hesitated. "The hour is late."

"It is," he readily agreed. "Too late for both of us."

She shook her head. Although she was no longer a virgin, she lacked the sophistication and experience of being a man's lover. "Your servants—"

"No one will disturb us. Everyone has retired for the evening." Comprehending her unspoken worries, the tension in his stance eased. "My servants are loyal and discreet. I promise, no one will speak of your visit. You have my word on it."

Tristan turned and she followed him up the staircase, the glass lanterns lighting their path.

"And what of my family?" she whispered, fearing her voice would carry.

"You will be home before your father summons the watch," he replied with his usual confidence.

As they climbed the stairs in silence, Imogene mused that it might have been more romantic if Tristan had swept her into his arms and carried her to his bedchamber. The thought made a lovely picture in her head, but she was a practical creature. In this dark interior, they would have more than likely stumbled and broken their necks.

Perishing in the Duke of Blackbern's town house would have been difficult to explain away.

"What is so amusing?"

Before she could respond, he opened a door and pulled her into one of the bedchambers.

"A fanciful thought," she said dismissively. Imogene remained near the door while Tristan strode to one of the unseen tables to light a candle. "Such an impressive staircase seemed to demand a more romantic ascension, do you not agree?"

The candlewick flared and illuminated the duke.

"Hmm, something along the lines of me carrying you up the stairs?" Tristan picked up the candleholder and joined her. He reached behind her and shut the door. His arm brushed against her side and the connection startled her. She heard him turn the key so no one could disturb them. "Too risky."

"I beg your pardon?" She felt his arm curve around her waist as he led her to the bed.

"Carrying you up the stairs in the dark. We would have broken our foolish necks."

Imogene laughed since she had come to the same conclusion. "I cannot refute your logic. It is one of many things that I admire about you."

Tristan placed the silver candleholder near the bed. "Admire? Or love? Are you in love with me, darling?"

Her sudden stillness had him almost regretting that he had asked the question. Tristan was usually more clever than this, and he blamed his loose tongue on the inferior wine he had consumed with Norgrave. He had been full of need and impatience since he coaxed Imogene into his coach, and for reasons beyond his comprehension, this evening he was determined to break down the remaining barriers between them.

Tristan stood behind her and placed his hands on her shoulders. He massaged the delicate muscles to ease the tightness and to offer comfort. "You can tell me anything. Your secrets are safe with me." He swept her curls aside so he could kiss the nape of her neck.

"What about me?" she softly asked.

His right hand slipped under her arm as he pulled her against him so her backside aligned to his front. Her closeness and womanly scent filled his nose. Her essence shot downward to his testicles. His cock, which had been partially erect since he had touched her in the coach, expanded and lengthened as he rubbed himself against her.

"Aye, Imogene," he murmured as his hand slowly moved upward, his nimble fingers unfastening the buttons on the front of her dress. He discovered once he had slipped his hand beneath the bodice that she had laced her stays in the front. "Your secrets and you are safe in my care."

It was a sincere vow. However, he buried his face in the curve of her shoulder to conceal his wince as he belatedly recalled the damn wager. He was determined to put an end to Norgrave's schemes, but it would not be a simple task. Especially, when his friend figured out that Tristan had claimed the lady whom he coveted.

"Yes."

Savoring the feel of her in his arms, he had forgotten about his question. "Yes?" he echoed, eyeing the bed and calculating how long it would take to undress her.

Imogene bowed her head. "I have never been very good at subterfuge. I assumed you had deduced my feelings weeks ago."

Tristan's chest tightened at her admission. The building pressure caused his heart to pound. "No, you are not a very good liar," he said, his voice growing hoarse with emotion. "Is it so difficult to speak the words?"

"Am I being foolish?" She expelled a breathy laugh. "I suppose hundreds of ladies have told you that they were in love with you."

Tristan thought of the women who had come in and out of his life. For many of them, his good looks, title, and wealth had been coveted as prizes. Others had only wanted his cock buried between their thighs. None of them had cared about him until he had walked out of their lives.

He turned her around, and used his fingers to lift her chin when she refused to meet his gaze. "No lady has ever truly loved me until you."

Imogene offered him a small smile. "Well, I have yet to admit it out loud."

He kissed her and nipped her lower lip to chastise her for torturing him. "Impertinent wench. Give me the words."

"I love you."

Tristan nodded and lowered his head until his forehead touched hers. His heart ached, and it took him a few minutes to recognize the emotion threatening to unman him as elation. "It took you long enough to admit it."

"Do you?" Imogene looked uncomfortable as she glanced away.

"Do I what?" he coaxed.

She swallowed. "Do you have feelings for me?"

The vulnerability and love he glimpsed in her dark blue eyes breached the cracks in the protective walls he had built around his heart since he had lost both his father and mother at a tender age. Her love filled him with strength, tenderness, and a fierce need to protect her. Love had a darker side. Tristan felt jealousy and fear. He could not bear the thought of losing her. "Aye, my lady. I have so many feelings churning in my chest that I am struggling not to get overwhelmed by them."

"You love me?"

"I need to show you," Tristan said, shuffling his feet closer. He was not the kind of man who openly confessed his feelings. It was simpler for him to demonstrate the depths of his affection for her with his body.

His lips touched hers with reverence. He kissed her as if he could keep her in his bed until morning. Their tongues teased and danced, a hint of the love play to come. He undressed her with the same deliberate slowness, worshiping every inch of her flesh he revealed. He traced the contours of her body with his fingers and tongue that sent her pulse racing and the folds between her legs drenched with her arousal. When he placed her naked on his bed, there was a primitive satisfaction in his gaze that she was as eager for their coupling as he was. He swiftly undressed and climbed on the bed.

Imogene's fingers closed around the shaft of his cock and she wordlessly pulled him closer. He covered her with his body, and his fingers sought the hot, damp flesh between her legs. He filled her with a single stroke.

Tristan began to move within her.

Love and lust battled for domination until a fine sheen of perspiration dampened their flesh and their bodies strained for completion. In perfect harmony, their cries of ecstasy blended as the delicate muscles of her sheath milked his cock as his release pumped in forceful spurts deep within her.

After a few minutes, he gasped, "So . . . love, eh?"

Imogene giggled and nodded.

He had never experienced such a soul-shattering release.

Before he had met Imogene, Tristan had bedded countless women, but he had never shared his body with love in his heart.

It was exhilarating and terrifying.

He and Imogene were running out of time. Soon, they would have to dress and he would escort her home, because she was not his to keep. It was a realization that he was gradually coming to hate.

"So this is not your first picnic here with Blackbern?"

A few days had passed since the night Tristan had brought her to his town house and they had spent several hours in his bed. Sated and exhausted from his enthusiastic lovemaking, Tristan had suggested that they return to the lake for an afternoon picnic. She was in love and was overjoyed that he was planning their next tryst. Imogene had not expected Norgrave to join them. From her duke's enigmatic expression, she could not tell if he was pleased or upset by their uninvited guest. Perhaps he could not think of a plausible reason to refuse the gentleman's request.

"Ah, no," she admitted as soon as she realized that she was on her own since Tristan appeared disinterested in offering the marquess an explanation. "After Blackbern ruined a picnic—"

"Utter lies," Tristan halfheartedly protested. "Do not listen to her, Norgrave."

"A picnic that I had planned with friends—" She blushed, recalling her quiet confession to the duke that she was dreadful when it came to subterfuge. "Blackbern was most definitely *not* invited!"

"Asher was one of the guests," Tristan explained to his friend. It was apparent that he did not view Lord Asher as one of her friends.

Good grief, was he jealous?

She opened her mouth and then promptly pressed her lips together. It had never occurred to her that Tristan viewed the gentleman as a serious rival for her affections.

Imogene was so distracted by the revelation that she had lost her place in the story. She brushed aside the thought with a wave of her hand. "Anyway, Blackbern was apologetic and he brought me here to make up for his rudeness."

She glanced over at Tristan and noted his arched eyebrow.

Have I revealed too much?

Tristan shrugged.

For reasons Imogene could not fathom, he was reluctant to admit to Norgrave that he had shared a part of his past with her. Considering what they had done near the old folly, perhaps it would have been wiser to keep her mouth shut.

Noticing her discomfort, a slow smile eased Tristan's somber expression. "Well, my lady, you might not have appreciated my presence, but Asher was very grateful," he teased, placing his hand on the small of her back as the trio strolled toward the lake.

The gesture did not go unnoticed by Norgrave.

"How long ago was this infamous picnic?" the marquess inquired.

"How long—oh, I don't know," she said, looking to the duke for assistance. So much had happened between them. "Tris—ah, Blackbern, do you recall the exact date?"

Imogene prayed her mistake was less obvious to her companions. She could not believe she had been so careless.

Tristan shrugged. "A few weeks ago, I suppose. Maybe longer. Does it matter?"

Norgrave shook his head. "Not at all." His gaze switched to his friend. "Blackbern has always had a problem with sharing. It was generous of him to drive you all the way out here to apologize for his boorish behavior. I cannot remember the last time I visited this place, and I have known him for most of my life."

"Do not sulk, Norgrave," Tristan said, his expression betraying his annoyance. "The land has been in the hands of tenants for more than a decade. I invited Imogene to join me so I could look the estate over before I rent it again."

"How convenient the lady was available on that particular day," his friend drawled.

Norgrave turned away so he did not see Tristan take a furious step toward him or Imogene's silent plea for him to halt as she divided her attention between the two men. With his back to the couple, the marquess nodded. "And a very cozy arrangement, indeed. I am positively jealous."

Since his words were closer to the truth than anyone wanted to admit, Tristan glared at his friend. "Come along, Imogene. We need to feed Norgrave before he decides to test his sharp teeth on my arse."

Chapter Fourteen

The minute the butler had announced the Duke of Blackbern was standing in their front hall and was requesting to speak privately with the Duke of Trevett's elder daughter, Imogene had forgotten about the letter she was writing and headed for the door.

"If you hope to catch that particular duke, I suggest that you strive not to appear so eager," her mother said, not even glancing up from her sewing.

"Yes, Mama. It is good advice," she said, deciding flattery was the best course to soften her mother's opinion toward Blackbern.

Imogene had not told anyone—not even her marriage-wary duke—but she intended to marry him. The last few weeks, she had demonstrated to Tristan that she was the perfect mistress; now it was time to show him that what he really needed was a duchess to fill his house with love and laughter.

She also had to convince her mother.

"I will pass along your regards to Blackbern," Imogene said, pretending not to hear the disgruntled sound the duchess made in her throat when she disagreed. She quietly shut the door and headed downstairs.

Tristan had his back to her when she descended the staircase. His attire suggested he had plans to travel. This was not a social visit.

"When are you leaving?"

He turned at her solemn question. His possessive gaze inspected every inch of her. It gave her hope that he would return to her. "Good afternoon, my lady. You look quite fetching in that dress. It puts color in your cheeks."

"I thought that was your favorite task," she teased.

"Unfortunately, I will have to delegate the pleasurable task to Norgrave and your other suitors." His demeanor was formal for the benefit of anyone who might be eavesdropping, but she noted the apology in his eyes. "I have neglected some important estate matters and they can no longer wait."

"How long will you be gone?" she demanded, resisting the urge to make him feel guilty over leaving her.

"Four days. Maybe longer." Tristan bent his head near her ear. "I shall miss you."

Imogene nodded, struggling not to cry. "Have a safe journey, Blackbern." Before he could step away, she kissed him on the cheek. "I love you."

He straightened and stared at her as if he could not quite trust his hearing. She swallowed the lump in her throat and the expanding pain in her chest when he did not echo her declaration. It was unfair to demand something he could not offer her freely.

To prove that she could walk away from him, she

smiled at him. "If I get betrothed, I will write you so you can return for the wedding."

Content that she had had the last word, she turned on her heel and walked to the stairs. Her foot had not touched the third step before Tristan had caught up to her, snatched her off the stairs, and kissed her hard enough that she would feel his mouth on hers an hour later.

"I will challenge any man who offers to marry you," he said, the violence in his eyes contradicting the gentleness of his touch. "If you care for any of these simpering fools, you will wait for my return."

He stalked off, not even interested in her response.

Imogene brought her fingers to her lips. Suddenly she grinned and her mood lightened. His threat was not the declaration she longed for, but he had days alone to improve on it.

Norgrave sought out Imogene as soon as he learned of Blackbern's departure.

Imogene's face warmed with affection when he entered the drawing room. "Lord Norgrave, how kind of you to pay us a visit!" She extended her hand, and he was pleased he had a reason to touch her.

He bowed over her hand.

"Lady Imogene," he murmured for her mother's benefit. "Your Grace, I trust you are well?"

"No worse than any other day, Lord Norgrave. Thank you for asking," the duchess politely replied.

He suspected the older woman did not approve of him. If so, he doubted Blackbern fared any better with the lady.

"Mama, with your permission, I would like to show

Lord Norgrave our gardens since it is a temperate afternoon," Imogene said, stepping in front of him as if she thought he needed her protection.

"An excellent suggestion," her mother murmured.

Imogene hesitated. "Would you care to join us?"

"I will have to regretfully decline. Of late, my left ankle has been troubling me." The duchess waved her and Norgrave off. "Enjoy your walk."

Once they were out of the drawing room, Imogene linked her arm through his. "I cannot believe you are here. How did you know I needed rescuing?"

He wondered how she would react if he stopped and kissed her. Since he did not want to ruin the moment, he resisted his impulses and patted her hand. "I am pleased to be of service, my lady, though I cannot fathom why you needed saving from your sweet mother."

Imogene laughed as they descended the stairs. "Mama is weary of the endless stream of suitors who have been filing through our drawing room. She laments that I have not narrowed my choices to one or two gentlemen."

"So few," he teased. "You are young and deserve to be courted by dozens of suitors."

As long as Imogene chose the right gentleman at the end of the season.

With Blackbern out of town, Norgrave intended to use the duke's absence to his advantage. He might have taunted his friend into agreeing to the wager, but his time with her had convinced him that the lady had value beyond a quick fuck. He had already surmised that Imogene had tender feelings for his friend, but he was confident that nothing would come of it.

He, on the other hand, had higher aspirations for the

future, and with Imogene at his side, he would achieve them.

"Perhaps I should have you speak to my mother and father," Imogene grumbled, obviously frustrated by her family's interference.

Norgrave believed that with a little effort, he could sway the duke and duchess to his side. "I am honored you view me as an ally."

They crossed the front hall.

"Of course," she said cheerfully. "You are a good friend."

Damn it, how could she not see that he was more than a friend? Once she discovered the shallowness of Blackbern's affection and scrubbed the stardust from her eyes, she would finally see the man willing to stand by her.

Imogene paused at the hall table to retrieve the bonnet she had removed earlier. As she picked it up, her reticule hidden underneath it tumbled to the floor. She muttered something about clumsiness and knelt down to gather up the items that had spilled on impact.

"Allow me," he offered, kneeling beside her. He picked up her reticule and suddenly stilled at what he had discovered beneath it. Before she could react, he grabbed the key.

She nibbled her lower lip in dismay. "If I may have it, I will—"

"I recognize this key," he said, holding it just out of her reach. His gaze was solely focused on the last item he expected her to have concealed in her reticule. "Did Blackbern give this to you?"

Imogene stared at him. Guilt shimmered in her eyes as she nodded. "I was not supposed to tell anyone."

His hand closed around the key. Blackbern was not careless with his possessions. Until this moment, Norgrave had been the only one who had a key to the duke's house. Even if Imogene did not fully comprehend the meaning behind the gesture, he saw it with brilliant clarity.

Blackbern had been lying to him.

At some point, his friend had won their little wager by seducing Imogene. Instead of gloating about it to Norgrave, he had given the lady the key to his mother's house.

Blackbern had finally fallen in love.

The realization roiled in his gut like an oily tar.

"I have not used it," Imogene confessed, his silence making her nervous. "Tri—Blackbern insisted that I keep it."

"Our friend is generous that way." It was a measure of his control that he stood and offered her the key instead of backhanding her with his closed fist. "Forgive me, my lady, I regretfully cannot enjoy your mother's gardens. I forgot about a prior commitment."

Uncertain, Imogene accepted the rest of the items he pressed into her hands. "You are welcome to call again, Norgrave."

"I shall return, Imogene. Perhaps I can help you cross a few suitors off your long list," he said, the smile on his face never reaching his eyes.

"I would appreciate any help."

Norgrave kissed her hand and turned away. It was not

until he had returned to his coach that he allowed his fury to surface. His dark thoughts were consumed with Blackbern and Imogene.

He had sorely underestimated his friend.

And Imogene.

Had the two of them laughed at his failed attempts to seduce her?

Norgrave slammed his fist against the glass window until it fractured into a delicate web of sharp splinters. The pain focused his thoughts and a plan of revenge began to form in his head.

When he was finished, Blackbern would rue the day he had betrayed their friendship. And Imogene—the duplicitous lady needed to be punished.

He was the perfect man for the task.

Chapter Fifteen

Imogene used her key to unlock the front door, and slipped into the house. She was confident that she was alone. Servants were hired to keep the town house clean and tidy, but the staff was gone by dusk since Tristan preferred his privacy. She shut the door, trying not to contemplate how many women had entered this dwelling at Tristan's invitation. Her chest tightened at the thought. How many of them had believed she alone had captured her handsome lover's elusive heart? How many had departed the house in tears, grieving that the passion they had shared with Tristan had burned itself out?

Am I doomed to a similar fate?

Until she had received Tristan's brief summons for her to join him at his mother's house, she had been unaware of his return to London. Imogene believed he genuinely cared for her, and perhaps he did in his own way. However, had she not been warned by numerous people that she should not trust the duke's fickle affection? He had loved countless ladies—many who were lovelier and richer than her—and none of them had kept his devotion for long. Perhaps that explained why she had felt a touch of unease at his summons. She had retained his interest longer than most, and a part of her had been waiting for him to grow bored with her. To tell her that it was time for her to let him go.

The warm light of several oil lamps greeted her in the front hall. Hours had passed since she had sent a response to his terse note, but she did not expect him to be waiting for her. His duties often delayed him, and he once told her that he liked entering the house, knowing that she was waiting for him.

What was so important that it had driven him to wait for her?

"Tristan?" she called out.

He did not respond. There was only the high-pitched wail of the wind as it gusted and blew through unseen crevices in the house, causing it to creak and shudder. She started at the sound of someone stepping on a loose floorboard overhead.

Tristan.

Perhaps the approaching storm had masked her arrival. Or he was simply waiting for her to join him. Imogene shook her head, unsurprised by his arrogance. She set down her reticule on the table. Tristan was too used to getting his way. Imogene opened a small drawer in the table and withdrew a candle. She pushed it into the empty socket of a candleholder, and used the flame from the nearby lamp to ignite it.

With the candle to light her way, she slowly climbed the grand staircase. She opened the door to the drawing room, but it was dark and empty.

"What sort of game are we playing this evening,

Tristan?" she called out, keenly listening for any sound that might reveal his whereabouts.

Unafraid, she moved through the house, opening and closing doors as she passed them. She expected to find him in the bedchamber to which he had brought her on several occasions, but to her chagrin, it was also empty.

With each step her annoyance was increasing. Imogene turned left to search the eastern wing of the house. She had yet to explore this portion of the house, since Tristan had other activities in mind when they met here. The door to the chamber at the end of the corridor was open and soft candlelight was a warm beacon in the darkness.

Imogene hurried down the passageway and crossed the threshold. The décor within the chamber was distinctly feminine, leading her to believe that this was the wing that Tristan's mother had occupied when she was alive.

"This was the last place I would have thought to search for you," Imogene said as she glimpsed his movements through the partially drawn curtains of the bed. "I left the house as soon as I could. Is something amiss?"

Imogene set her candle down on the nearest table and followed him to the other side of the bed. Her hand fluttered to her mouth to smother her gasp.

It wasn't Tristan who had summoned her. Lord Norgrave straightened as he stood to greet her. "No, my dear. Nothing is amiss. In fact, everything has worked out quite perfectly."

Confused, she stepped closer and peered at the bed.

She half expected to find Tristan reclining against the pillows. "I do not understand. I thought—"

He nodded, his eyes filled with kindness. "You believed that Tristan sent the note. I regret that I resorted to a little trickery to gain a private audience with you. Tristan has distinctive handwriting, but I learned to imitate it many years ago. People who have known him longer than you have been fooled by my skills."

"So this was a prank?" she asked, a hint of a smile teasing her lips.

"I suppose you could call it one." He walked to her and clasped her by the hands. Norgrave brought one hand to his lips and pressed a kiss on her gloved knuckles. "Are you amused?"

She laughed, noting he had not released her hands. "Of course. You had me completely fooled. I am certain Tristan will find all of this humorous. When is he expected?"

Instead of answering her question, Norgrave led her to the bed and invited her to sit on the mattress. Above all people, Tristan trusted this gentleman so Imogene saw no reason to protest.

"I was enjoying some brandy," he said, retrieving his abandoned glass. He took a sip and contemplated her over the rim of the glass. "Would you like to join me?"

Imogene wrinkled her nose. "No, thank you. It is too strong for my stomach," she said, recalling the night when Tristan practically poured the awful stuff down her throat to calm her nerves.

"If you like, I suppose I could find a bottle of wine," he said, his eyes resting on her face with a fierce intensity that made her uneasy.

Imogene silently wondered how much of the bottle the marquess had consumed as he waited for her. "There is no need to go to the trouble. I really cannot stay," she said, rising from the mattress. "Please pass along my regrets to Tristan."

Norgrave placed his glass of brandy on the table he had been leaning against. He stepped in front of her to prevent her from leaving. "There is no reason to bother him. He doesn't know you are here."

"Oh," she said faintly. "I see. You have used your key."

It wasn't a question, but he nodded as if it was. "I've had it for years. While Tristan thought the place too grand to use it as his residence, he was reluctant to sell it. Some years, he leases it to families who can afford his exorbitant demands, but lately he has discovered other uses for it."

Imogene felt her cheeks heat with embarrassment. Norgrave knew she and Tristan were lovers. Had he told him? It made little sense since he had appeared eager to keep their relationship a secret.

"Tristan told me that he often comes here to be alone."

Norgrave chuckled. "Is that why he gave you a key, too, Imogene?" He shook his head. "Do you know how many balls Tristan has hosted in this old house? If only the ghosts in this house could speak. I am not referring to the refined balls you have enjoyed during your stay in London. I speak of the decadent, drunken orgies that continued for days. The glorious nights when both Tristan and I buried our cocks in so many eager wenches, our ballocks were bruised for a sennight."

Imogene backed away from him and bumped up against the edge of the mattress. The marquess spoke with deliberate crudeness to upset her. Tristan had never denied that he was a scoundrel. Out of kindness he had tried to shelter her from his unsavory past, but he could not escape it completely—not when London was littered with his flirtations and former lovers.

"You speak of the past, not the present, my lord," she said, anger putting an edge to her voice.

"Do I?" Norgrave purred, pleased by her reaction. "I recall not too long ago when a pretty courtesan was kneeling at your lover's feet, her talented mouth wrapped around Tristan's—"

"Enough!" she pleaded, closing her eyes as if she could banish the image the marquess's words invoked. Her eyes snapped open. She was furious that she was allowing Norgrave to bait her. "I am well aware that Tristan is no saint. In some circles, he is not even viewed as a gentleman. Is there a point in discussing his past with me?"

Beyond hurting me?

"I do not mean to distress you, my dear. In truth, I admire you greatly. You are beautiful and full of compassion. I thought it was imperative that you understood the man who claimed your virginity."

She glanced away.

"Ah, yes . . . I know all about it. Naturally, Tristan does not keep secrets from me. He told me all about his fascination with you. It was amusing, really. For a man who has spent most of his adult life steeped in sin, your innocence beguiled him. I hope you do not begrudge him sharing all the scandalous details with me."

"Why would I mind?" she softly countered, struggling not to drown in the hurt rising up to choke her. "As long as you found it all so *amusing*."

He lightly grasped her chin and encouraged her to meet his earnest gaze. "Not all of it, sweet Imogene. It pains me to tell you that Tristan cannot be trusted with your heart. I am certain you are already aware that he tires of you and is seeking a way to end your relationship."

Hearing her private fears uttered by this gentleman gave her pains in her chest. Norgrave had to hold her up as her knees weakened and her shoulders slumped in defeat. "You did not summon me over a prank. Is that why you are here, my lord? Are you his messenger?"

"I fear so, my poor girl." His face tightened with anger. "I am often asked to clean up his messes. As his closest friend, it has been my honor to serve him, until this day. Not when I have to gaze upon your sorrowful expression. It shames me to be a part of this. Tristan is a coward and a bastard for hurting you like this."

Imogene stared at the marquess with tear-filled eyes. If she allowed those tears to fall, her devastation would be complete. She refused to shame herself further in Lord Norgrave's presence.

"Thank you for telling me the truth, my lord. You can tell Tristan"—she inhaled, feeling as if she was drawing in slivers of glass instead of air—"His Grace that his message has been delivered and that he is free. I will not bother him again."

She shifted in the marquess's embrace, her sole thought focused on escape. "Please, I beg of you . . . let me go."

"What a damnable situation," he muttered, pulling her closer. "Here." He reached for his glass of brandy. "I insist you swallow every drop. You have had quite a shock, and I feel like a bounder since I am responsible."

Imogene made a wordless protest when Norgrave pressed the glass to her lips. She didn't want the brandy, but the gentleman was stronger. The brandy burned a trail down to her stomach. The glass was empty in less than a minute. She felt oddly lightheaded, but he hadn't given her much choice in the matter. She was unable to take a deep breath until she consumed the entire glass.

"I have to leave," she said, her voice sounding odd to her ears. "I do not want to be here when he returns."

Probably with a new lover in his arms.

"You have nothing to fear. I told you, Tristan is the one who sent me. As always, he will leave the task to me. He won't interfere."

Imogene pressed the empty glass into his chest. Norgrave grabbed it and set it aside. She thought of the note she had sent Tristan. Of course he would not be coming to the house. He had sent his friend to collect the key and send her away.

"Good." She swayed against Norgrave. "Then I shall be on my way."

"I cannot leave you in this condition, my dear. There's no telling what trouble you might encounter on the streets this time of night."

His touch was firm, but soothing. Imogene laid her cheek against his chest. The warmth of his body comforted her. He smelled good, too. She closed her eyes and pretended for a moment that the strong arms holding her belonged to Tristan.

Imogene pulled away from him. "I was counting on—it no longer matters. A hackney coach will take me home. If you can secure one for me, you will be free of me as well, Lord Norgrave."

Norgrave's fingers gripped her waist so she could not step away from him. "What if I do not wish to be free?"

He kissed her.

Her head still spinning from the marquess's revelations about Tristan and from the brandy he had poured down her throat, Imogene did not protest when Norgrave hauled her against him and channeled all of his passion into that kiss. His actions, while she assumed they were inspired by genuine feelings, left her bereft for the man who hadn't had the courage to tell her that he was finished with her. She felt his hot breath as he kissed her mouth, the line of her jaw, and her throat in a desperate attempt to elicit some kind of response from her.

The marquess was handsome, witty, and he had shown her kindness. Imogene willed herself to respond, but she felt nothing. She had given everything to Tristan. A hysterical bubble of laughter rose like bile in her throat as she tried to push him away.

"Norgrave . . . I cannot . . . please stop," she said, stirring in his embrace that was beginning to feel as restrictive as her stays.

"Now that he has discarded you, I no longer have to hide my feelings, Imogene." His hand slid up her arm and cupped her face. His mouth was merely inches from hers. "Tristan might have claimed you first, but you will find that I am a generous lover. Before long, I will make you forget—"

He thought his confession would please her, but she

sensed that she was overlooking something important. Tristan had mentioned that his friendship with Norgrave was complicated, and often jealousy had driven their competitive natures. "It does not bother you that Tristan was my lover?"

Norgrave scowled. "You are not the first lady to surrender her maidenhead to Tristan. He can be quite charming to gain a lady's favor." He tried to kiss her again, but she turned her face so his lips brushed her cheek.

Once again, the marquess's words did not align with what she had been told. Tristan had confessed to her that her innocence had troubled him. Out of habit, he generally avoided young ladies who had marriage-minded mothers and he had been chagrined at himself that he had succumbed to temptation.

Either Norgrave or Tristan was lying to her, and she was too hurt and confused to deduce which one had been telling her the truth.

"Forgive me, my lord," she said, feeling the weight of regret that he might have misunderstood her actions. "You are generous to overlook what many would view as a flaw in my character. Nevertheless, I have no intention of being any man's mistress. Not the Duke of Blackbern's. Not yours."

She pushed away his hands and managed three unsteady steps before he grabbed her and whirled her around to face him.

"You are upset with Tristan, and deservedly so. Just give me a chance to prove myself," he entreated, his hands moving up and down her arms in a soothing fashion. "Here and now. You won't regret it."

His fingers bit into her flesh when she tried to pull away.

"I already do," she said, struggling as he tugged her closer to the bed. "I thought we were friends, Norgrave."

"We are, my love. This evening we will become good friends," he promised, but his leering gaze made her feel unclean.

Imogene slapped him. Horrified, she gaped at him. She had never struck anyone in her life, but the marquess seemed to be impervious to her pleas and struggles. Norgrave froze. His eyes flared in fury, and she instantly regretted her actions. His stillness was even more frightening than his unwanted caresses.

Before she could apologize, he lunged at her. They collided with the table. The empty glass slid across the table's surface and shattered when it hit the floor. He captured her arms and shook her.

"You ungrateful chit!" he raged. "No one strikes me. Certainly not some silly little girl who ruined her good name by playing the eager whore for Blackbern."

"It was never like that," Imogene shouted back, even though she knew he was not the only one who would see her affair with Tristan in such an unflattering light. "I love him! He may no longer want me, but that doesn't change how I feel. There will always be a part of me that loves him, and neither you nor Tristan can take that away from me."

Norgrave's handsome face darkened and twisted in fury. "Let's just see about that, shall we?" He shoved her onto the bed, but he was on top of her before she could crawl to the other side of the mattress. "Oh no, love.

There's no escape for you. I promised that I would be a generous lover, and I intend to see it through even though you don't deserve it."

He seized the front of her bodice and tore it open. Imogene fought him in earnest. She used both of her fists to strike him on the face, neck, and shoulder, but he quickly subdued her by pinning her arms above her head. He roared in pain when she managed to get one hand free. She could scratch him, but she jabbed her fingers into his right eye.

"Why, Imogene, Tristan never told me what a little tigress you are in bed," he said, through clenched teeth. "I adore rough fucking."

He slapped her hard enough to rattle her teeth. Her cheek burned.

"Norgrave, I beg you . . ." Her eyes filled with tears as she realized that she did not have the strength to stop him. With each passing second, her limbs grew weaker as she struggled to push him away.

"Already eager for my touch," he taunted, kissing her exposed breasts.

He used the weight and length of his body to secure her to the bed. One hand pinned her arms over her head while the other hand—her stomach roiled as her mind interpreted the sounds of him unbuttoning his breeches. Her legs were partially exposed during her fight to wriggle away from him. Norgrave took advantage by roughly kneading her bare thigh.

"You have lovely legs. I can't wait to mark all of your white skin with my teeth," he murmured, biting the soft swell of her breast.

Imogene tried to scream, but only managed a pathetic

yelp. The weight of his body was squeezing the air out of her lungs. She could only take shallow breaths. The touch of his fingers between her legs energized her struggles. Tears streamed down her cheeks as she silently tried to cope with the violence being committed to her body.

A part of her understood that she meant nothing to Norgrave. She was an unwilling pawn to be used, broken, and discarded. The person he was trying to hurt was Tristan, and she mentally wailed at the injustice of it all.

"You have nothing to prove, my lord." Her mouth trembled. "Remember? You said yourself that Tristan no longer cares what happens to me."

Norgrave's hand between her legs stilled. He stared down into her tearstained face, looking as lost as she felt. "This isn't about him. This is about us. Our future together. In spite of your tarnish, I could do worse for a wife. I predict your father will pay me handsomely for marrying his reckless daughter, especially when I tell him that there is a possibility that you are carrying my child."

"He will never grant you his blessing—not when I tell him everything!"

"You sound like a petulant child." He pressed his fingers into her body to remind her who held the power. "Your father is a man of the world. He will want to avoid any scandal. After all, think of your younger sister's future. Why should her marriage prospects be ruined because of you?"

Imogene turned her face away, and sobbed.

He leaned down and tenderly kissed her cheek. "Don't fret, my dear. I can make you feel pleasure. In time, you will be eager for my touch."

Unable to conceal her disgust, Imogene raised her head and vomited. Some of it splashed on his coat and shirt. Appalled, Norgrave released her and scrambled backward off the bed. He did not bother covering himself. The sight of his rigid manhood spurred her to move. She crawled off the bed and landed hard on her knees. She gritted her teeth against the pain and struggled to stand.

"Oh, you can't escape me so easily," Norgrave said, sounding grimly amused.

Imogene reached for a shard of the broken wineglass just as he turned her over onto her back. Blindly, she struck out at him. The sharp edge of the glass cut him near the corner of his left eye and down his cheek.

With a roar, he knocked the piece of glass from her hand. "Look what you've done. You will pay for this!"

Heedless of the blood running down his face, Norgrave's fingers found her neck and squeezed until she saw tiny bursts of light. She tried to pry his unyielding fingers away as she gasped for air, but her gloves slipped. Her vision began to dim.

"Don't faint on me," he said, his sneering face inches from hers. Drops of blood struck her face like hot rain. "We are just getting started and I don't want you to miss a minute of it."

Chapter Sixteen

A trickle of unease went through Tristan when he discovered the front door unlocked. One of the servants
could have been careless, but he dismissed the idea. His
thoughts shifted back to Imogene's message.

> *You have not given me much notice.*
> *I will slip out of the house when it is safe to do so.*
> *I will try not to be late. Imogene*

There was nothing alarming in her message except
for one important fact. Imogene was responding to a
message Tristan had not sent her. She had left the safety
of her family to seek him out, and if this was one of
Norgrave's pranks, he vowed to seek retribution for the
man's mischief.

"Imogene?"

She didn't respond. Someone had lit the lamps in the
front hall. Tristan walked to the table where he noticed
her reticule. On top was the key he had given her. He
picked up the key and frowned. She had no inkling of
the true meaning behind his gesture. It was a sign of

trust. The old house belonged to him, and by giving her the key, he was granting her access to a part of himself. She had been free to explore the treasures within, and to his surprise she had unlocked hidden doors within his mind and heart that he had not been aware existed.

He was not a careless fellow, and had not handed out keys to every female who had caught his eye. There was only one other person who had a key, and that was his closest friend.

Norgrave.

Tristan slipped the key into a pocket and he picked up the lamp. He had no idea how long Imogene had waited alone in the house. Perhaps she had fallen asleep in the bed they had shared. Even now, she could be dreaming of their lovemaking. The notion of waking her from her slumber and slowly loving her with his body quickened his stride as he climbed the stairs.

The rest of the house was cast in shadows so he headed for the bedchamber. A brief glance revealed it was empty.

Where the devil is she?

Concerned, he pushed away his lustful thoughts and began shouting her name. He heard a soft whimper when he checked the wing that once belonged to his mother. He rarely used this portion of the house. Even in his darkest moments of depravity, he had been incapable of desecrating his mother's possessions.

The door to his mother's bedchamber was ajar, and the glow of candlelight revealed he had found his errant lover. Relieved by his discovery, a trickle of annoyance crept into his voice when he entered the room.

"Imogene, did you not hear me call your name? The

door is unlocked and I thought the worst—" His throat dried when he saw the disheveled state of the room.

There were several overturned chairs and broken glass on the floor. The bedcovers had been pulled back as if someone had been searching for something. Careful of the glass, he circled around to the other side of the room where a single lamp burned. It was then that he saw her huddled on the floor next to the bed. She had her knees drawn up to her chest and her hands covered her face as she silently sobbed.

"Dear God. Imogene!" He rushed to her side and dropped to his knees.

Imogene had been unaware of his presence until he touched her. He regretted his actions the moment she pulled her hands away from her face and started screaming. She struck out blindly as she shrank away from his hand.

"Imogene, it's me!" he shouted at her, willing her to look at him. Her dark blue eyes were unfocused and wild. Her scream faded into soft mewling sounds. When he caught her chin to gain her attention, he noticed the ugly bruises on her face. The dried blood at the corners of her mouth.

Someone had hurt her. He blamed himself for not getting to the house quicker. Ignoring her attempts to push him away, he pulled her into his arms and held her close. "Hush, I'm here," he whispered over and over as he rocked her like she was a child.

Her body was stiff as he held her. He stroked her back, and took note of every detail. Imogene had been struck in the face. The thought of anyone laying a hand on her had him seething with the urge to return the favor. She had been crying, but the swelling near her eyes had nothing to do with her tears. Her hair looked as if she had pulled out all of the hairpins in haste. The front of her dress was torn and there were smudges and stains on the fabric that looked like drying blood.

"Did someone break into the house?" he murmured into her tangled hair. She shook her head and continued sobbing. "How badly are you hurt? I need to know, darling. Should I summon a physician to examine you?"

Imogene shuddered in his arms. "No!" she cried. "Just leave me here."

"Someone must have addled your wits if you think I will abandon you." She flinched when he kissed the side of her head. "I regret that I am too late to confront your attacker. I came as soon as I saw your message."

"Why?" She lifted her head and it was then that he noticed the bruises around her neck. "Were you eager to watch him at work or did you expect to find my body?"

The sorrowful shadows in her dark blue eyes revealed the depth of her suffering. A part of him was desperate to believe Imogene had surprised a thief, but her presence here this evening had been planned. Her abuser had tricked her and lured her with a message that had not been written by Tristan's hand.

"Who would I be watching, Imogene? Norgrave or someone else?" he demanded. "I have already deduced he was the reason why you are here. Did you and Norgrave surprise a small band of thieves? Where the devil is he? Is he summoning the watch? Is that why he left you alone?"

His friend had some rough edges, but Tristan could

not believe Norgrave was responsible for Imogene's battered condition. And, if he was innocent, then why had he abandoned her? The watch could have been summoned later. There was nothing in the house that could not be replaced.

Instead of replying, she wiped her eyes with her fingers. Her hands were bare, but he noticed there was dried blood on them. He captured her hand and pried open her fingers. There was a nasty cut on the palm of her hand. The bleeding had slowed. He retrieved a handkerchief from his waistcoat and placed it over the wound.

"We need to clean it or you will get an infection."

Imogene shook her head, but she held the handkerchief in place by making a fist.

"I need you to talk to me, darling," he said, striving for a soothing tone that he didn't feel. He was determined to hear the entire ordeal from her lips, even if it took the rest of the night to coax it out of her. "When I read your note, I knew something was wrong because I didn't send you a message. The one you received wasn't written by my hand. I could think of only one man who was capable of duplicating my handwriting, but I don't know the reason behind it."

"He told me it was a prank," she said after a few minutes of silence.

"Who?" She was in his arms, but she might as well have been miles away. "Was it Norgrave?"

Imogene glanced away. "Did you send him? He told me that he was here on your behalf. That . . . that you sent him because you were finished with me."

Damn Norgrave's black soul to perdition! Tristan's

arms tightened around her. Finished with her? How could she believe such a lie when she was all he thought about when they were apart? "Norgrave lied to you, Imogene. I started this affair between us. I damn well would have had the courage to face you if I wanted to end it."

Her brow furrowed in puzzlement at his anger. He was offended that she thought so little of him.

"The things he said . . . I thought . . . I believed . . ." The color drained from her face.

Imogene was making very little sense. "What did you believe?"

"I let him ruin everything," she said, more to herself than him. Her face crumpled as she sobbed into her fist. "I did not tell him that I sent a note to your house. If what he told me was true, I did not think it mattered. Is that why you came? You believed his lies, too?"

What lies?

He did not understand exactly what had transpired before his arrival, but the pain and confusion in her voice was breaking his heart. He picked her up and held her close to his chest as he stood. "Imogene, love, I have not spoken to Norgrave. How could I? I left town. Remember? You need to be resting on a bed, not—"

Imogene practically strangled him as she wound her arms around his neck. "No! I cannot, please, I cannot."

Tristan thoughtfully glanced at the bed and the bed-chamber. His initial impression had been that a robbery had taken place and the chamber had been ransacked. When he imagined his friend alone in the room with Imogene, the confrontation became more intimate and sinister. His intense gaze lingered on the bedcovers that had been pulled back and were twisted. The linens were soiled with smudges of blood and other stains he could not identify. Her bloody gloves had been discarded at the edge of the bed.

Dear God.

"He's a dead man," Tristan said. The fury simmering in his gut rose as it threatened to consume him. Imogene had her face nestled against his shoulder as she attempted to hide from him and the devastation of Norgrave's attack.

Without asking her permission, Tristan carried her out of the bedchamber. He did not need a lamp to find his way to the bedchamber he had shared with Imogene. Grimly, he understood what she was trying to tell him—that she was ruined because of what Norgrave had done to her.

The immoral lice-ridden bastard.

He placed her gently on the bed. When he tried to step away to light a candle, she clung to him.

"Do not leave me!" she begged.

Tristan struggled to swallow the lump that had formed in his throat. "Love, I'm not. We are staying long enough for me to find a cloak for you and then we will be on our way. You need to be examined by a physician. I need to know—" He cleared his throat. "You've been hurt and I need to know how badly."

The strain on his neck was unbearable so he sat down beside her. She crawled back onto his lap and he welcomed the chance to hold her again, while he struggled to strap down his emotions for her sake.

"I do not know if I can let anyone . . ." She trailed off,

her voice so faint he had to bow his head to hear her. "Everyone will know what was done. My father. There will be a scandal. Verity. Is it fair that my sister pays the price?"

Tristan listened, trying to make sense of what she was telling him. Norgrave obviously was counting on her to never speak of his attack. How did he hope to keep it a secret? Did his friend think he would hold his silence once he learned the truth?

I wasn't supposed to find out.

Imogene had said that Norgrave was unaware that she had responded to his note. If Tristan had not followed her to the house, she would have continued to believe the blackguard's lies. She would have spurned all of Tristan's efforts to speak to her, and for the sake of her family, she would have never told anyone what had transpired in this house.

"I am to blame for all of this," he murmured, sickened and desperate to avenge her. "Norgrave would have never touched you if I hadn't desired you. If I had left you alone—"

"After our first meeting, I longed to see you again," she whispered back. "I was shameless enough that I would have chased after you if you had not sought me out."

He closed his eyes and wished he could have arrived in time to stop his friend. "Imogene, we cannot stay and pretend nothing has happened. Norgrave has to pay for his crime. I need to alert the watch."

"No," she said flatly. Imogene stirred in his arms, but she did not push him away. "Do you think to find justice in the courts? If you have him dragged in front of a magistrate, he will tell everyone that I was a willing participant. He will point out that I had a key to your house, and no one will blink an eye when he announces that both of you were my lovers. Naturally, he will be contrite and offer to marry me to spare my family the scandal. Even if my father protests, the magistrate will find it an acceptable resolution for all parties."

Tristan cursed. He had not considered that Norgrave might be forced to marry Imogene if the truth became public knowledge. Norgrave had never expressed any interest in marriage, however, there were advantages to marrying a duke's daughter. Had this been Norgrave's plan all along?

"I cannot marry him, Tristan," she said starkly, trembling in his arms. "I could not bear it."

"Neither could I," he grimly replied. "However, I cannot keep silent and feign friendship with the man who has hurt you. Don't ask this of me."

She brought her fist to her mouth to smother her sobs. "Then you condemn me to a fate far worse than death."

"Not if I can help it," he said, tenderly shifting her from his lap to the mattress. "Do you trust me?"

Tristan winced at her hesitation. Of course she did not trust him. He had failed her in so many ways.

Imogene grasped his hands when he attempted to move away. "I want to trust you. Is it enough?"

Tristan concealed his disappointment with a slight grin. He couldn't complain since she was granting him more than he deserved. "I will prove to you that your trust isn't misplaced. It begins with us leaving this house."

"I cannot go home," she said, her shadowed gaze following his movements as he lit a candle and then moved to the wardrobe to search the drawers for a cloak. "I have little skill for deception, and besides, my dress—"

"I have a plan." Tristan's mind was racing as he weighed their options against the risks.

Where is that damn cloak?

He opened and shut drawers, revealing his frustration and impatience. He needed Imogene covered from head to toe. She was trembling as if she was cold so she would likely welcome the warmth of a thick cloth. It would also conceal her identity. If luck was on their side, no one would see them leave the house.

"If not my home, where will we go? Your private residence?" she said in disbelief.

Tristan had considered bringing her to his house. She would be safe there, but the risk of her being recognized increased. "Not that I would mind settling you in my residence, but I thought our goal was to avoid a scandal."

"Then where?"

"My aunt's house," Tristan said decisively. He grunted with satisfaction when he pulled a cloak from one of the drawers. Draping the fabric over his arm, he picked up the candleholder and returned to her side.

Imogene was clutching one of the pillows to her chest. "Do you think it is wise to involve her?"

"She will be discreet," he promised. "We could do worse for an ally."

Tristan set the candle down, and shook out the cloak and wrapped the fabric around her. He refrained from telling her that his aunt would also insist that Imogene be examined by a physician to assess her injuries. There was no reason to heighten her fears.

Norgrave would have to be dealt with. Imogene was vehemently against having him hauled in front of a magistrate for his crimes, but there were other ways to punish the bastard, and Tristan was personally going to deliver the message.

Chapter Seventeen

Imogene was lost in a sea of misery and pain.

How amazing that it was Tristan, her beautiful and strong reluctant knight, who had emerged out of the darkness and wrapped his arms around her to stop her from slipping under the surface of the dark waters of despair, her mouth and lungs filling with the warm, salty liquid of her tears. He had kept her from drowning.

She loved him, and she hated him. Distrust twisted her wounded heart, but as he cradled her in his arms within the shadowed interior of the coach, she knew he was determined to save her. Her knight might be tarnished and his honor in shreds, but he understood duty. The need to protect her from further harm burned in him as brightly as his thirst for vengeance. He blamed himself for Lord Norgrave's attack. Whether it was fair or not, a part of her blamed him, too.

"Are you still with me?" Tristan murmured into her hair.

"Y-yes," she stammered, slipping her hand underneath his waistcoat until it splayed over his chest. In spite of his calm demeanor, his heart was pounding in his chest.

"Good. Hold on to the fact that you are strong—and brave. You'll be in good hands under my aunt's care. She'll know what to do," he vowed.

She did not know which one of them he was trying to convince.

Imogene closed her eyes, letting Tristan's warmth sink into her body. She was so cold and there was a deep ache that seemed to radiate from her bones. Flashes of color exploded beneath her eyelids. At first the patterns were indistinct, and nonthreatening. Suddenly, the Marquess of Norgrave's face came into focus. His normally genial expression hardened and twisted until she no longer recognized him.

"Will you tell Blackbern the truth? I wonder. Are you that brave?"

Imogene gasped and straightened, pushing the man holding her away.

"What is it?" Tristan demanded, his tone harsh because she had startled him.

"I . . ." She brought her hands to her face and took a few deep breaths. "I must have fallen asleep. It was just a dream."

Tristan tentatively reached out and placed his hand on her back. When she didn't flinch from his touch, he rubbed her back in a soothing manner. "More like a nightmare, I think." He fell silent as he carefully chose his next words. "Darling, can you tell me about it? The dream. I do not expect that you are ready to talk about what happened in the house. Not yet anyway."

Imogene wasn't certain she would ever be able to speak of it. Her hands fell away from her face, revealing that her cheeks were dry. She had cried for so many hours, she did not know if she had any tears left. "I do not recall much. I was not even aware I was dreaming. I just saw *him*."

His hand rubbing her back froze. Tristan cleared his throat as if it was dry. "Norgrave?"

Imogene nodded. "I felt his breath on my face and I opened my eyes. He asked me a question and then I awoke." She pulled the edges of the cloak together to banish the cold, but it didn't help.

"What did the bastard say to you?"

She sighed. "It was a dream, Tristan. Nothing more."

He shifted, crowding her so that she could not avoid him. "The hell it is. I want to know what he said that had you crying out in fear."

Imogene was tempted to lie, but the man beside her always seemed aware of her feelings. "He wanted to know if I would tell you the truth."

The confines of the compartment seemed to vibrate with the fury Tristan was attempting to shield her from. Instead of punching the nearest wall of the coach, he rubbed his jaw. "There is darkness in Norgrave, but I never thought him capable—" He grimaced and shook his head.

Shame clung to her like an unpleasant scent. "You still do not understand. How could you, when I am unable to believe or accept it?"

"Then tell me," he coaxed.

She closed her eyes as his fingers grasped her upper arms. He turned her until she faced him.

"You can tell me anything."

Imogene blinked at the abrupt sting in her eyes. His tenderness was her undoing. Perhaps she had a few tears left, after all. "You have to understand. I tried to stop him." She brought her hand to her nose and sniffed. "He was too strong. Too determined to hurt—"

"You," Tristan said when she struggled with her words. He cupped her face with his hands. "I know, love. You don't have to explain."

"No, he was trying to hurt *you,*" she said in a swift rush of words. Her stomach ached as if a poison festered there and she needed to be rid of it. "He taunted me, daring me to tell you because it was the one thing you would never forgive."

"The sin is on *him,* Imogene." Tristan's eyes looked like obsidian in the dim glow of the coach's lanterns. "You did nothing wrong."

"No, it is you who do not understand! When he—" She gazed helplessly at him as she thought of the terror she had felt when he pushed her onto the bed and shoved his hands between her legs. Gulping air, she turned away from him and pressed her forehead against the cushioned wall of the coach.

"Imogene?"

"Norgrave forced me to experience pleasure." She struck the wall with her fist, her fury renewed at his devious cruelty. "I was prepared for the pain. I welcomed it, but he stripped everything from me and then told me that I had to live with the knowledge that I secretly desired him. It is a lie, of course, but he planted doubt within me even as he filled me with his seed."

Imogene glanced over her shoulder when she heard the soft, ragged sound. Her gaze locked with Tristan's, and there was nothing left to be said. His dark blue eyes were luminous as tears filled his eyes. He did not turn away, but allowed her to see them fall freely down his cheeks.

"I want to kill him for what he has done," Tristan confessed, his voice hoarse with suppressed anger. "What you've said does not change my feelings. The sin is his to bear, Imogene. I know you have doubts." His composure broke, and his features contorted as if he was in pain. Quickly recovering, he continued, "But with time, you will come to understand that Norgrave is a master when it comes to manipulation. He made you feel pleasure against your will, because he knew the anguish of it would linger in your thoughts. He will only succeed if you let him."

The coach slowed. He inhaled sharply and scrubbed his face to wipe away the evidence of his tears. In the dim lighting, he looked older than five-and-twenty. The door opened, and Tristan pulled the hood of the cloak over her head to conceal the bruising on her face. "Can you walk to the door or should I carry you?" he asked, giving her a choice.

Imogene felt battered and dazed. A part of her prayed that she was asleep in her bed and that when she opened her eyes, the horror of what she had endured would fade. Tristan said she was strong and she desperately wanted to believe him. "If you carry me, it might draw unwanted attention. I can walk . . . just give me a moment to compose myself."

He looked as if he wanted to protest, but he managed a brief nod before he descended the steps of the coach. Imogene remained seated for a few minutes. She could hear Tristan and the coachman talking, but they were speaking too softly for her to discern their words. Taking her time, she adjusted the hood so the fabric hid her features. She could not understand why he had brought her to his aunt's house. The only reason why she had not argued with him was that she could not face her family. Not yet. She needed more time to figure out how to explain everything to her mother and father.

Tristan poked his head through the doorway. "Are you ready?"

Imogene held out her hand, and he immediately grasped it. Belatedly, she noticed that she was still clutching the handkerchief he had given her to stanch the blood from the cut on her hand. Not all of the blood on her dress was hers. The marquess had seemed oblivious to the damage done to his face. The long furrow she had made with the jagged shard of glass had been deep enough to leave a scar. He would bear her mark for the rest of his life.

With the help of Tristan's steady arm, she disembarked from the coach.

Tristan deliberately set a slow pace that Imogene could manage. She leaned against him, and he could sense that she was weakening with each step. He was moody and impatient, and he longed to scoop her up into his arms and carry her into his aunt's house, but he understood her need to find her own way.

The front door opened, and the blazing light from within bathed their faces. He could hear his aunt's voice as she issued orders to everyone within hearing distance. His aunt was preparing to depart for the evening.

"Tristan," the countess exclaimed, finally noticing his and Imogene's approach. "This is a most welcome surprise. We are getting a late start on our evening and were just on our way out." She peered at the cloaked figure standing next to him. "Who is your companion?"

Unexpectedly, Imogene's strength ebbed and she sagged against him. When her knees gave out, he swiftly caught her and picked her up.

"Forgive me, I feel unwell," she mumbled, her face still obscured by the cloak's hood.

"Good grief, is that Lady Imogene?" his aunt asked. "Is she ill?"

He did not bother answering his aunt's questions. "Rest. You did well," he murmured to Imogene. Without waiting for an invitation, he strode by his aunt and entered the house. "I need a bedchamber prepared for her."

Tristan pushed back the hood, and his aunt gasped when she noticed the bruises on Imogene's face.

"Forgive our intrusion, Lady Ludsthorpe," Imogene said, politely ignoring the older woman's alarm. "It was not our intention to interrupt your evening, but Tristan insisted on bringing me here."

He had to give his aunt credit. She quickly recovered from her shock at Imogene's appearance and took charge of the situation. "He was wise to bring you here," she said sincerely. "Tristan, why don't you carry Lady Imogene up to the drawing room? She can have some tea while her bedchamber is being prepared."

While his aunt slipped away to make her excuses to

her family on why she was not joining them, Tristan carried Imogene upstairs and placed her on the sofa.

"You do not have to coddle me like a child," she said crossly. "What your aunt must think of me!"

At the moment, the countess probably believed the worst of him, but he wisely held his tongue. "I like coddling you, and there is nothing about you that gives me the impression that you are a child." He absently bent down to kiss her on the cheek, but she shied away from him.

Tristan silently cursed his carelessness. "Do not fret about my aunt. She is a generous soul, and she will open her house to you until you are ready to summon your mother and father."

The butler entered the drawing room with a heavily laden tray.

"Ah, there's your tea. It will warm you during my absence."

"Where are you going?" she demanded as she started to rise from her seat.

"Sit and drink your tea. I intend to speak to my aunt. Our disheveled appearance on her doorstep requires an explanation," he said, gently coaxing her back onto the cushion. "I will return shortly."

As he suspected, his aunt was waiting for him as he exited the drawing room. He shut the door so their conversation could not be overheard by the lady within.

"Thank you for taking in Imogene," Tristan said, genuinely grateful to his aunt. "I wanted to take her directly home, but the notion of her parents seeing her current state was too upsetting. It seemed prudent to keep her calm."

His aunt jabbed her finger into his chest. "Are you responsible for that poor girl's condition? She might be covered in one of my sister's old cloaks, but I noticed she has dried blood on her dress."

"So naturally you assume I am to blame," he snarled, more than happy to give his anger a target. "Do you take me for a fool? If I was the one responsible for ravishing her, why would I bring her to *my* family?"

"Ravished?" his aunt said, clutching her necklace in distress. "Are you certain?"

"Imogene was tricked and has been brutally mistreated. I have yet to get the entire tale out of her, but I have heard enough to understand that she needs more than a tender heart."

"I'll send a footman for a physician."

"I have already given my coachman the task. It is someone I trust. His hands are steady, and he will be discreet. I need your assistance in convincing Imogene to accept his help."

"This is a travesty. Do you know who hurt her?"

"It was Norgrave."

The countess swayed, and Tristan worried that she might faint. "Norgrave. Your friend is the one responsible? I cannot believe it."

"There is no doubt that Norgrave lured Imogene to my mother's house, so he could—so he could—" He swallowed the rest of his words, unable to speak the thought out loud.

"Tristan, Lady Imogene's mother and father must be told. You cannot keep this from them."

"I am aware of that, madam," he said, in clipped tones.

"As for the marquess . . ."—his aunt clasped and

unclasped her hands—"he must be brought in front of the magistrate for his crimes. I can send a servant—"

"No." He stepped in front of her to block her from heading downstairs. "I will deal with Norgrave."

"I understand how you must feel. After all, he is your friend."

"He was my friend," Tristan said coldly. "Will you look after her during my absence?"

"Nephew, does the woman sitting in my drawing room know you are planning to kill her attacker?"

Tristan met her gaze unflinchingly. "You do not approve? I'll admit it seems rather bloodthirsty, but revenge tends to be dark and messy. Besides, someone has to send him to hell."

The countess made a fretful noise in her throat. "My dear boy, you are not thinking clearly. What good are you to Lady Imogene if you are languishing in prison? She would not approve of you throwing your life away. Allow me to send for the watch."

"No watchmen. Nor will I be sent to prison." *Not if I am careful.* "I spoke rashly. There are ways of dealing with depravity that do not require bloodshed," he lied with practiced ease. He kissed her sweetly on the forehead.

His aunt remained unconvinced. "Tristan," she said, a warning in her voice.

"I have to leave," he said, refusing to be swayed. "Offer Imogene my apologies, though I doubt she will accept them. The physician will be here soon. Tell him to send the bill to me."

"Stay. Your lady needs you," she entreated.

Tristan did not bother to deny that Imogene belonged

to him. She had rushed into his life and knocked him off his feet, altering his world forever. "Not now. Imogene needs compassion and I am too full of vitriol to be of much help. I will return when I am able."

He brushed by his aunt and headed for the stairs. "Send word to the Duke and Duchess of Trevett. Imogene will not thank us for it, but her family should know that she has been hurt. Tell them." He braced his hand on the ornate post at the top of the stairs and thought. The last thing he desired was for Imogene's father to challenge the Marquess of Norgrave. "Just send word that there has been an accident. Explanations can be made when they arrive."

"And what shall I tell Lady Imogene?"

Tristan regretted that he was leaving her without kissing her farewell. He had chosen his path and he would not allow anyone to dissuade him from confronting his friend. "Tell her that I will return."

Satisfied that Imogene was in good hands, he hurried down the stairs where the butler was waiting to open the front door for him. Retrieving his hat from the male servant, Tristan stepped out into the night.

Imogene heard the muffled sound of a door closing. Still wearing the cloak Tristan had wrapped around her, she scrambled to her feet just as the door opened and Lady Ludsthorpe hurried into the drawing room.

"I have been dreadfully rude abandoning you to take your tea alone," the countess said, her right hand moving from her waist to her throat in a nervous gesture. "Pray, remain seated. How are you feeling? Shall I pour more tea?"

"No, thank you," Imogene said, her eyes shifting to the empty doorway. "Where is your nephew?"

"Oh, dear me, I do not know where that boy has wandered off to," the older woman said with false cheer. "Perhaps Tristan wanted a word with Lord Ludsthorpe before he departed to one of his clubs. Or he might be downstairs raiding the stock of brandy in the library. I do not know about you but I would not mind a sip or two."

Lady Ludsthorpe sat down abruptly next to Imogene on the sofa.

"I dislike brandy."

Her stomach churned as her thoughts drifted back to Lord Norgrave pouring brandy down her throat—of the glass shattering and Imogene sitting beside Tristan's aunt with dried blood on her hands. The elegantly attired countess was a reminder that her dress was in tatters. All she wanted to do was pull the hood over her head and hide, but she did not wish to insult her hostess. The lady probably thought her behavior quite odd as it was. She brought her hand to her face and smoothed the hair from her cheek.

"I hope you do not mind that I took the liberty of having the servants heat some water for a bath. You will feel better once you have washed and put on fresh clothing."

It was going to take more than hot water and soap to make her feel clean. Her arms and wrists ached from the marquess's fingers as he had held her down. Imogene did not realize she had whimpered until she noted the compassionate tears in Lady Ludsthorpe's eyes.

"It was wrong of Tristan to bring me here."

The lady gently clasped Imogene's hand. "I do not always approve of the decisions my nephew makes, but he was correct to bring you to me. If you are done with your tea, I will show you the bedchamber I had prepared for you. Many of our guests have proclaimed it the best room in the house."

Imogene found herself gently maneuvered from the drawing room to the bedchamber upstairs while the countess prattled on about her adult children, Lord Ludsthorpe, and the new cabinet she had recently ordered for the library. She had always marveled at Tristan's talent for coaxing the people around him to do what he wanted, but he clearly had been taught by the best.

"You must be overly warm in that old cloak. Why don't you remove it, and we will find something more comfortable."

Her hand tightened around the fabric she was clutching, preventing the countess from peeling back the flaps. The condition of the dress was more revealing than the bruises on her face. "Lady Ludsthorpe—"

"Ruth. You may call me by my given name, or simply Aunt Ruth. Over the years, I have collected a fair share of nieces and nephews who are not related to me by blood. It would also please me if we were friends."

Somehow she had undone the clasp and pried the woolen fabric from Imogene's fingers. The cloak fell away and dropped to the floor. The countess bit her lower lip as concern filled her brown eyes. "Oh, dear, I do believe the dress is beyond repair. With your permission, I will have it torn into rags and burned. We will find you another dress. Among my three daughters, I am positive we have a dress that will fit you."

Imogene would like nothing more than to see the dress she was wearing burned until it was ash. "You are too generous, my lady." At the older woman's chastening glance, she amended, "Aunt Ruth."

A soft knock at the door had Imogene taking a step backward.

"Yes?" Lady Ludsthorpe called out.

"Madam, the physician has arrived," the butler said from the other side of the closed door.

"You never mentioned that you had summoned a physician." Imogene crouched down and gathered the discarded cloak. She clutched it to her bosom as if it could conceal the damage done. "Is this why Tristan vanished without a word? Is he responsible for bringing the man here?"

The countess took the cloak from her. "Do not be angry at my nephew. He is worried about you. If Tristan had not sent for his man, I would have asked our family physician to tend to your wounds."

"What was done to me cannot be cured with tonics and bleeding, Lady Ludsthorpe!" she said, knowing she was being unreasonable. With the butler and the physician standing just outside the bedchamber, she felt trapped. "I beg of you, please send him away."

Having raised five children, the older woman was familiar with tantrums. "Be sensible, Imogene. You must be examined for the sake of your health. Think of your family . . . and Tristan. He blames himself for failing to protect you from Norgrave."

Imogene's expression was sullen as she glared at the countess. "Tristan is not responsible for the marquess's actions."

"A logical assumption, I concur. However, my nephew has known Norgrave since they were boys. They have watched over each other for most of their lives. It was simple to overlook the flaws in his friend's character because love and loyalty blinded him."

Until this evening, when he had discovered the depths of Norgrave's depravity.

Was he angry enough to confront his friend? Tristan had been so attentive since he discovered her curled up on the floor of his mother's bedchamber. Imogene could not believe he would abandon her. More likely, he was waiting downstairs in his uncle's library.

Still, she could not resist asking, "Ruth, where is your nephew?"

"I do not know," was her evasive reply, which had Imogene's eyes narrowing with suspicion. "He promised to return to you, and he is a gentleman who keeps his word. We can discuss this further after the physician has inspected your injuries."

Imogene stared at the door as if she expected to see Norgrave at the threshold. She shuddered, but to the countess's immense relief, she nodded.

Lady Ludsthorpe gave her an approving look. "All will be well, my dear. You'll see. I will even stay so you will not be alone."

She straightened her shoulders. Tristan had called her brave. If she could not do it for herself, she would find the courage for his sake. "I would like that very much."

Chapter Eighteen

Tristan expected to spend half the night searching for Norgrave, but it had only taken three stops and a bribe to one of his servants to discover the man's whereabouts. He had rented several rooms at his favorite club, the Acropolis, where he indulged in forbidden pleasures and satiated some of his more perverse appetites.

His name and another bribe granted him entry into the private club. While he was not a member, over the years, he and Norgrave had ended many evenings at the Acropolis. When he was younger, the lavish decadence of the establishment and the willing participants encouraged him to explore the darker side of his nature. It had been intoxicating and addictive, so much so, that he began to distance himself from this particular vice, while Norgrave had only been drawn deeper into this world.

No one paid attention to him as he climbed the stairs. Norgrave had selected one of the finest rooms in the establishment. He had told the proprietor that he was celebrating and had asked for three companions for the evening. Tristan did not have to deduce the reasons for his former friend's good mood.

Tristan used the spare key the proprietor had given him to unlock the door to the chamber.

Music filled the air. The marquess was indeed in high spirits. He had hired musicians who were playing a lively tune. A large table had been carried in and it was heavily laden with food and bottles of wine. The food and drink encouraged other patrons to join the festivities. Tristan counted at least eight females in various states of undress. There were four men in the room, too, but he did not recognize any of them.

A bare-breasted blonde weaved toward him. "'Allo, stranger! My, you are a handsome one," she said, offering him a drunken leer. "The bed is already occupied, but I know of an alcove."

The woman had consumed too much wine to be reasonable. Tristan removed her curious hand from the front of his breeches and gallantly kissed it so she would not be offended. "I have some other business I must attend to first, why don't you wait for me in the alcove?"

Her eyes were mere slits. With luck, she would fall asleep and forget all about him. "It will cost ye, but you will not regret it."

"I rarely do," he murmured, but the drunken temptress was already staggering away to do his bidding.

Tristan headed for the double doors that would open into the bedchamber. He opened one of the doors and stepped inside. Fully naked, Norgrave was standing next to the bed with his back to the door. Although he could see only glimpses of her, the marquess was not alone. He had positioned a woman facedown on the mattress. The energetic, rhythmic thrust of the man's hips did not deter Tristan from entering the room and shutting the door. Wearing only a thin chemise, another woman was reclining on the long sofa while her female companion's dark head was nestled between her thighs.

She glanced back and smiled at Tristan's approach. "My lord, you did not tell us that you've invited your friend."

Norgrave's head snapped in his direction. Without slowing his pace, he said, "Blackbern, I was not aware that you had returned. Join us!"

It wasn't the marquess's lack of modesty that disturbed Tristan, it was the glimpse of the ugly cut on his face that was disquieting. He thought of the blood on Imogene and the bed, the wound on her hand. She had not accepted Norgrave's abuse meekly, and he had not walked away unscathed. A surgeon had stitched up the deep sections of the gash. The side of his face was swollen and discolored, and an infection might spare him the trouble of murdering the coldhearted scoundrel.

His former friend grunted and his shoulders rippled and bowed as he spilled his seed into the woman. It was not the first time that he considered Norgrave arrogant and reckless. Tristan wondered how many bastards the man had sired. The thought that Imogene might be carrying the marquess's child fueled his fury.

Norgrave slapped his lover on her arse and she cried out in surprise before she crawled to the other side of the bed to avoid another slap. "Be a dear, and get my friend a drink. He prefers brandy."

"I did not come to drink with you," Tristan said, his gaze shifting to the two women on the sofa. "Perhaps we should speak privately."

"Why? I have no secrets." The marquess slipped his

hand into the sleeve of a red silk banyan with blue flowers and worked his other arm into the other. He did not bother to fasten the buttons down the front. Tristan glanced down at the man's turgid cock with a raised brow. The man's confidence was something he once envied, but now he felt nothing but disgust.

Norgrave plucked the glass of brandy from the woman's hands as she walked by him. "Well, if you don't want the brandy, then I will claim it."

Whether it was intentional or not, his double entendre spurred Tristan into action. His fist connected with the man's jaw, sending him backward and into the fireplace mantel. He heard the three women cry out in surprise and alarm, and there was movement behind him.

Norgrave's pained expression relaxed into speculation as he rubbed his sore jaw. "Leave us."

The women hastily slipped out of the bedchamber, but neither of the two men observed their departure.

"You're bleeding," Tristan said dispassionately. He walked over to the table and picked up a linen napkin that had been discarded. He tossed it at the marquess. "That is a nasty gash."

"Would you believe I cut myself shaving without a mirror?" Norgrave pressed the cloth to his cheek.

Tristan lunged and seized the loose cloth flaps of the open banyan. He slammed Norgrave against the mantel. "You must have been astounded when Imogene fought back. It's a pity she didn't cut your throat, though there is a certain justice to her marring your handsome face, don't you think?"

Tristan tightened his hold and pulled him closer so

he could pivot the marquess away from the fireplace. He sent him careening into a table.

Norgrave toppled over the table and spun around to confront him. "Have you lost your head? Whatever the lady told you is a lie."

"I know about the message you sent Imogene. Duplicating my handwriting was simple enough. You knew it was the only way Imogene would agree to meet you. What you didn't count on was that she replied to the note she thought I had written to her."

A dry chuckle rumbled in Norgrave's throat. "Did you actually see the note that she claimed I wrote in your handwriting? You have it all wrong, my friend. Imogene is making fools out of us both. I regret telling you this since you are fond of the minx. Nevertheless, the lady invited me to join her at your mother's house. If she wrote you, she did so with the deliberate intention of pitting us against each other."

He stalked toward his former friend. "I went to the house and found her, you filthy piece of excrement. You cannot lie your way out of this."

Norgrave picked up a vase and wildly swung it at Tristan's head. It missed breaking over his skull, but it struck him in the shoulder. The vase broke on impact, and he felt one of the sharp edges slice into his shoulder. With a roar, he collided into the marquess and they both fell to the floor.

For a few minutes it was a balanced battle with no clear victor. However, the man who always prided himself in abiding by the rules was no longer interested in playing fair. He grabbed Norgrave by the testicles and twisted. The man bleated like a wounded goat, too blinded by the pain to even roll away.

Tristan drove his elbow into the man's stomach. He wanted to beat the man to death with his bare hands. He managed to hit him again, before the man kicked him away.

Norgrave staggered to his feet and sneered. "I never knew you were such a dirty fighter, Tristan. Shouldn't you be issuing a formal challenge and demanding that I choose my seconds?"

"No challenge," Tristan rasped, his collarbone throbbing from the blow. "You have no honor to defend. I suppose I will have to be satisfied with beating you bloody."

Norgrave landed a brutal punch, and Tristan's vision dimmed at the edges. He grabbed for the banyan, and gravity caused them to fall. The marquess landed on top, and he took advantage of his position. Tristan twisted his head to evade the man's fists, but he took several blows to the face and shoulder. From the corner of his eye, he espied a small shard from the shattered vase within reach and he grabbed it. The piece was too fragile to be lethal, but the shallow cuts across Norgrave's abdomen gained him his freedom.

"Enough!" the marquess barked, his hand lifted in surrender.

Tristan could not claim a clear victory. Both of them were gasping for breath and bleeding from numerous cuts. His face was already beginning to swell from the other man's punches. Fortunately, the marquess looked worse. The gash on his face was bleeding noticeably. He would need a surgeon's needle again before the night's end.

"I need to know why."

"Why what?"

"That damn wager, Norgrave," Tristan shouted. "What angered you more—the notion that I was no longer interested in playing your bloody games and saw you for the manipulative bastard that you are, or that Imogene picked me instead of you?"

"If I were you, I would question the lady's loyalty. Did she tell you about our time together?" he softly taunted.

"Spare me your lies." Tristan wiped the sweat from his brow with his sleeve. "I can never forgive you for what you have done. From this day forward, our friendship is over. If you speak of this night to anyone or utter Imogene's name, I will grant you the challenge you seek, and there will be no mercy. Sword or pistol, I will kill you."

Tristan had delivered his message. He headed toward the door. If they were lucky, everyone was too drunk or nervous to summon the watch.

"You are casting our friendship aside over a *woman*?"

"No, I am no longer your friend because I despise you!" he yelled back. "You twist and corrupt everything that touches your life."

Norgrave was outraged that his dearest friend was choosing a woman over him. "You will come to regret this decision. Your lady has a secret, one that she will never disclose. Do you hear me, Blackbern? Your lady took my cock with the eagerness of a Covent Garden whore. It was my name she cried out when she found her womanly pleasure within my arms." He bared his teeth when Tristan froze and slowly looked in his direction. "The next time you coax her onto her back, you will wonder—which one of us will she be thinking of when she closes her eyes."

Enraged, he slammed his fist into the marquess's damaged cheek, ruining the surgeon's handiwork. Norgrave was unconscious before his knees struck the floor.

Tristan turned on his heel and silently walked out of the room.

The Duke of Trevett was waiting for him in his uncle's library. The older man quietly scrutinized the swelling and bruises on Tristan's face. Without a word, he walked over to Lord Ludsthorpe's desk and poured brandy into a glass and handed it to him.

"Is he dead?"

Tristan slowly shook his head. "He probably will wish I had killed him when he looks at his face."

"How much do you know about what happened?"

The duke pinched the flesh between his eyebrows. "Your aunt told me what she could. I gleaned the rest from the physician."

Tristan thought of the fear he'd seen in her eyes, and the blood on her dress. "It is not my place to ask, but I need to know—were her injuries beyond the physician's skills?" he gruffly asked.

The older man sighed. "No more than one might expect, but worse than those who love her can bear. However, my daughter is young and healthy. In time, she will heal."

The knot in his stomach loosened. "Are you planning to pressure the magistrate to bring charges against Norgrave?"

"I have been apprised of my daughter's concerns," the

duke said tersely. "While I would relish the sight of seeing the scoundrel in iron chains, I do not wish to distress Imogene. If Norgrave courts public opinion to press his suit for marriage, our family is prepared to weather the scandal. My daughter is beyond his reach."

The two gentlemen sipped their brandies.

It was the older duke who broke the companionable silence. "Tell me, is there any chance that Norgrave will die from his wounds?"

Tristan would have thought it impossible, but his mouth curved into a brief grin. "There is always a possibility."

The duke nodded. "If you do not mind me saying so, you look as if you could use the services of a physician."

Tristan chuckled, and then winced in pain. "I will heal in time, too." He needed to see Imogene. He had promised to return, and he wanted to assure her that Norgrave would never trouble her again. "Is Imogene awake?"

"Not likely, son. The physician gave her something to ease her discomfort and help her sleep. My duchess and your aunt are watching over her. You can speak to her when she awakens."

Tristan swallowed his protest. If Imogene was resting, he did not want to disturb her. "I feel I should inform you of my intentions. If your daughter will have me, I plan on marrying her."

The Duke of Trevett reached for the decanter of brandy, and refilled their glasses. "It seems appropriate since you have already seduced my daughter." He noticed Tristan's discomfort and smiled. "Norgrave wasn't the only man I was longing to see in chains."

Tristan could hardly blame the man. "I understand that you find me unworthy. That your duchess had high hopes of finding a foreign prince or king for Imogene."

The older man's thick silvered eyebrows climbed north to meet his scalp, but he remained silent.

"I confess, my intentions have not always been honorable, but I fell in love with your daughter. I have never felt—" He cleared his throat and tried again. "As my duchess, she will never want for anything. I will protect her and vanquish anyone who dares to hurt her, even at the cost of my life."

"A noble vow. What if I refuse to offer my blessing?"

The duke sounded more curious than angry. Tristan had not considered what he would do if her family rejected his offer of marriage. "If Imogene will have me, then I will marry her without it."

Her father's eyes gleamed with approval. "Blackbern, you are a swaggering, disrespectful fellow. If you had given me a different answer I would have been disappointed. Aye, if Imogene agrees, you have my blessing. You have already proven that you are willing to risk your life in my daughter's name."

An hour later, he said his farewells to the Duke of Trevett and his uncle. He left the duke to apprise Lord Ludsthorpe of the evening's events. Tristan had collected his hat, and had planned to slip out the front door. The sudden arrival of his cousins had lured his aunt from Imogene's bedside. The longcase clock had chimed the three o'clock hour minutes earlier. At this rate, everyone would still be awake at dawn. The sight of his bruised face brought the older woman to tears. She hugged him and cried on his shoulder, and seemed loath to let him go until one of her daughters needed her assistance.

With everyone separating and heading to their bedchambers, Tristan found himself standing just outside Imogene's bedchamber. He had learned from the lady's father that the duchess was watching over her daughter. She would not welcome visitors at this late hour. Still, he could not resist a quick peek to assure himself that she was safe.

Tristan quietly twisted the doorknob and slipped inside the bedchamber. A single oil lamp lit a corner of the room. His gaze immediately sought out the Duchess of Trevett, and to his amusement the dragon was asleep. Her head bowed, the older woman sat near the lamp with an embroidery basket at her feet. The book she had been reading was still open on her lap.

With admirable stealth, he crept past the duchess. Her soft snores gurgling in her throat assured him that she was sound asleep. He moved toward the bed. As her father had predicted, Imogene was not awake. Tristan knelt at the side of her bed and studied her serene expression. She looked younger, and the shadows concealed the bruise on her cheek. He laced his fingers with hers and brought her hand to his lips.

"You own my heart," he whispered, kissing her hand. Tristan bowed his head and silently prayed for her recovery to be swift. "Sleep well, my love."

Imogene's fingers squeezed his hand, and he lifted his head to find her staring at him. Her eyelids drooped as she fought not to fall asleep.

"You came back," she said softly.

"Hush, you will awaken the dragon," he teased, though he was careful to keep his voice low. "I promised I would, did I not?"

Imogene blinked rapidly, and then squinted at Tristan. "Your face. You and Norgrave fought."

She reached out, and he leaned closer so she could stroke his cheek. "It was inevitable. I could not stand idle and permit his crimes to go unchallenged."

"You fought him in a duel?" She tried to sit up.

He glanced at the sleeping duchess as he gently pressed Imogene's shoulders back against the pillows. "Why use a sword or pistol when my fists were sufficient?"

"Did you kill him?"

"No," he said, striving to lighten his tone. "You and my aunt would not have approved. Nevertheless, I have conveyed a clear message to Norgrave. He is aware that I will challenge and kill him if he troubles you again. I have also cut all ties with him. He is dead to me."

"I am sorry, Tristan."

"Don't be," he whispered back, his eyes eloquent in their sorrow. "My only regret is that I had not ended our friendship sooner."

Norgrave would have left you alone if not for me.

"You loved him."

Tristan shook his head. "I do not think I truly loved anyone but myself, until I met you. I love you, Imogene. When you are ready, I want us to marry."

She glanced away, and he felt her silent retreat as if it was a blow to his heart. "I am getting ahead of myself. We will discuss this again when you are stronger."

"I love you, too."

"Aye, I know," he said, her declaration giving him hope. Tristan caressed her face. "I would sleep at your feet like a faithful hound, but I doubt the dragon would approve."

Imogene rewarded him with a smile. "You have to stop referring to my mother as a dragon."

"Why?" He stifled the urge to groan as he wearily stood. "It's meant as a compliment."

He fully expected the duchess to breathe fire when she learned of his intentions to marry Imogene, but it was a battle best reserved for another day.

"Go back to sleep." Tristan kissed her fingers. "You have not seen the last of me, my lady."

"Mmm . . ."

He released her hand when she nodded and dutifully closed her eyes.

As he retraced his steps, he was too distracted to notice that the duchess was no longer snoring. It was only when he shut the door that the lady opened her eyes and stared at the door in quiet contemplation.

Chapter Nineteen

Imogene sat on the edge of the large marble fountain her mother had installed in the back garden a year earlier. The duchess had purchased it from an old medieval ruin, and thought the artifact was essential to her *jardin d'amour* or "garden of love." For a fortnight, it was her favorite place for contemplation as her bruises healed and the passing days put distance between her and Norgrave's betrayal.

Not that she could completely banish the marquess from her thoughts.

Her mother had been quite vocal about returning to the country. She thought Imogene required fresh air and the rural landscape to hasten her recovery. To her astonishment, it was her father who disagreed. He had argued that an unexplained departure in the middle of the season would be fodder for the gossips. It was already known that Blackbern and Norgrave had done their best to kill each other at one of London's most unsavory establishments, the Acropolis. She overheard her father tell her mother that one of the stories being bandied about centered on Tristan catching Norgrave bedding one of his old mistresses. Many blamed the violence on too much drink and vice. Others cast a speculative eye toward Imogene, since many members of the *beau monde* had witnessed the men's friendly competition to gain her favor. Even though there were numerous debates on the reasons for the brawl, everyone agreed on a single point. Blackbern and Norgrave were no longer friends. The bond that had been forged in boyhood, and strengthened by camaraderie, loyalty, and, yes, even love, had been severed by a single act of violence.

Those who were acquainted with both gentlemen placed wagers at their clubs, and patiently waited for the next explosive confrontation. So far, neither man was being very accommodating. Tristan had not altered his routine. If anyone questioned him about the bruises on his face, he rudely ignored them. Norgrave had not been seen. Most assumed that he was recovering from the injuries that he had received during the fight.

Imogene had also gone into hiding. When asked about her absence, her family explained that a stomach complaint had put her in poor health. Even Tristan's aunt had added credibility to the lie, by telling everyone that Imogene had collapsed at her residence and a physician had had to be called. The Ludsthorpes were protecting her when she had expected to be shunned.

"I thought I might find you here," Tristan said, his expression indulgent as he approached her. He clasped her extended hand, and he kissed her knuckles.

She sensed he desired more than a chaste kiss on the hand, but he released her hand. Since the night he had slipped into the bedchamber and whispered that he loved her, he had been attentive and patient. His daily visits were something she looked forward to. Even her family did not seem troubled that Tristan had become a part of all of their lives. He had played cards with the duke at his favorite club, flirted outrageously with Verity, and to her amazement had secured two dinner invitations from her mother.

Tristan sat beside her on the narrow edge of the fountain. "You will freckle if you keep forgetting your bonnet."

"I like the feel of the sun on my face," Imogene admitted. "Will you love me less if I do freckle?"

He scratched at his earlobe and appeared to take the question seriously. "It is something to ponder."

She offered him an exasperated sideways glance. "Tristan—"

"It is a travesty to mar the beauty and perfection of your nose." In one fluid move, he wrapped his arm around her waist and pulled her body against his as they stood.

"It was not even a genuine question." Imogene huffed.

"Everything about you is a subject that I happen to take very seriously. Even your imaginary freckles." Tristan leaned down and placed a small kiss on her nose. "You are important to me."

"I am aware of your feelings, Your Grace," she said, wishing he looked less somber when he gazed into her eyes.

The corners of his mouth lifted at her formality. His blue-gray eyes twinkled with mischief. "Not all of them. If you did, you would be rushing into the house." He sighed as he savored the feel of her body. "I have missed holding you in my arms."

"I feel the same." Imogene breathed in his warm scent and leaned into him. She had deliberately kept Tristan at a distance and they had both been hurt by it. "I needed some time."

"I know, my darling." His hands slid up and down her back, his hand dipping and cupping her backside. "Everything happened so quickly between us, and then Norgrave . . . I understand."

"I do not blame you."

"Of course you don't," he replied, unable to conceal the shadow of guilt from his expression. "You are generous, and see the good in everyone you meet. You probably saw the decency in Norgrave, even though he does an admirable job of burying it."

Tristan's remark struck with uncanny accuracy. She gasped, and turned away.

"Imogene." He touched her on the shoulder. "Forgive me. It was a thoughtless observation. In my defense, my tongue doesn't always consult my brain."

She had hurt him, too, so it was easy to forgive him. "You were not wrong. About your friend."

"My former friend," he corrected.

"Regardless, I believe you are correct." Imogene missed his warmth. She edged closer to him. "Norgrave must have a sliver of compassion in him, otherwise I doubt you would have been his friend for so many years."

Tristan brushed a kiss against her lips. He retreated before she could react. "See? Generous. Norgrave does not deserve your forgiveness."

"He does not have it," she countered sharply. "I may never grant it, but I doubt he wants it."

Tristan had chosen her, and it was a betrayal that the marquess would never forgive.

"I assume the dragon has mentioned my aunt and uncle's upcoming ball," he said, abruptly changing the subject. He refused to allow her to brood over the past.

On separate occasions, she had been approached by her mother and father about the ball. Verity had already selected the dress she planned to wear to the ball. "Next Wednesday, I believe?"

"The guests will be family and close friends. The duke mentioned your mother has ordered a dress for you since it's a special occasion."

"Tristan," she said, glaring at him because he was doing what he did best—pressing her to get his way. "I have not decided if I will attend."

"If you cry off, it will be awfully humiliating for me when our family announces our betrothal. I do not know if I will be able to recover."

"You think you are so clever," Imogene muttered.

"Not particularly. If I was so intelligent, you would already be my duchess."

She rolled her eyes. The man was persistent. "So our courtship has come to an end?"

"I have had your family's blessing for weeks, Imogene." His blue-gray eyes darkened as concern furrowed his brow. "Unless you have reconsidered. Perhaps you do blame me—"

"No," she said firmly. "I do not recall most of what I said to you the night you arrived at the house. My head was muddled, but I have had time to discern the truth from the lies that I was told."

"Excellent, then we can proceed as planned and announce our intentions to marry the night of the ball."

"Why?"

Tristan grimaced, plainly frustrated by her reluctance. "Love, my lady. Is that not reason enough?"

"Sometimes," she conceded. "I just . . ."

"Talk to me. You have doubts that I love you?"

Imogene shook her head. "Are you marrying me because of Norgrave?" she blurted out, relieved that she finally had the courage to ask the question that had been troubling her for weeks.

He stepped back as if she had pushed him. "What has brought this on?"

Imogene could see that she had angered him. If his answer was not so important to her, she would have let the matter drop. "Do you not see? You have been protecting your friend, cleaning up his messes for so long that you do not realize it. If you are feeling guilty about not protecting me, and have proposed marriage as some sort of misguided penance, then I must refuse. I am not ruined. If there is a scandal, my family and I will weather it. You told me that I was strong. I doubted you the night you told me, but I have come to see that you are right. I do not require a noble sacrifice from you."

"I do not believe it!" Tristan muttered something unintelligible under his breath. "Your head is still muddled if you think I would marry out of guilt or to rectify a wrong. When I found you huddled on the floor in my mother's bedchamber, I stopped denying my feelings for you because I realized I could have lost you. If marriage is a sacrifice of my freedom, then I gladly surrender it. I love you, Imogene. I want to build a life with you. Perhaps you do not feel the same about me?"

Tristan inclined his head. "Forgive me for intruding."

"You are leaving?" Imogene trailed after him. She did not want to part from him in anger.

He halted, but did not turn around. "For now," he said curtly. "You have been so concerned about my feelings that you have not contemplated your own."

"I do not have to—I love you, Tristan."

He sighed. "I have neglected my duties so you will not see me until my aunt and uncle's ball."

"Are you punishing me?"

Tristan pivoted and marched up to her. "No, I am giving you time to miss me."

He grabbed her by the upper arms and pulled her forcefully to him, his mouth muffling her exclamation. His kiss was unlike the chaste kisses she had grown accustomed to the past fortnight. It was rough, carnal, and her blood heated as he kissed her to vent his anger. If he had tossed her over his shoulder and carried her upstairs to her bedchamber, Imogene would have gone willingly.

This was the duke she had fallen in love with.

"Tristan," she said, swaying slightly when he ended the kiss.

"I will settle for nothing less than marriage, Imogene," he said, letting his arms fall to his sides as he stepped away from her. "You know I am not a patient man. But I am trying . . . for you."

At dinner, her mother accused her of sulking. Imogene could not deny the charge so she delicately shrugged and continued to push the food around on her plate. Her exchange with Tristan was a lead weight on her heart. She had unintentionally hurt him. Her duke was offering her everything she had secretly wished for, but a part of her seemed incapable of trusting her good fortune.

When her melancholy increased as nightfall descended, Imogene kissed her mother and announced that she was retiring early. However, sleep was elusive. Lying on the bed, she refused to think of Norgrave, but she could not banish the night from her thoughts. He had been rough, but he had behaved as if he was her lover rather than her attacker.

"Blackbern will never marry you, Imogene," the marquess taunted. "You have betrayed the man whom you claim you love, and you will continue to do so."

"You are the one who betrayed him, not I," she cried.

Norgrave did not react to her words. "You chose the wrong man," he said, sounding disappointed in her. "However, I am willing to forgive you."

She flinched when he tried to stroke her cheek.

"Fight me if you must. Eventually, you will come to accept the truth."

Afraid to provoke him further, Imogene bit down on her tongue to keep from speaking.

The marquess's lips twisted into a mocking smile. "Even if Blackbern deigns to touch you again, it will be my face you will see when you close your eyes. My hands on your breasts . . . my mouth between your thighs giving you pleasure."

Imogene pulled the sheet higher as she shuddered. Norgrave had been wrong about Tristan, but he had been correct about one thing. She thought of him often. It angered and confused her, leaving her to wonder if she would truly be free of his torment.

She rolled over onto her side at the soft knock at the door.

Someone opened the door and peered in.

"Imogene, are you awake?" her sister asked.

"Yes." She sat up on the mattress. "Is something wrong?"

"I came to ask you the same question." Verity entered the chamber. She placed the branch of candles she was holding on the table near the bed. "You seemed distracted at dinner this evening. Did you and Blackbern quarrel this afternoon?"

"Why do you ask?"

Verity shrugged. Not waiting for an invitation, she sat down on the bed. "He has made a habit of lingering in the garden with you, but today he departed with barely a word to anyone. Mama noted that your duke appeared to be upset."

"I thought Mama was ignoring Blackbern?" Imogene asked, deliberately using his title in front of her sister. She had done her best to shelter Verity from the more scandalous details of her relationship with the duke, and Norgrave's attack. Her mother and father had also agreed with her decision.

Verity leaned back until her head rested on the pillow. "The duke is wearing her down. The last time he called her dragon, I swear, she smiled when his back was turned."

"He once told me that he would win our mother over," Imogene admitted. "At the time, it seemed like an impossible task, but I should not have doubted him. One would have to be dead not to fall for his flattery."

"Including you?"

"Yes," she said softly. "Including me."

"So does this mean you will be marrying the duke?" Before Imogene could ask Verity why she had come to this conclusion, her sister went on to explain. "A few days ago, I overheard Papa tell someone that he expected that you and Blackbern would be posting banns soon. And this afternoon, I came across Mama and the housekeeper while they discussed the recent entries in the kitchen ledger. Mama said that the next few orders would be higher than usual, on account that you and—"

Imogene rolled over and tugged the end of her sister's braid. "Good grief, you little sneak! How many times do I have to tell you that it is rude to listen at doors? One of these days, you are going to overhear something that you will truly regret."

"How else am I supposed to find out what is going on in this house?" Verity demanded. "No one tells me anything. And before you deny it, I know all of you are keeping something from me."

She didn't evade her sister's intent gaze. In the candlelight, her sister looked older. While Imogene had been distracted with her own concerns, Verity had been maturing into a young lady. "Why do you believe everyone is keeping secrets? Did you overhear something not meant for your curious ears?"

"What about the night Mama and Papa were summoned to the Ludsthorpes' town house?"

Imogene rolled onto her back and covered her eyes

with her forearm. She resisted the urge to groan in frustration. Of course, it would have been too much to hope that her sister had been blissfully unaware of that horrible night.

"What about it? You are aware that I had fallen ill, and Blackbern was worried. He brought me to his aunt's house, and Mama and Papa were summoned. The physician thought it was prudent that I stay in bed for a few days. You know all of this," she said, feeling exasperated and annoyed that her sister wanted answers that she was reluctant to give.

"Mama was so upset. She and Papa argued."

Her eyes widened with alarm. "What did you overhear?"

"Nothing. They were speaking too softly, but I could tell they were talking about you." Verity bit her lip as if she was stalling. "Maybe Blackbern."

Relief washed over Imogene. Although her sister was suspicious, she had not stumbled across the true reasons that had brought her to Lady Ludsthorpe's door. "Verity, naturally, Mama and Papa were concerned. I had slipped out of the house to meet the duke and I fell ill in his company. Needless to say, my actions and Blackbern's part in this have forced him to formally declare his intentions to our family."

While there were certain omissions she wished to take to her grave, she had not lied to her sister.

"What about Lord Norgrave?"

Imogene started at the marquess's name. "What of him?" she warily asked.

Her sister shrugged. "He appeared to be quite earnest in his courtship of you. Since he is Blackbern's closest friend, he must be disappointed that he did not win your affections."

Imogene stared off into the darkness, her mind drifting to the last time she saw him. The marquess's light blue eyes seemed to glow with determination and triumph as he held her down. She ruthlessly banished the dreadful memory from her thoughts.

"I have no inclination to inquire after Lord Norgrave's feelings. However, you may be correct. He and Blackbern have had some sort of falling-out, and the gentlemen have ended their friendship."

"They fought over you?" Verity asked, excited over the romantic prospect that the two men had fought for Imogene's hand.

"I am not privy to the details," she hedged. "And I would consider it a great favor if you do not pester the duke about it. The marquess was once loved as a brother, and even though they have severed all ties, I am certain Blackbern mourns the loss of his friend."

"So they *did* fight over you."

Imogene groaned. God save her from a stubborn sister. "Even if my affection for the duke instigated a fight between them, Norgrave and Blackbern were on this destructive course long before they encountered me." She huffed and rolled back onto her side so she could scowl at her sister. "Now that I have satisfied your curiosity, let this be the end of it."

Verity was silent for several minutes. Imogene could almost hear the younger woman's thoughts clicking and whirling like the mechanical workings of a clock. She did not have to wait long before another question emerged.

"You never answered my question." She ignored Imogene's exaggerated sigh. "Why were you and the duke quarreling this afternoon? Does it have something to do with Lord and Lady Ludsthorpes' ball next Wednesday?"

"If I answer your question will you cease your annoying habit of eavesdropping on private conversations?"

"I promise," her sister hastily vowed.

"On your honor?" she added, doubting her sister would be able to pass by a closed door without pressing her ear to it.

"Imogene!" Verity exclaimed, taking offense. "I promised, did I not?"

"I shall be cross if I hear of another incident."

"Oh, for goodness' sake, if you believe I lack honor then I shall swear upon yours." Her sister folded her arms across her chest and waited.

"Very well. Blackbern revealed that our betrothal will be announced at Lord and Lady Ludsthorpe's ball."

"This is marvelous news! Oh, Imogene, how did he ask for your hand?" Excited, she sat up and clasped her hands together. "Did he drop to his knees to declare his love? Recite poetry? Or better still—"

"The duke did none of those things," Imogene said, her voice rising over her sister's to silence her questions.

She rubbed at the mild ache forming between her breasts. Was it disappointment that she was feeling because the flowery declarations of love she had dreamed of as a young girl had vanished with a single act of betrayal? Instead of love shining in her beloved's gaze, she had glimpsed sorrow and rage, and a thirst for vengeance. He had returned to her bedside with his friend's blood on his hands, his heart and emotions as tattered as hers. It was not the sort of love she had expected, but they were bound together in blood, pain, and sacrifice.

"Perhaps you are too young to understand, but I do not need poetry or garrulous speeches to comprehend the depths of Blackbern's feelings toward me. He has made his intentions clear for quite some time. I was the one who had doubts."

"Is that why you quarreled with him?"

"In part." Imogene blinked away the sudden sting of tears. "I fear that I am unworthy to be his duchess."

She gasped in surprise at Verity's impulsive embrace.

"Oh, you silly goose," her sister teased. "Blackbern obviously disagrees. You and he are perfectly wonderful together. You worry for naught. You were born to be his duchess." She pulled away as an unpleasant thought occurred to her. "Unless . . . do you love him?"

"So much so, I might burst from it."

"Then all will be well, sister."

Imogene nodded. With Verity at her side, she could almost believe it.

Chapter Twenty

Norgrave was not sulking. Nor was he a coward.

He viewed his self-imposed seclusion as a tactical decision. His face and body still bore the healing wounds and pains from Blackbern's attack, and he was not prepared to explain the reasons why his closest friend tried to beat him to death. There had been witnesses to their brawl, and concerned acquaintances had knocked on his door to ferret out the details. He had turned everyone away. *Let them all wonder,* he thought. Without the unpalatable truth, Blackbern appeared to be the villain.

It was a title his traitorous former friend deserved.

They had been as close as brothers, and somehow a woman had come between them. Worse yet, the duplicitous blackguard had chosen Imogene—discarding a lifelong friendship and brotherly love.

Love.

Even pondering the word made him sneer. Blackbern had fallen in love with her. The notion might have amused him if he had not quietly succumbed to her charms as well. Or perhaps he merely saw the advantages of seducing and keeping Imogene for himself—especially now, when Blackbern seemed so determined to ruin him financially. The man had claimed his pound of flesh, but he was not satisfied. Now he was determined to pauper him.

"For what, I ask you?" Norgrave abruptly stood and strode to his desk to retrieve the decanter of brandy. "The pleasure I found between her legs was not worth our friendship." He splashed brandy into his glass. "Not worth my bloody fortune!"

Rage bubbled up within him. Needing an outlet, he threw the crystal decanter at the nearest wall. It shattered quite nicely.

"Milord?"

Unsteady on his feet, Norgrave turned at the sound of his butler's voice. "What is your opinion, Starling?" he asked, gesturing to the wet pattern soaking into the wallpaper. "The walls could benefit from a little decorating, do you not agree? Since you are here, you might as well bring up some more brandy."

"Yes, milord," the servant said, inclining his head with a respectful bow.

At his hesitation to do his master's bidding, the marquess snapped, "Did you have something else to say to me?"

"Forgive me for intruding, milord. You have a visitor."

It was probably his damn solicitor again. Of late, the man brought him nothing but complaints and depressing news. "Send him away," he muttered, taking a sip of brandy from his glass.

"It is a lady, Lord Norgrave." At the savage look of pleasure on his master's face, the butler took a step back.

"However, I can see that you are indisposed. I will tell her that you are not receiving visitors this afternoon."

Well, this was most unexpected. Had Imogene been so reckless as to confront him without her protector? Or perhaps, during their weeks apart, she had discovered that she had chosen the wrong man. "Her name, Starling. Come, man, give me her name."

"Lady Charlotte Winter, milord," he said, unable to prevent his concern for the lady from leaking into his normally unflappable tones. "Shall I send her away?"

Disappointment burned in his stomach as he silently fumed. Why the devil was the chit chasing after him when he had politely conveyed his disinterest? Her looks were passable and the lady possessed some intelligence. However, when compared to Imogene, Lady Charlotte was merely a pale imitation. He was not the kind of man who settled for second best.

Norgrave was on the verge of telling the servant to show her the door. He hesitated as his mercenary nature emerged. The lady was the beloved daughter of an earl who had the King's ear. His current situation with Blackbern had placed him in a defensive posture. He needed money and allies.

"I will see her."

If his butler disagreed with the decision, he hid it well. "Very good, milord." Starling closed the door behind him.

Norgrave set down his glass of brandy on the desk. He scrubbed his face and belatedly realized he had not shaved. Also, he was pleasantly drunk. His inebriated condition was not a problem since he doubted he was sober during any of his previous exchanges with Lady Charlotte. He glanced around the library, wondering where he had discarded his banyan. Greeting a lady in informal attire created an intimacy that might be misinterpreted.

He had not decided if this was to his advantage.

The door opened and Starling announced Lady Charlotte. She stepped into the room, her gaze sweeping the room until she noticed him standing near the desk. Attired in a bronze silk dress, she looked like a sleek robin. The pleasure in her hazel eyes faded and caution dimmed her enthusiasm as she took in his disheveled attire and the condition of his face.

Norgrave crossed the room to greet her. "Lady Charlotte, how unexpected." He bowed and she curtsied.

"Forgive my intrusion, Lord Norgrave," she said, sounding uncertain. "Your butler said that you were receiving visitors."

His informal attire and neglected grooming was making the poor lady nervous. "Actually, I have been turning away most visitors for weeks. When Starling told me that you were waiting in the front hall, I decided to make an exception."

"You honor me, my lord." She stood before him, her hands and reticule clasped in front of her. "You have been injured."

He lightly touched the wound Imogene had given him. The mending flesh felt hot and tight as he smiled absently. He would bear the lady's mark for the rest of his life. In many ways, the scar bound them in a manner that holy words and a ring could not.

"It is nothing," he said dismissively. "What providence has brought you to my door, my lady?"

She blushed, and the heightened color on her cheeks added to her beauty. "I—no one has seen you in weeks. There were rumors that you were ill, and it appears the gossips were correct for once."

Norgrave wondered what other rumors were connected to his name. According to his solicitor and a few friends, Blackbern did not seem to be mourning the loss of their friendship. Imogene had been notably absent, but the speculation about her was tied to his former friend. Blackbern had been seen in the company of the lady's father, and the older gentleman seemed to view him favorably. Some believed it was a matter of time before a formal offer of marriage was announced.

Honorable bastard.

Norgrave had expected Blackbern to be angry about his claim on Imogene, but he also expected him to sever all ties to the lady. The duke would comfort himself with the knowledge that his cooling affections would protect her from the marquess's future advances, but the truth was, his former friend abhorred emotional entanglements. In the past, he had yielded to all of Norgrave's challenges because the women had meant nothing to him.

And yet, Blackbern appeared to be more dedicated to Imogene than ever. His actions were unexpected and exasperating.

"As you can see, I am quite healthy," he said cheerfully, masking his dismay that all of his calculated moves regarding Imogene might not come to fruition if Blackbern was determined to claim her for himself.

She refused to meet his gaze. "And what of the gash on your face?"

"A humiliating accident," he smoothly lied. "Understandably, I do not wish to speak of it."

"Of course."

Such an agreeable little bird, he thought, as he took her hand and led her to the sofa. "So you missed me?"

"Oh!" Lady Charlotte's eyes widened in shock as he accurately deduced the true reason for her visit. "I"— she gulped and stammered—"yes. I have missed our brief chats."

Norgrave could not recall the subject of a single conversation he had shared with the chit. It was nothing personal. The only topic he enjoyed centered on him. Like all vain creatures, he had lingered and basked in her worshipful glances, while he sought more spirited challenges.

Like Imogene.

He discreetly studied Lady Charlotte, and considered the possibilities. In truth, she was a poor substitute for the lady he desired. Nevertheless, her family had connections that could be used to stave off Blackbern and his allies. If he controlled his somewhat depraved appetites and temper in her presence, she could be useful.

He leaned in subtly, and tenderly took up her hand. "I must confess that I have missed our chats as well."

She smiled broadly at his admission. "Then I am happy I did not talk myself out of visiting you this day."

"How many times did you have to dissuade yourself from behaving recklessly?"

"Too many times, my lord. I have lost count," she breathlessly admitted.

Lady Charlotte was appallingly easy to manipulate. Norgrave predicted he would be bored with her by the end of their visit. Fortunately, he had a respectable stock of wine and brandy in the cellar. With enough brandy coursing through his system, he might even believe the lady was Imogene.

"Ah, have I mentioned that I have a weakness for reckless ladies?"

As Lady Ludsthorpe's ball drew closer, Imogene expected the butler to announce the Duke of Blackbern's arrival, but he had kept to his word and he had stayed away from her. Instead he courted her from afar. Not a day went by without their butler or the housekeeper presenting her with a new gift from her betrothed. In the beginning of their blossoming friendship, he had offered her heart-melting kisses and his beautiful, flawless muscled body before he thought to offer her his heart. Her hesitation to believe that his love was genuine had struck an unintended blow. He might have deserved her disdain if she had learned of his and Norgrave's wager a month ago, but his tender care after Norgrave's cruelty had been a balm to her wounded soul. If she did not quite trust her instincts, she only had to look to her family. They had accepted him into the family, and now everyone was waiting for her to come to her senses.

If only her decision was based solely on hurt feelings.

Imogene had already forgiven Tristan for agreeing to the wager. She understood that his decision to pursue and seduce her had started out for selfish reasons; however, his presence had deterred Norgrave from carrying out his nefarious plans. If the marquess had been a good man, the wager might have ended with Tristan as the declared winner. To her deepest regret, Norgrave was not a graceful loser. Nor did he plan on allowing her to escape unpunished for choosing the wrong man.

If everything had gone as planned perhaps she would have walked away from both gentlemen—heartbroken, albeit wiser.

Imogene smiled at the absurd thought. Tristan had no intention of allowing her to escape him. Even though he was keeping his distance, a day had not passed without a messenger knocking on their front door with a note or a gift from the exasperating man.

"I did not court you as I should have," he had written in his first note. *"Pray accept my tokens of affection and dream of me, darling."*

Tristan had sent her a yellow-green canary in an iron and ivory birdcage on the first day, and enameled scent bottles with her favorite fragrance on the second. On the third day, a pair of silver shoe buckles with paste stones arrived, followed by a ruby and pearl pendant attached to a gold and enamel chain, a small garnet ring, and a delicate hand-painted fan. He included his calling card with each gift, and had written three words on the back.

I love you.

"If you do not marry him, perhaps I will," Verity had said as she tried on the garnet and gold ring. "Blackbern is handsome and generous . . . not to mention, he has excellent taste."

Imogene had written him a note after the arrival of each gift, asking him to call on her in person, but her requests were ignored. She was running out of time.

Imogene knew what Tristan wanted. If she expected him to beg, she would continue to wait in vain. A gentleman—even one in love—had his pride. So with Lady Ludsthorpe's assistance, she had left the sanctuary of her home and arrived at the duke's private residence.

His butler, McKee, looked almost relieved to see her. She stepped into the front hall, and was surprised when the countess did not follow.

"I have done my part in bringing you here. I believe you and Tristan can handle the rest," Lady Ludsthorpe said, raising her hand in farewell. "With the ball tomorrow, I have a dozen tasks to accomplish this afternoon."

That fact alone made her gesture even more priceless. "Aunt Ruth?"

She halted as her thoughtful gaze sharpened with expectation. "Yes, dear."

"Thank you," Imogene said.

The countess's expression brightened. "You will be a nice addition to our family, Imogene. If Tristan is too busy to escort you back to the house, then send one of his servants to fetch our coachman. I promised your mother and father that I would look after you, and I will not hear of you hiring a hackney coach. Do I make myself clear?"

"Yes, madam," Imogene said, still smiling even after the butler had shut the front door.

"McKee, where will I find the duke?"

"I believe His Grace is on the terrace. He was practicing with his sword, and asked not to be disturbed."

She did not have to guess why Tristan was honing his sword skills. Clearly, he had time both to court her and plot his revenge against Norgrave. "Oh, I see." Imogene bit her lower lip in consternation. "He is not expecting me. How angry do you think he will be if I interrupt his training?"

The butler shook his head. "His Grace has a standing order with the staff that you are allowed entry at any hour."

Imogene was stunned by McKee's revelation. Tristan valued his privacy. Before her, he had never brought one of his lovers to his town house. "When did he issue this order?"

"Well, I cannot recall the precise date, my lady." He gave her an apologetic glance. "However, I believe His Grace issued the order after your first visit."

So much had transpired since that night.

For a few minutes, Imogene could not speak because she feared she would break down in tears. For a man who rarely trusted anyone, he had opened his private house wholly to her. Although she had been unaware of this, his order revealed more about his feelings than he had been willing to admit at the time.

"C-could you show me the quickest way to the back terrace, McKee?"

Chapter Twenty-one

Alone, Tristan silently advanced and retired, allowing his foil to be his voice as he thrust and parried with his imaginary opponent. He had discarded his coat and waistcoat more than an hour ago, and his linen shirt clung to him like a second skin. His legs and arms moved as gracefully as a dancer's, his muscles attuned to the lethal weapon in his hand. If Norgrave had been foolish enough to step in front of him, Tristan would have thrust the point of his sword into the man's heart without hesitation.

"Tristan?"

For the first time, his foot shifted sideways and his step faltered. He straightened, allowing the hilt of his foil to rest against his hip. "Imogene." He said her name with reverence. She had come to him. Granted, he had not given her much choice since he had not replied to any of her invitations to visit her. He had promised to keep his distance, and it had been difficult to stay away.

He nodded to McKee, and the servant silently disappeared into the house. As he stared at her, his gaze taking in every detail, his initial joy cooled as he realized that she might have come for less pleasant reasons. "You look well," he said, stepping closer.

"You." She gestured at the forgotten foil in his hands. "The manner in which you moved. You looked beautiful and deadly."

"And you, my lady, are simply beautiful," he said. Tristan longed to take her into his arms and kiss her senseless, but he feared that she might flinch from his touch. "I have missed you."

"Did you? Then why did you not respond to any of my requests?" she demanded, and he could sense that she had been hurt by his actions.

"I did not ignore your invitations out of indifference or to punish you," he said, his voice sharper with frustration. "I told you that I would stay away so I would not say something stupid like—"

"Like what?"

"Like making demands when I want you willing and in my bed." Tristan stepped away from her to retrieve a small towel from a nearby table. He used it to mop the sweat fom his face, and then he draped the towel over his arm that held the foil. "Come inside. Your skin is too fair to be outside without a parasol."

He placed his hand on the small of her back and gently guided her back indoors. McKee immediately appeared when they entered the house, and he collected the damp towel and foil from the duke.

"Shall I serve refreshments in the drawing room?" the butler inquired politely.

"We will ring for them later," Tristan said, as he became aware that he was not dressed to entertain anyone in his formal drawing room. "Come with me, Imogene."

He led the way, confident that she would follow since she would assume that they were heading for the drawing room.

As she ascended the steps, she asked, "Are you planning to entertain this evening?"

"Why do you ask?" he replied, glancing over his shoulder.

Imogene gestured to the four maids cleaning the front hall. "No reason in particular," she said swiftly as if she was uncertain of her welcome since she had shown up at his door without warning. "I just noticed—this house must require a large staff."

"It does. However, I asked the housekeeper to bring on more staff this week." When he reached the landing, he leaned against the banister. "Do you want to know why?"

"Only if you wish to tell me," she teased him back, taking the time to playfully trail her finger across his chest as she walked by him.

The small intimate gesture triggered a strong need to pull her against him, but he resisted. Patience, he thought as he caught up to her. "Isn't it rather obvious? The servants are readying the house for its new mistress."

The fact that the news caused her to abruptly halt and her mouth fall open did not bode well.

"You do recall my aunt is preparing a ball on our behalf—our betrothal ball?" he said, trying not to sound as irritated as he felt. "Or perhaps marrying me is not very important to you?"

"Oh, Tristan," she said, looking a little sad. "It is nothing like that. It is just—"

"What is it precisely?" he asked, feeling annoyed at

himself that he had already managed to ruin her playful mood by mentioning their betrothal.

Her hands parted in a gesture to encompass her surroundings. "All of this. I have thought of you . . . of marrying you. I had not given much thought to what it will mean to be the Duchess of Blackbern, my responsibilities . . . to this house and your other estates. To be honest, all I thought of was you."

Her explanation doused his anger. Tristan clasped her hand within his and brought it to his lips. He pressed a kiss to her gloved hand. "It pleases me that you have thought of nothing else but marrying me. As for the rest of it, we can figure it out together."

Imogene nodded, though she did not seem entirely convinced that it could be so simple. It was incomprehensible to her that all he desired was her.

"Wait, are we not going to the drawing room?" she asked, when he directed her toward the stairs again.

"There are too many servants wandering about. I do not want us to be disturbed."

She remained silent until they had reached the door of his bedchamber. "What if the servants see us?"

Tristan snorted, and opened the door. "Imogene, the entire household knows I intend to marry you. Considering my illustrious reputation, no one will be scandalized that I wish to visit with my soon-to-be-duchess in my private quarters." He stared at her, almost daring her to refuse him by declaring that there would be no marriage. The time apart from her had not quelled his fears. In spite of her father's assurances that the lady would offer her consent eventually, he had not slept well since he had left her alone in the Trevetts' gardens.

Unable to think of a proper rebuttal, Imogene stepped into the bedchamber. Feeling as if he had won this first battle, Tristan did not bother concealing a little smirk as he closed the door and turned the key in the lock. If he had his way, he would keep her in bed until his ring was on her finger.

Since it had been too dark to explore on her first visit, Imogene took her time walking into Tristan's private quarters, her curious gaze noting the colors he had chosen, the walls, each piece of furniture, the thick rug beneath her feet, and the draperies framing the windows. Aware of his quiet scrutiny, she felt it would be rude not to compliment him on his bedchamber.

"Very charming," she said, her gaze flicking to the bed. "I highly approve of your choices."

Even though she was nervous, it had not escaped her notice that this room represented a very private part of the duke. He might have bedded countless women, but he did not share this bed.

Until her.

"It eases my mind that you approve," he said, placing his hands lightly on her shoulders so he could give her a chaste kiss on the cheek. "McKee would have been upset if I ordered everything to be tossed into the street."

Slightly stunned by contemplating the waste and expense of such an action, she did not even protest when he guided her to the bed and applied enough gentle pressure on her shoulders to encourage her to sit on the mattress. "You would have thrown everything out if I did not approve?"

His beautiful mouth curved upward. "Well, perhaps

not everything. You will have your own private rooms that you may decorate to your taste; however, I expect you to share my bed each night. It makes sense that you should feel comfortable here."

Tristan turned away from her, and walked to a chest of drawers. The top panels parted to reveal a hidden washstand. It was more sophisticated than the one she used in her bedchamber. There were four narrow drawers in the front, but he leaned down and an unseen drawer on the left held a chamber pot. The one on the right was a wooden ledge a person could use as a seat to wash one's legs and feet. He picked up the pitcher and poured enough water into the basin to wash the sweat from his outdoor exertions. After everything she had experienced, he still managed to make her blush. Her pulse increased at the realization that he intended to wash in front of her.

To confirm her suspicions, he tugged the ends of his shirt out of his breeches and pulled the garment over his head. Imogene should have given him a modicum of privacy by averting her gaze, but she stared at his muscled back in rapt fascination. The times he had removed his shirt in her presence, she had only viewed his incredible physique under candlelight. With the afternoon sun filtering through the windows, he was giving her a chance to study and admire the gentleman who appeared so eager to marry her.

Imogene resisted the urge to leave her soft perch and go to him. She wanted to trace the intriguing contours of muscle and bone with her fingers. If she was daring, she would press her lips to his back and taste the salt on his flesh with her tongue. Unintentionally, she must have made a soft sound of longing, because Tristan suddenly glanced at her, his eyelids narrowing.

It was then she became aware that she was leaning forward with her hands clenched into fists at her sides. Hoping he would not notice, she slowly straightened her spine and relaxed her fingers. With a careless grin and a nod, he offered her his back again.

Fiendishly clever devil.

Tristan was deliberately trying to seduce her by giving her a tempting view of his body.

Imogene heard a drawer open and close. He muttered something under his breath that she did not quite catch. There was a splash of water as he dropped a cloth into the basin.

"I beg your pardon?" she asked.

"What?"

Tristan glanced back and frowned as if he had forgotten that she was there. Imogene did not believe it for one second. The duke was aware of her as much as she was of him. The warm air in the room carried the heady scent of his masculine essence and her subtle floral fragrance. She raised her eyebrows, letting him know that she was not fooled by him.

"Oh, right." He sat down on the narrow ledge to remove his shoes and stockings. "Now that we are alone, I am curious to know the purpose of your visit. Not that I am disappointed. I am overjoyed to see you, darling. I just did not expect to see you until the ball."

His position gave her a good view of just how enthusiastic he was about her presence. The impressive bulge in the front of his breeches revealed he was aroused, but he made no effort to close the distance between them.

"Ah . . . the reason," she said, clearing her dry throat. Perhaps she should have asked McKee to send up some tea, after all. "Why have you not replied to any of my notes?"

Tristan stood, and her gaze lingered below his waist. In fact, his manhood seemed to swell under her frank perusal. He grimaced and turned away. His hand went to the buttons at his waist. She imagined his current state of arousal must have been quite uncomfortable in its tight confines.

Imogene held her breath as she waited for him to remove his breeches. Would he? Her nipples puckered in anticipation. A part of her was surprised by her reaction. After Norgrave's attack, she had felt nothing but anger. Even Tristan's kisses had not awakened her body. She had worried that such feelings were beyond her.

Her discovery was wondrous!

Her eyes moistened with joy, but she was done with tears. Even though he was unaware of it, Tristan had helped her rediscover a part of her that she thought she had lost. Or maybe he was. The duke was a clever man. She would not put it past him to have manipulated her unexpected visit to his own benefit.

And hers, as well.

"I wanted to give you a chance to miss me." His shoulders rippled as he soaped the small towel in his hands. He wrung out the excess water and commenced to casually wash himself.

"I have," she said, her throat threatening to close up on her as she became overcome with emotion. "I wanted to thank you for all of your gifts. I love each one of them."

Imogene held up her right hand, even though he had his back to her. "I wear the ring. It fits perfectly."

Just like him, she thought sadly.

Whether he sensed her distress or merely wished to see his ring on her hand, Tristan glanced over his shoulder. His playful expression sobered when he saw the tension in her face. He tossed the wet cloth back into the basin and walked toward her.

Dropping to his knees, he clasped her hands. The soap with which he had scrubbed his chest, arms, and armpits smelled of sweet almonds. "Imogene. What is it? You did not come to simply thank me for the gifts, did you? You have already conveyed your pleasure and thanks in your notes."

Imogene stared at his strong hands covering hers and trembled. Although she had not spoken about her fears to anyone, he was correct. She had come to him for another reason.

"You are safe in my care, Imogene," he said, using the sincerity in his voice and eyes to ensnare her wary gaze. "I want nothing but truth spoken between us."

His admission coaxed a breathy laugh from her. "Then you do not know women as well as you claim, Your Grace."

Her smile had him grinning in response. "You may be right, my lady." His forehead furrowed as he tried to deduce on his own what troubled her thoughts. "Am I rushing you into your marriage bed, Imogene? Do you have doubts about me . . . about us? Of what we can be together?"

She turned her face to his hand when he caressed her

cheek, and leaned into his touch. "If only our troubles were so simple."

Tristan stilled, his entire body filling with sudden tension. "Have you come to persuade me to not announce our betrothal at the ball?"

"Not precisely," she said, knowing she was being evasive when he deserved honesty from her. "I will leave the final decision up to you."

The relief blossoming across his face was a dagger in her heart.

"Then I shall give you my answer. I want us—"

She silenced his words by touching her fingers to his lips. "Not until I give you the truth you wish to hear." Imogene sighed. "Tristan, I believe I am with child."

His expression became guarded. "Are you certain?"

"No," she said, feeling defensive. For all of his promises, she could not guess his feelings on the subject. "I am no expert in these matters, and I refuse to approach my mother. You are the only one I have shared my suspicions with."

"You think this child is Norgrave's," he said flatly.

"It is a possibility," she said, her voice sounding hoarse even to her ears. "He was the last man to—"

Tristan held up a hand to stop her from finishing her thoughts. He swiftly stood and began to pace in front of her. There was a wild look in his eyes, but she knew his anger was not directed at her.

He stopped and glared down at her. "When was the last time you bled?"

Imogene winced at his bluntness. "I do not know." She gasped when his fingers caught her wrists and she was pulled onto her feet. "M-maybe the week we arrived in London. With everything that happened, I was not as attentive as I should have been."

He nodded, almost absently. "Then the child is mine."

"You do not know for certain—" His hot, furious gaze had her swallowing the rest of her argument. "You asked for truth between us, Tristan. Do not ask me to dissemble about what took place in your mother's house. You know there is a chance the child could be Norgrave's."

"I have not forgotten," he shouted at her. Tristan refused to release her hands when she attempted to pull away. His fingers tightened over her wrists, but he was not hurting her. "Listen to me. Since you collided into my life, you have bewitched and maddened me. I have done reckless things, and have not always been careful when it comes to you. Not when I claimed your maidenhead, or the other times when I bedded you. If you are with child, it is my babe sleeping in your womb. I would wager my estates and title on it."

"Can you understand how difficult this is for me? I want this child to be yours," she yelled back at him, matching his temper. "I would give anything . . . *anything* . . . for there to be no doubt."

Tristan cupped her face, and lightly touched his forehead to hers. "Oh, darling, how long have you carried this burden by yourself?"

"Since the night it happened," she said, his tenderness almost her undoing. "He taunted me about the possibility and it took root in my brain. He said other things—" She could barely look him in the eye.

"Let me guess," he said, practically spitting out the

words. "Norgrave told you that I would abandon you once I learned that you carried his child."

"Yes."

"Imogene, the bastard lied. Norgrave told you what *he* would have done if he learned his lover carried another man's child. He does not speak for me, and he never will again." Tristan cuddled her against his chest. "You should have told me about the baby sooner."

"I am not positive, but there are signs," she murmured against his bare chest.

"Then it is good that I am already planning to marry you." He rubbed her back in a soothing fashion. "I am looking forward to watching you get as fat as a hen with my child."

Imogene sensed Tristan was still furious at the marquess, but he somehow managed to keep his darker emotions from her because she needed to be comforted. "What if you are wrong?"

"I am not. You still do not understand," Tristan said, impatience flashing in his gaze. He placed his hand on her belly. "I claim this child as mine. Anyone who hints otherwise will become my enemy who will face ruin by my hand. Our son will never doubt even for a moment that I am his sire."

"So you have decided that I am carrying your heir?" she asked, her heart lightening at the conviction ringing in his vow.

"Of course," was his arrogant response. Tristan's eyes took on a sensual cast as he reached for the buttons on her dress. "And if you are not with child, you soon will be."

"You are not—we cannot—not with all of the servants

strolling about," she protested, but the duke was no longer listening.

"I am—we can," he countered firmly.

It seemed Tristan had decided the only way to wipe out her lingering doubts was to coax her back into his bed. She wondered if that had been his plan all along when he had escorted her upstairs to his bedchamber.

In silence, he undressed her. His touch was light but confident, as if the duke spent his days undressing women, which was probably closer to the truth than she preferred. Imogene glanced down at her legs, and was grateful the bruises on her body had faded. When he had finished, she felt vulnerable and a little foolish standing naked in front of him, but the front of his unfastened breeches revealed that he was aroused. If she had any doubts, he swiftly allayed them by stripping down until he was as naked as she was.

Imogene reached out and touched the light yellow bruising on his ribs that had not completely faded. He had been injured worse than he had let on when he had gone after—no, she thought, that odious man had no place in the room with them.

The rising desire in Tristan's heavy-lidded gaze showed that he was wholly focused on her. On all the things he wanted to do to her.

"My love," she said, sighing.

"Say it again," he entreated, standing so close she could feel the heat rolling off his body. He was fully aroused, his majestic staff jutting forward. The thick crown brushed against her hip bone, causing her to shiver.

She cleared her throat. "My love."

"Aye, that is what you are to me," he said as he leaned

orward and kissed her lightly on the lips. His face dark-
ned with intensity. "My heart. My love. I should have
poken the words more often instead of just showing you
vith my body, assuming it was enough. If I had, maybe—"

Both of them had made mistakes.

"Hush," she said, deliberately rubbing her hip against
iis manhood and enjoying how he sharply inhaled as if
he movement wavered between ecstasy and pain.
'Leave it in the past."

"You are right," he muttered, annoyed at himself for
llowing his regrets to intrude. "No more talking."

Imogene felt the palm of his hand on the small of her
»ack, and in a fluid, almost dancelike move, he guided
ier backward until her legs bumped against the bed, and
hen she felt her backside sinking into the mattress.

Tristan caged her with his arms, his knee positioned
»etween her legs keeping him on his feet. "Beautiful,"
ie said, staring at her with so much heat and love in his
·yes that she believed him.

Trusted him.

Perhaps she always had on an instinctive level. If she
iadn't, she would have never encouraged him or allowed
iim to coax her into exploring her undiscovered pas-
,ions. He had been a temptation she could not resist.
Ier tutor in the carnal arts and her lover. He would soon
»e her husband and the father of her children.

Had they already created a child together?

Her womb clenched at the heady thought.

Laid out on the mattress like his personal banquet,
mogene gazed at Tristan as he stared down at her with
iungry anticipation. Straightening so he could gain use
»f his hands, he combed his fingers through her hair. He

plucked out every hairpin and wasn't satisfied until her hair was splayed out like a golden sun on the mattress.

It was just the beginning, and she was not certain she could withstand the torment. He seemed oblivious to his arousal, but she was keenly aware of the hot rigid length. As he touched her hair and teased her mouth with his lips, the heavy length brushed against her flesh, and burned her like a brand. She would have squeezed her thighs together to ease the warm tingles building deep within the core of her. His fingers had not touched those sensitive folds, and still she was already wet. Her body was readying itself for the union that they both were craving.

Tristan appeared content to take his time, and it was driving her half mad. Excitement and longing were entangled with a healthy dose of lust.

"My lovely duke," she murmured dreamily. "Have I told you how pretty you are?"

"A few times," he said. His fingers and mouth had moved on to her collarbone and shoulders. "However, I never grow weary of hearing how much I please you. Vanity is a hungry beast, and it must be fed often. Will you feed me and our son with these?"

He posed the question so casually, she had not deduced his intent until his mouth closed over her breast. Imogene tensed and arched her back slightly to meet the demands of his mouth. Pleasure shot through her as straight as an arrow, its target the very heart of her intimate heat. She squirmed against this sensual onslaught, the demand that he cease his teasing and take her was a persistent tickle in her throat.

"Will you?" he pressed, roughly suckling on her niple. The exquisite pain was almost her undoing. Her breasts had been sensitive for weeks, and under Tristan's calculated ministrations, they were inflamed.

"Yes," she hissed.

"Of course you will. You have always been generous, and have never denied my whims," he said, his breath coming out in hot puffs.

Tristan had tethered his own needs to give her pleasure, but he was chafing against his self-imposed restraints. Imogene silently wondered what she could do to send him over the edge.

It seemed only fair.

He nibbled his way down her flat stomach, and teased her navel with his tongue. "I cannot wait to see you swell with my child," he said, inhaling deeply to take in the subtle fragrance of her desire for him.

He pressed a firm, loving kiss to her belly. A kiss meant for their child.

Imogene's face crumpled as she struggled not to cry. She was overwhelmed by his acceptance and love.

As if sensing her distress, Tristan was determined to distract her. He shifted lower until the backs of her legs rested on his shoulders. Parting the feminine folds, his mouth was pure magic as he kissed the inner sweetness of her vulva.

Imogene could not muffle her cry of surprise, and her shoulders lifted off the mattress. Her beautiful lover's mouth was skilled and thorough as he teased the small fleshy knot and was rewarded with another raw moan of pleasure. Her thighs tightened as he used his fingers and tongue to send her body spiraling toward the blinding gratification she had only found in his arms.

"Again," he rasped, nipping her inner thigh. "The taste of you is as intoxicating as a mulled wine. I want to drink deep, and keep drinking until I'm drunk on the taste of you."

To prove it, his mouth descended again. Imogene glimpsed a mischievous grin on his lips as he anticipated her response. She found her release—a second and third time. Someone screamed, and to her embarrassment, she realized as she trembled from the lingering quakes that it was her.

Her duke raised his head and their gazes met. From his smug expression, he was quite pleased with himself. He was never going to let her live this down.

By her fifth release, she was panting and could barely move.

"No more," she begged. "If your goal was to melt my bones, you have succeeded. I congratulate you on your devious scheme. If you continue, I will be unable to leave this bed on my own."

Tristan had the audacity to laugh at her. Imogene offered him a weak smile. She could not begrudge his mischief, when he looked so happy and unfettered from the rage that had been burning in his eyes since he had found her in his mother's bedchamber.

"You have deduced my wicked intentions," he said, slowly rising to his feet. She laughed as he placed wet kisses on her stomach before crawling up the length of her body until they were face-to-face. "If I had my way, the nights without you in my bed would end this day. I consider it my duty to keep you boneless and satisfied."

"Can a person die from too much pleasure?" she asked.

"My darling lady, give me some credit. I will never

give you too much pleasure . . . you have my promise that you will always have just what you require," he said, his eyes glowing with amusement and something she could not quite define.

Imogene had her answer a minute later. Her eyes flared as she felt the head of his manhood press against the nest of damp curls between her legs. Without any hesitation, she shifted her right leg so he could—*there*.

She was so drenched, Tristan slipped easily within her. He made a soft growling sound of approval as she felt her body stretch around his manhood. Before she could marvel at how perfectly they fit together, he began to move within her. Slowly, at first. His mouth closed over hers, and she could taste herself on his lips, She arched her back, savoring the feel of her erect nipples raking his chest.

"Christ, Imogene—I do not know if I can hold on. You feel—" He clenched his teeth as if he was in pain, and his pace quickened.

Imogene understood the wildness driving him. She wrapped her legs around his hips, and slightly lifted her hips, silently inviting him to not be gentle. His eyes widened in surprise, and she saw flashes of relief and approval cross his face. He clasped her by the hips, and began to thrust at such a frenzied pace that she understood at once that he had been holding back for her sake.

"Are you mine?" she gasped, amazed that the lethargy that had overtaken her was fading as she felt the fires he was building within her.

His eyes were glazed with lust and his expression was fierce when he uttered, "Aye, love." Tristan thrust deeply. "Yours."

Anyone walking past the bedchamber door would have overheard his strangled shout of elation as he surrendered to the blinding pleasure. Tristan tugged her hips closer and buried his face against her neck as his seed filled her in copious pumps. Imogene cradled him in her arms, and this time she let the tears flow.

When his breathing had calmed, Tristan lifted his head and was distressed at the sight of her tears. "You have been crying."

"Tears of joy, Your Grace," she said, smiling up at him. "Every time I think our lovemaking cannot be bested, you prove me wrong."

He laughed, which caused his manhood to twitch deep within her. Sobering, he braced his weight on one arm as his other hand slipped lower until his palm covered her belly. "Has our love play disturbed my son?"

Imogene was not fooled by his casual tone. Tristan wanted to know if he had banished her fears. If a child had been conceived, the duke was the sire. He had no doubts. "Your son is fine, Your Grace."

If she was wrong about her delicate condition, she was positive her days and nights in Tristan's bed would swiftly remedy her error.

"Good. Do you have any objections to our announcing our betrothal tomorrow evening?"

A wave of shyness washed over her. It was ridiculous considering that she was naked in her lover's bed. "Not a one."

If Imogene resisted, she suspected Tristan would keep her in his bed until he seduced the correct answer from her lips. It was a pleasurable notion. However, she was too tired to fight him. "I am yours if you will have me."

He gave her a roguish grin. "Oh, I will, darling. Again and again."

Tristan spent the rest of the afternoon rewarding her for making the right decision.

Chapter Twenty-two

In a short time, Norgrave's life had become positively domestic.

He smiled indulgently at the woman admiring the amethyst necklace he had given her in front of the small mirror mounted on the dressing table. Clad only in a chemise, Lady Charlotte made a charming picture. It was a pity he did not have any skill with a pencil.

Since the day she had entered the proverbial lion's den, he had relieved her of her maidenhead and done things to her virginal body that he had only experienced with whores. The gradual corruption of innocence had held his interest for days. Sometimes she had been eager. More often than not, she had fought him, and that is when he closed his eyes and pretended that she was the defiant Lady Imogene, her eyes damp and filled with what she perceived as betrayal. In those brief moments, he could almost believe he loved her.

Lady Charlotte was never mad at him for long. He knew how to break down a lady's resistance and convince her that his passion for her had caused him to handle her roughly. The necklace and other small tokens of affection had assuaged all hurts. If she had not believed she was in love with him, she would have wondered how he had procured the necklace so quickly. He had several that he kept in a locked box for such situations. This particular one had already been offered to another lady. When she realized that he had only given her the necklace as a parting gift, she had hurled the jewelry at his head and marched out of the room. Her fit of temper had prompted him to chase after her. He had shoved her onto her knees and mounted her with savage enthusiasm. When his seed had been spent, she had been eager to see the last of him.

"Oh, Cason, it is the most beautiful necklace I have ever owned," Lady Charlotte said, returning to the bed that they had just shared.

Norgrave grasped her hand. "If it is, then your father has been miserly with his affection. A few months ago, I noticed one of his mistresses was wearing a similar necklace and the center stone was the size of a pigeon's egg."

The blonde frowned. "My father is devoted to my mother. He would never take a mistress."

"Ah, little innocent." He pulled her back into bed, and rolled her onto her back. "I grant you, the gentleman is discreet. Nevertheless, from the looks of his latest one, I predict you will have a new half-sibling in four months."

Lady Charlotte's expression grew mutinous. "I do not believe you."

"Are you calling me a liar?" he silkily asked.

Already familiar with that particularly dangerous inflection, she shook her head. "Of course not, my love.

Forgive me for implying that you are spinning tales. It is just . . . my father."

Since she apologized so prettily, he decided to be benevolent. The necklace was an indication of his boredom and he was content to let her go before he ruined her completely. His convalescence was over, and he was hungry for a lover who enjoyed the pain he could inflict on her.

"I understand, my dear," he said in soothing tones. "We place those we love on such high pedestals. It hurts when they do not live up to our expectations."

Lady Charlotte nodded, but the seeds of doubt were already sprouting. Norgrave did not know if her father had a mistress or not. He did not truly care. Her blind devotion to her family irritated him. Now she would always look at her father and wonder if he was a liar and an adulterer.

"What time is it, do you think?"

"After two o'clock, I suppose," Norgrave said, stifling a yawn. "Why do you ask?"

"I must return home," she said as she touched the necklace. "My family and I are attending Lord and Lady Ludsthorpes' ball this evening. Rumor has it, the Duke of Blackbern will be announcing his betrothal to Lady Imogene. Not that it is much of a surprise. It is obvious to everyone that the duke is in love with her."

Lady Charlotte's voice faded into the distance as the blood roared in Norgrave's ears. He abruptly sat up in an attempt to ease the pain in his head. Blackbern intended to marry Imogene. He caressed the healing wound on his cheek as if it somehow brought him closer to the lady who had marked him. Blackbern was marrying the chit? He had never shown any interest in marriage. What Norgrave had done to Imogene should have sent his former friend scurrying away from the lady. Instead, Blackbern had tried to kill him and now he was marrying the lady who Norgrave considered his. Damn it all, the infuriating man was ruining everything.

"Cason, are you listening?" Lady Charlotte asked, her face clouded with unwarranted concern.

"What are you blathering about?" he snapped, and she recoiled at his impatience.

"I asked if you were planning to attend the ball this evening?" she said, unaware that her news had soured his mood. "I know there has been friction between you and the duke. However, betrothals are a cause for celebration, and a time for the two of you to put aside your differences."

"Was that the only reason that you wanted me to attend?"

There was something in his tone that had her edging away from him. "I—I thought you might pay your respects to my mother and father."

His hard smile heralded a brewing storm. "Have you told them that you begged me to fuck you?"

Lady Charlotte flinched as if he had struck her. "No! How could you describe what we did so crudely? What is wrong with you?"

What is wrong with me? I am not Blackbern.

The lady was far from finished with her tantrum. "You told me several times that you loved me. You gave me this lovely necklace. I would have never allowed you to touch me if I thought you did not—"

"Pray, shut your mouth," he said with biting politeness.

"Due to your limited skills, I can only think of one or two things you are capable of doing with that tongue."

She gasped and backed away from the bed.

Oblivious to his nakedness, he stalked her. "Is there an hour in the day that you are *silent*? I can barely form a rational thought with you prattling on and on."

Lady Charlotte's hands went to her neck and fumbled for the clasp. "If you feel that way, then you can keep your precious necklace. I no longer want it."

"Do you plan on tossing it in my face?" He sneered. "Strive for something original. The last chit I bribed into my bed with that necklace threw it at me when I told her that I had grown tired of her."

"You mean—" The tears that filled her hurt gaze left him unmoved. Her lips trembled. "Do you feel anything for me, Cason?"

"Only that you were a means to an end, my dear lady," he said carelessly. "Dallying with you relieved the boredom, and for an hour or two, I even entertained the notion of marrying you. I could do worse and with the proper training you would make an adequate wife." He shook his head. "Then I came to my senses and realized that I could do better. Keep the necklace or leave it. I no longer care."

He turned his back on her.

It was the final straw. Lady Charlotte screamed and charged Norgrave. There was mild surprise on his face, when he pivoted and she raked her fingernails across his face. He cried out in pain as part of the scab on his cheek was ripped away. Blood coursed down his cheek.

"You bloody bitch!" he roared. Norgrave backhanded her in retaliation. The blow sent the lady crashing into the dressing table. The top of her head cracked the small rectangular mirror.

"Did you honestly convince yourself that you were worthy of a man like me?" he shouted at her.

Lady Charlotte glared at him as she straightened. Her cheek was red from his blow. She tore the necklace from her throat and threw it at him. "I hate you . . . I hate you . . . I hate you!" She said the words over and over as she struck his shoulders, face, and chest with her fists.

Norgrave roughly grabbed her, and they fell to the rug. He landed on top, and quickly gained the advantage because he had no qualms about using his strength. To shut her up, he slapped her across the face. By the fourth slap, he was fully aroused and the lady was whimpering.

"Your spirit is astoundingly inspiring, Lady Charlotte," he said, rolling her onto her stomach and pulling her up so she was on her hands and knees. She tried to crawl away, but he held her in place. Norgrave spat into his hand and grabbed his cock. He pushed the head into the cleft of her buttocks. "Perhaps I am not quite done with you, after all."

All of the servants halted at the sound of a woman's screams. It was not an unfamiliar sound in this household, but everyone knew their master had been amusing himself with a lady of quality. She was young and her obvious distress caused several of the footmen to take a courageous step toward the stairs.

"See to your duties or face getting sacked without references," the butler curtly said. He glared at all of them until they wandered off.

Alone, Starling cast his concerned gaze at the empty

stairs, and shook his head in dismay. He hoped the lady's screams could not be heard from the street. Lord Norgrave would be furious if the watch knocked on the front door.

If anyone made inquiries, he would handle them. He always did. Over the years, he had become quite proficient at cleaning up his lordship's messes.

Tristan waited at the bottom of the staircase for his soon-to-be-bride. After standing in line for several hours beside Lord and Lady Ludsthorpe as they greeted guests and well-wishers, Imogene had slipped away for a few minutes of privacy. His uncle had teased that Tristan should expect to spend the rest of his life waiting for the females in his life, but he did not mind as long as Imogene eventually made her way back to him.

Everyone was waiting for them to enter the ballroom. At the appropriate time, the Duke of Trevett would announce to family and friends Imogene and Tristan's betrothal. He had already given her a ring, but he had his grandmother's ring tucked away in his waistcoat pocket. It was a yellow gold ring with seven rose-cut diamonds, the largest stone in the center with two medium-sized diamonds on either side and the smallest stones nestled above and below the row. The ring would initially be loose on her slender finger, but she would be grateful for the ill fit once their child rounded her figure.

And he was convinced she was pregnant.

The knowledge made his cock twitch, which was embarrassing when they had a ballroom filled with people waiting for them. Besides, the damn thing should be sated. He and Imogene had spent the entire afternoon in his bed, and when he was not making love to her, he had taken his time exploring her body. He noted her breasts were slightly fuller and more sensitive to his caresses. There was a glow to her skin and her appetite for all manner of things had increased. Not that Tristan was complaining. He loved the subtle changes, and he looked forward to discovering new ones.

Tristan could not wait until he could place the palm of his hands against her round stomach and feel his son shift within Imogene's womb. And this child was his. His instincts were never wrong. This child and Imogene were his family, and he vowed to protect them with his life if necessary.

As for Norgrave, he could go to hell. He and his manipulative lies would never touch Imogene again.

The front door opened. Tristan's expression brightened at the sight his friend Lord Jasper.

The earl sent him an apologetic look as he handed his hat and walking stick to the footman. "I know I am late. Have I missed the big announcement?"

"It was a near thing, but you have arrived just in time. It is good of you to come." Tristan and the earl embraced. "What the devil happened? Lame horse?"

"Nothing like that. I was delayed at the club, and you would not believe the juicy bit of gossip I have just heard," he said, his face flushed as if he had run the entire distance.

"What has happened?"

"I have news about a certain gentleman." Jasper's brown eyes gleamed with excitement. "As far as I am concerned, come morning it will most likely bury the wonderful news of your upcoming nuptials to Lady

Imogene, but it cannot be helped. Not when the calamity that has befallen him is very much deserved."

Tristan's expression became shuttered. It was easy to deduce the gentleman was Norgrave. If someone had finally put a bullet or sword in the scoundrel, he would offer a toast to the assassin.

"Is he dead?"

The earl laughed. "No, but I am certain he wishes he was." He stepped closer so they could not be overheard. "There was a time when you called this gentleman your friend."

Tristan crossed his arms over his chest. "No more, so nothing you say will offend me."

"Then you are quite aware of his preferences when it comes to lovers, and that his carnal appetites can be unsavory to the uninitiated."

Sick dread pooled in Tristan's gut. "I am."

Jasper gripped one of the balusters. "While this gentleman was recuperating from an unfortunate accident"—his steady gaze revealed that he knew who was responsible and that he was merely uttering the gossip that was circulating through the *beau monde*— "he encountered Lady Charlotte Winter. A friendship bloomed between them, though the couple did their best to keep it a secret."

Tristan swore under his breath. Lady Charlotte was a sweet, gentle creature. Like Imogene, she could not fathom the darkness that resided in Norgrave. Nor the pleasure he derived from hurting others.

"No lady would fare well under this gentleman's care," he predicted.

"Lady Charlotte discovered this unfortunate fact for

herself. This unpleasant business has no place at your betrothal ball, but I thought you should know the details that have been passed on to me. The poor girl was beaten and abused in the most heinous fashion. To add further insult, the bastard stuffed her in a hired coach and ordered the coachman to return her to her family."

Tristan shut his eyes. "Merde." He could imagine the pain and terror the lady must have suffered at the marquess's hands. "He gets bolder with each victim. This is too public for her family to hush up. Has he been dragged before a magistrate or did the family put a bullet in Norgrave's black heart?"

"Regrettably, he has escaped both fates. Once Lady Charlotte's brothers learned of her lover's cruelty, they went straight to his house and a violent brawl ensued. Norgrave was beaten until he was unconscious and his legs were broken. Though it is still uncertain that he will survive his injuries, the lady's family solicited favors to secure a special license to spare the humiliation of Lady Charlotte possibly giving birth to his bastard. She is his countess, and mayhap in the coming days, his widow. Either way, Norgrave has been punished for his sins."

"For the lady's sake, I hope the devil claims him," Tristan muttered, feeling nothing but pity for the new Lady Norgrave. "He would make a poor husband for any lady."

"Aye, my thoughts exactly," Jasper said. He released the baluster. "I should go in and pay my respects to your aunt and uncle. "Will you walk with me?"

He shook his head. "I am waiting for my lady."

"You are a lucky man." The earl clasped his hand on Tristan's shoulder. "I will greet your lady properly later."

Tristan waited until Jasper walked away to join the other guests. "How much did you hear?"

He glanced up the staircase and saw Imogene poised on the steps. Her face was pale, but her gait was regal and steady as she descended the remaining steps.

"I did not mean to eavesdrop. You and Lord Jasper were deep in conversation and I did not wish to interrupt." Her eyes were dry, but she shivered when he placed his arm around her. "Poor Lady Charlotte."

Uncertain what he could do to comfort her, he kissed her. It calmed him when she kissed him back. "It is not your fault. Everyone knew the lady was smitten with him. If her own family could not keep her away from him, then there was nothing you or I could have said or done to prevent this outcome."

Looking a little lost, she nodded. "I know. I was fooled by him once, too."

Helpless rage rose up like bile in his throat. Tristan hoped the lady's family had the forethought to castrate Norgrave. Gazing at Imogene's forlorn expression, he wished he had done the deed himself.

"He has stolen enough from us, Imogene. Are you planning to let him ruin your betrothal ball?"

The question seemed to bring her up short. Determination shimmered in her blue gaze. "Of course not!"

Tristan offered Imogene his arm. "Then let us be off. I cannot wait to tell all of London that you will soon become my duchess."

She rewarded him with a smile. "Between my parents

and you shouting the news from the rooftops, I highly doubt it is a secret."

Imogene halted before the closed doors. "Do you intend to tell everyone about the baby?"

"In a month or two will suffice." He did not have the heart to tell her that when their child arrived months early, everyone would know that she had been a willing participant in his wicked seduction. By then, she would be happily married and very few would care that she had anticipated her marriage bed.

He would deal with the people rude enough to point that fact out to her.

"Have I told you that I love you?"

Imogene laughed. "Not in a few hours. If you can wait until after the ball, you can sneak into the bedchamber Aunt Ruth has prepared for me and tell me in private."

"A lady after my own heart."

The footmen opened the double doors and the ballroom beckoned.

"I already have it, Your Grace," she said smugly.

Tristan grinned. He did not deny the charge. His future bride had an annoying habit of always being right.

Epilogue

Seven and a half months later . . .

She was suffering and it was all his fault.

Tristan dropped the glass of brandy his father-in-law had pressed into his hand minutes ago at the muffled scream behind the closed door. The glass shattered at his feet, but he was oblivious. Imogene needed him, but he had been ordered by the females attending his duchess to stay away.

"Tristan, you have done your part, let her do hers without you hovering over her like a thundercloud. Imogene will worry about you when she should be saving her strength for the birth," had been his aunt Ruth's calm response when he had initially refused to leave his wife's side. His aunt had been sympathetic to the fear she noted in his wild gaze, but nothing he had said would alter her decree.

"You should be waiting for the good news in your library, Blackbern," his father-in-law grumbled. "For my daughters' births, I left the house and distracted myself by playing cards at my club."

With Imogene so close to giving birth, Tristan had

been reluctant to stray far from the house for weeks. It had been the middle of the night when he had awakened with Imogene standing beside the bed. She had taken the time to light a branch of candles so he could see her clearly. Her chemise was damp with sweat and her hands had been splayed over her swollen abdomen that felt like an impenetrable shell when he touched it.

"Your son is coming, Tristan," she had told him.

Twelve hours had passed since she made her stark announcement.

"Your nerves are sturdier than mine. I would lose a bloody fortune if I played cards, Trevett," he said, glaring at the closed door while a servant picked up the broken glass and mopped up the brandy.

"Why do you think I suggested it?" Imogene's father said, cuffing him on the back of the head with undisguised affection.

"What was that for?" Tristan demanded harshly.

"I am not senile, Blackbern, and I can count on my fingers." The duke shook a finger at him. "If I had learned early on about the kind of mischief you were indulging in with my elder daughter, I might have paddled her backside before I tucked her away in one of my country estates to keep her out of your reach."

Tristan snorted at the obvious falsehood. "And deny yourself the pleasure of a grandson to spoil? I doubt it. And, just to clarify, your daughter threw herself at me first. Your duchess will confirm it. You cannot blame me if I was shrewd enough to recognize a rare find when I had it wriggling against me and decided to keep her."

He aimed a finger in the older man's direction. "You should be thanking me."

"I do in my prayers every day, son." He clamped a hand on Tristan's shoulder and for a few seconds his fingers tightened. "My lower back is beginning to ache so I am heading downstairs. Are you sure you do not want to join me? If I pour enough brandy down your throat, you might actually feel better for it."

Tristan shook his head and waved him off. He crouched down and settled on the floor so he could be close to the brave woman who was strong enough to bring his son into the world.

He let his forehead rest against his forearm and murmured a few whispered prayers. The past seven and a half months with Imogene at his side had been incredible. He loved her so much, and as the end of her pregnancy drew nearer, his anxiety had increased. Since he did not want to upset her, he had kept his fears to himself.

If I lose her now . . . how will I go on?

"Tristan?"

He blinked and stared blankly at his mother-in-law. Then he noticed her tears. He scrambled to his feet. "Is it Imogene? Is something wrong?" he asked, while his rising panic made him clumsy.

The dragon smiled at him and then did something most unexpected. She grabbed his face and kissed him firmly on the lips. "Imogene is fine and she is asking for you. Go inside, while I find my husband to share the good news."

Tristan rushed into the room and discovered a very

pale Imogene sitting in their bed. Someone had dressed her in a fresh chemise and a sheet had been pulled over her legs. She cradled their child in her arms. He ignored his aunt and the midwife as he strode directly to his duchess's bedside.

Imogene.

Their gazes locked and he could not conceive of loving her more than he did in that moment. She pushed back the blanket to reveal a thick cap of dark hair. "You have a son, Your Grace," she softly said. "I cannot fathom why I doubted you. You always get your way."

He supposed anyone who was listening would assume he and Imogene were referring to a friendly debate on whether they would have a boy or girl. Although they never spoke of Norgrave, he had been unable to completely banish her worries.

"I do my best." Tristan sat down on the mattress beside her. He tentatively stroked his son's hair. The texture felt like down, and his relief that Imogene and his son were healthy threatened to unman him.

"It was kind of you to give me my heir first. I do not know about you, but I am not sure I can go through this again," he said, half serious. The women behind him chuckled knowingly, but there were tears in his eyes as he stared down at the miracle they had created together.

Imogene clasped his hand and squeezed, quietly assuring him that she was fine. "In time, your son will want brothers and sisters to play with and torment. Will you deny him?"

And me? Imogene's expression seemed to ask.

If she desired more children, how could he deny his duchess when she had given him everything? Tristan laughed as he leaned forward and kissed his wife. "Not at all, darling."

Hours later, Tristan and Imogene introduced their son to his family. They had given the new Marquess of Fairlamb the name Mathias Ellis Rooke.

Coming soon…

Look for the next Masters of Seduction novel by
bestselling author
ALEXANDRA HAWKINS

You Can't Always Get the
Marquess You Want

Available in April 2016 from St. Martin's Paperbacks